as i descended

as i descended

ROBIN TALLEY

HARPER TEEN
An Imprint of HarperCollinsPublishers

HarperTeen is an imprint of HarperCollins Publishers.

Library of Congress Control Number: 2015959762
ISBN 978-0-06-240924-9

Typography by Torborg Davern
20 21 22 23 24   CPIG   10 9 8 7 6 5 4 3 2 1
❖
First paperback edition, 2020

For Julia, even though she prefers Hamlet

as i descended

ACT 1

in

thunder

1

THE CHARM'S WOUND UP

The Ouija board was Lily's idea.

Maria warned her not to go through with it, but Lily didn't listen. She went onto eBay while Maria was at soccer practice and bought the prettiest board she could find. A "genuine antique," she called it.

Only when she showed it to Maria and Brandon that night she pronounced it "gen-you-wine," showing off the Southern drawl everyone teased her for. Soon after that they opened the bottle of cheap white wine left over from Delilah's eighteenth birthday party, and every five minutes either Brandon or Maria would utter the words "gen-you-wine an-TEEK!" and collapse into giggles.

Lily pretended to take offense the first few times, but by her last Styrofoam cup of Chardonnay Lily was adding an extra *I* to every word she said. "Sit" became "See-it." "Drink" was "dree-enk." When she started calling Maria "Mariah," like Mariah Carey, Brandon confiscated her cup.

Maria had been worried about Lily all day. She wasn't normally this loud, or this giggly. And Lily never drank—she didn't even like to take her painkillers. Normally she sat at the edge of the party sipping seltzer and watching their friends with her hawk eyes to make sure no one spilled anything on their plush dorm-room carpet.

Part of Maria wanted to declare the evening over, escort Lily back to their room, put her in bed, and keep an eye on her for the rest of the night to make sure she didn't do anything else out of the ordinary.

But Maria couldn't focus on Lily right now. Not with that Ouija board sitting next to her.

This board was the real deal. Maria could feel it. It wasn't any of that plastic Milton Bradley crap. This board meant business.

It was after lights-out in the dorm, so the three of them kept their laughter to whispers. Everyone was supposed to be in their rooms tucked into bed by ten p.m. if they didn't want to get written up by one of the dorm monitors who prowled the halls.

None of the staff ever checked the old dining hall, though. Most of the students never ventured here after dark. There were rumors about the room. Scary stories the younger kids whispered about at sleepovers.

Maria had seen enough to know those kinds of stories were

usually bullshit. The truth was a lot scarier than anything little kids could imagine.

But Lily had thought the old dining hall was the perfect place for their first séance, and Maria had given up arguing about it. Lily was smart—smarter than Maria; they'd both known that much from the beginning—but she didn't know the first thing about what that Ouija board could do. She'd begged, though, and begged some more, and she'd smiled sweetly and said pretty things, and finally, Maria had given in.

Maria probably should've put up a fight. It was just that she hated fighting with Lily more than almost anything. It was always better when she knew she could glance over at Lily and be certain her girlfriend would smile that warm, secret smile she saved just for Maria.

Besides, it might not work. It had been years since Maria had last tried to talk to the spirits. Maybe they'd forgotten her.

By the time they'd poured out the last of the wine, Lily and Brandon were giggling so much Maria wondered if they even remembered the board still sitting in its cardboard box. Maria could never forget something like that. Her eyes were on Brandon—he was telling them about the giant beetle he'd found in the flowers Mateo had given him for their two-week anniversary, and his epic screams that had brought the dorm monitors running, convinced he was having an epileptic fit—but through it all, the board kept humming to her. The longer it went on, the more Maria ached to know if the spirits really did remember.

So when Brandon wrapped up his story and Lily pulled the

candles out of her bag and said, "Shall we begin?" Maria didn't hesitate. She was ready.

Brandon shrugged and took another swallow from his cup. Maria lit the candles while Lily set up her phone's audio recorder.

Maria hadn't wanted to do this, but there was no going back now. Not while Lily was giving her that smile.

Not while the board was still humming to her.

Brandon covered his yawn as Maria lined up the candles, following instructions Lily had found on some website. Brandon was designated the note taker and given a pad and pencil. His job was to copy down whatever the planchette spelled out.

Brandon had played with Ouija boards enough as a kid to know it wasn't going to spell out anything more than a few fart jokes, so he didn't mind this job. Plus, as an added bonus, this way he got to keep drinking. At their usual parties, when all the popular seniors got together to drink and flirt in someone's room after lights-out, Brandon never got in more than a few swallows. The other guys were always grabbing his drink out of his hand and then pounding Brandon on the shoulder too hard, howling laughter as they thanked him and guzzled his beer.

Lily pulled the board out of its packaging. It was bigger than Brandon had expected. At least two feet wide. You could tell it was old from the cracks in the paint and the worn-smooth edges of the wood. But it was still nice-looking, with artsy paintings in the corners for the sun and moon and fancy calligraphy on all the letters and numbers. The words "YES" and "NO" were carved into the corners in a fancy font. At the top was an elaborate drawing of a single eye, wide-open, with a deep black pupil, and at the bottom, the words "GOOD BYE" was drawn next to a closed eye.

Brandon didn't care one way or the other about Ouija boards, but those eyes were still creepy. No matter which way he leaned in his seat, it felt like that one at the top was watching him.

Lily slid the board onto the table and set the wooden planchette gently on top. It was flat and heart-shaped with another deep black eye carved into the wood, right below the hole that was cut to show which letter the planchette had chosen. Brandon took another sip of his drink and avoided its gaze.

Lily took out the poem she'd printed from the website and began to read. Her giggliness from before was long gone, and she was using a deep, serious voice, like something she must've seen in a horror movie. Before she'd finished the first line, Brandon had to bite his cheek to keep from laughing out loud.

> "'Tis time, 'tis time.
> *Round about the talking board,*
> *Candles burn, the charm's own chord.*
> *Open, locks, whoever knocks.*
> *We, the living, offer you vox.'"*

Brandon stifled his laughter while the girls reached into the center of the table. Each of them laid two fingers on the planchette. Since he was the only one not absorbed in the utter seriousness of the thing, Brandon was the only one to notice the dorm's two cats, Rhett and Scarlett, nosing their way into the room from the staff kitchen.

Brandon could've sworn he'd locked that door when he and the girls first came in. The main door that opened into the hallway, too.

Oh, well. He must've remembered wrong. He'd had kind of a lot of wine.

Brandon seemed to be the only one who'd noticed it was getting colder, too. Three candles grouped in front of him flickered, their flames turning blue, as though they felt the chill. Brandon shrugged on the Acheron Academy soccer team sweatshirt Mateo had left in his room the night before.

Neither of the girls looked up at the movement. They both had their eyes fixed on the board. Maria wasn't even blinking.

Several minutes passed without anything happening. Brandon yawned again. He should really be studying for the physics quiz tomorrow, but it had been so long since Maria had wanted to hang out with him alone. Well, alone plus Lily.

Brandon had always liked Lily. Or tried to, anyway, for Maria's sake, once he found out the two of them had taken the whole roommate thing to the next level. Lily was pretty. She was smart, too, and she was nice enough, if you were talking to her about things like homework or teachers or what she was going to major in, which were the only kinds of things Brandon ever talked to her about.

But there was something strange about Lily. Something he'd

never been able to put his finger on. Something that made him want to avoid getting stuck alone in a room with her.

Lily put up with him, but only for Maria's sake. So did most everyone in that crowd. Being best friends with Maria had lots of benefits. She was the second-most-popular girl in school. After Delilah, obviously.

Though to Brandon's surprise, in the past couple of weeks since he'd started hooking up with Mateo, things had been looking up for him on the popularity front. He'd been excited to finally have a boyfriend, of course—it still made him grin to think about it—but he hadn't realized it would make the others treat him differently, too. Brandon had always lived on the periphery of the popular crowd, but Mateo had set up a permanent residence right in the middle of it years ago.

But then, that was Acheron's social universe. When you were fat and gay and on financial aid and you spent your free nights alone in your room watching old *Battlestar Galactica* videos, most of the blond-haired, blue-eyed Old South plantation owners' great-great-great-great-great-grandkids didn't have much reason to bother with you. Unless you were hooking up with one of their own.

Of course, Brandon *was* a blond-haired, blue-eyed Old South plantation owner's great-great-great-great-great-grandkid, too. He'd just had the misfortune of being born several generations after the family money had withered away.

Meanwhile, Maria and Mateo both had the Spanish names, dark eyes, and brown skin that would've kept them off those Old South plantations—unless they'd come with a price tag.

The irony had never been lost on Brandon. But sometimes he actually found it preferable to think the reason he didn't fit in at Acheron was that he was poor, or that he was gay, or that he was fat. It was better than thinking the problem was the fact that he was . . . him.

Anyway, he liked hanging out with his friends. Some of the straight guys he'd gotten to know through his work-study job in the athletics office were cool to him, and as long as he had Maria, he could deal with the rest.

Maria was the best friend he'd ever had. The only one who'd really mattered. He could never have lasted at this place if it hadn't been for Maria, giggling with him at room parties and muttering jokes into his ear during pep rallies and sneaking into his room after lights-out to whisper under the covers while his roommate snored in the next bed.

Tonight had been a fun night. Up until the girls had gotten all serious about talking to ghosts or whatever.

The planchette on the table hadn't budged an inch. Lily was watching Maria from across the table, her eyebrows lifted. Brandon suspected she was getting bored too.

Maria had her eyes closed. She was sitting so still Brandon wondered if she'd fallen asleep.

Maria was awake. More awake, in fact, than she could ever remember being.

She should've done this a long time ago.

Lily and Brandon were the only two people Maria trusted in

the world, but she knew even they had never quite believed her when she'd told them about the things that happened when she was a kid.

That strange connection she used to feel. The shapes that used to flit in the corner of her eye. It had been years since Maria had felt that sensation.

She felt it now. Every cell in Maria's body was buzzing.

The feeling was warm. Potent. Almost arousing. But sharp, too, somehow.

It wasn't a pleasant feeling, but it wasn't painful either. It was—necessary. Vital.

Maria never wanted to stop feeling it.

She'd give up anything—anything but Lily—if only she could keep feeling this.

She was intensely aware of everything that was happening in the room. The cats watching them from the foot of the table, tails twitching. Lily's growing impatience on the other side of the planchette. Each tiny movement of Brandon's lips and throat as he slurped the remains of his wine.

She was aware that the room's temperature had dropped at least five degrees since Lily placed the planchette on the board.

And she was aware that they weren't alone anymore. If they ever had been.

Maria opened her eyes.

"What is your name?" she said.

Brandon giggled at the sound of Maria's slow, solemn voice. This wasn't how Brandon was used to hearing her.

Then, Brandon had only ever heard Maria speak to the living.

She closed her eyes again and put Brandon out of her mind. She blocked out everything but her questions for the spirit in the room with them.

Who are you?

What is your name?

What do you want from us?

The wooden planchette quivered under her hand. Maria opened her eyes.

Lily sat up straight in her seat. Her fingers were pressing down too hard on the planchette, but that shouldn't matter. If the spirit wanted to communicate, it wouldn't care about a little extra weight. In Maria's experience, spirits didn't care about much of anything the living did or didn't do.

The planchette slid toward the row of letters at the top of the board.

"Okay, which of you is doing that?" Brandon said.

Maria ignored him. The room was getting colder.

Something hissed in the corner. Maria didn't move, but Lily jumped and Brandon yelped. Then he let out a forced chuckle and said, "It was one of the cats. Don't mind me. I'm just quietly losing it over here."

The planchette settled over the *M*.

"*M*," Lily read. "Brandon, write down *M*."

"Shh," Maria said, as softly as she could. Lily should've known better than to talk while she was touching the planchette.

Maria couldn't let herself get distracted. It had been years since she'd last tried to contact something, but she hadn't forgotten the basics.

"Please continue, spirit," Maria said out loud, ignoring Brandon's muffled laughter. "Your name begins with *M*. What comes next?"

The planchette didn't move. But the cats did.

They'd been watching the girls' hands on the board, but now, in an identical movement, their heads rose, arcing, their eyes fixed on a single point in the air Maria couldn't see. Neither cat made a sound, but their heads followed the same path over the table and across the room. Then they stopped, staring into the far corner of the ceiling.

The hair on the back of Maria's neck prickled. Lily and Brandon shivered. The air around them was frigid.

Maria followed the cats' gaze. The antique chandelier's illumination didn't reach that corner. The shadow on the ceiling wasn't shaped the way you'd expect a shadow to be, with clean edges that followed the path of the light. Instead, it was jagged on one side. As if something were perched in that corner, clinging to the wall, hunched up on knees and elbows.

Maria closed her eyes again and willed her heart to stop pounding. Showing fear was the surest way to anger a spirit.

Maria knew how to do this part.

She'd known ever since she first glanced into the old mirror that hung on her grandmother's back porch when she was five. Maria always liked to play on the porch when they went to visit her grandparents, even though no one else used it and it wasn't kept up anymore. The wind blew fiercely back there, even on calm days. The half-wild garden that ran along that side of the house had grown over, and vines crept up onto the rotting wood floor. It didn't have much furniture anymore. Just an old swing that Maria's nanny, Altagracia, warned her never to play on in case the rusted chains gave way.

And the mirror. An old cracked glass hanging from a nail that jutted out of the brick. The mirror needed a good polishing, but it never seemed to swing on its perch, no matter how bad the wind got. Maria didn't know why her grandmother kept the mirror out on the porch, but it was always there. Even in winter, when the glass frosted over.

Whenever Maria played out back, sooner or later she'd glance toward the mirror. Every time, she felt it. It started on the back of her neck, then slid down her spine and along her arms and legs, giving her goose bumps regardless of the weather. Every time, she'd go over to the mirror and stare into it.

She never saw anything except her own reflection, but it felt like something was tugging at her. Pulling her forward. Before she got old enough to know better, Maria used to think something was trying to pull her *into* the mirror itself.

Once she looked into the mirror, she never moved. She only stood there, gazing at her own face until Altagracia called her to come inside.

Maria drew in a deep breath and forced herself to shake the memory. The mirror on the porch was a long time ago.

She couldn't forget where she was right now. She couldn't lose focus.

She couldn't risk getting lost in the mirror again.

"If you're here," Maria said, her gaze locked on the planchette in front of her, "if you have anything you'd like to tell us, please do. We'd like to listen."

Above them, something knocked three times.

Loudly. The sound thundered in their ears and lingered, echoing.

"What the hell was that?" Brandon said.

"Probably a sophomore playing some dumb game," Lily said.

"It didn't sound like any sophomore," Brandon said. "It sounded like somebody knocking at the gates of hell."

The planchette quivered.

Lily and Brandon were both sitting forward. Brandon had his pad ready, a big *M* scrawled in the middle of it. The planchette moved faster than it had before, coming to a stop over the *A*.

"*M, A*," Brandon read. "Bet it's the ghost of Marie Antoinette. Ask her if she can get me the answers for the history test next week."

No one laughed.

Brandon kept talking anyway, his voice pitched higher than usual. "By the way, does anyone else smell something baking?"

The planchette was still moving.

The next three letters were *R, I, A*. Then the planchette stopped.

"That's not funny, Ree," Lily said. "I thought we said we were going to take this seriously."

Maria took her hand off the planchette. She was sweating despite the chill.

"I didn't do that," Maria said.

Lily sat back in her chair, her wide-set blue eyes narrowed, her forehead creased. "Then is this something that happens sometimes? Is your ghost coming back from the future to mess with us or something?"

"Couldn't it be someone else named Maria?" Brandon interrupted. "Why don't we ask its last name?"

Lily rolled her eyes, but from the look on his face Maria knew Brandon wasn't joking. She wondered if he'd seen the cats too.

Maria wished she could be alone so she could do this right, but that was the thing about Acheron: solitude didn't exist inside these old white walls.

Maria didn't want to touch the planchette again. Her desperate need to connect with the spirits had evaporated the moment the board finished spelling out her name.

Plus, she could smell baking, too. It smelled like empanadas. The kind Altagracia used to make on Sunday afternoons.

Maria used to like that smell. Tonight it made her nervous.

But it was dangerous to leave a Ouija session unfinished. She remembered that much from the "games" she'd played as a kid. Once you'd opened a link to the spirit world, you had to close it. If you didn't, the spirits would be free to roam as they pleased.

Maria put a fingertip back on the planchette. Lily did the

same. The dusty chandelier over their heads swayed gently and soundlessly.

Except—even with all the windows wide-open, there was no breeze. Not tonight. The air in the room was heavy and still. Heavy, still, and cold.

The old dining hall was on the first floor of their dorm, right next to Maria and Lily's room, but it wasn't used anymore. A massive cafeteria had been built in the new student life center on the other side of the hill years before any of them had come to Acheron. This room was much too small for actual dining anyway. It was the size of a small classroom, with just one long wooden table and a straight row of stiff-backed chairs on either side.

Until tonight Maria had only ever been in this room for a minute at a time, cutting through it on her way to the staff kitchen to rinse her coffee mug or avoid one of her so-called friends. But for all the years Maria had lived in this dorm, every time she'd been in this room—and sometimes when she'd only passed by the door in the hall—she'd felt it. The tingly sensation she remembered from staring into that mirror on the porch.

That was why Lily had suggested this room for their first session with the board. That, and because the old dining hall had never been renovated.

The Acheron campus was a converted old plantation, one of the oldest in Virginia. Most of the school buildings were new, but their dorm, where all the high school students lived, had been the plantation's big house, where the master and his wife and children lived. It was huge and ostentatious—a typical plantation house—and it had been remodeled and expanded over the years, with new technology put in and more rooms added to the wings. This part of the house, though, was original. For all any of them knew, the table they were sitting at was the same one where Acheron's original owners, the Siward family, had been served dinner by their slaves. The room had high ceilings, a huge fireplace, dusty landscape paintings in moldy frames, and a diamond-patterned wood floor that had probably been beautiful before it was scraped raw by generations of chairs. In the far corner was a rocking chair too rickety for anyone to sit in. The lower-school students liked to spook each other, saying they'd walked by the old dining hall late at night and seen the chair rocking with no one in it.

The nicest artifact in the room, though, was the ancient chandelier over their heads. It had surprised them all by lighting up when Brandon climbed onto the table and pulled the cord, shaking up enough dust they were still sneezing an hour later.

The shadow in the corner of the ceiling was ten feet from the chandelier. It wasn't moving, but Maria could still see those bent knees and elbows. Crouched. Waiting.

Waiting for what?

The planchette started moving again before Maria could ask the spirit another question.

"What's it doing?" Brandon said.

Maria didn't know. She'd never seen this happen before.

The planchette slid into the top right corner of the board.

That didn't make sense. There weren't any letters or pictures there.

It slid to the bottom left corner. Then the top left. Then the bottom right.

"What does that mean?" Lily said.

A faint hum buzzed in Maria's ear. It didn't sound like it was coming from the board this time. It was as if someone was humming a tune.

"Who are you?" Maria whispered. She kept her voice low. No one but the spirit needed to hear. "What happened to you?"

The planchette slid toward the dead center of the board. Then it moved fast, so fast Maria and Lily had to sit up in their chairs to keep up with it. It slid out in an arc, then down, then over, in a figure eight. Then another figure eight. The same pattern, three times, four, without stopping.

"How the hell are you *doing* that?"

Brandon really couldn't tell. The girls were both biting their lips, leaning over the board as if they were trying to keep up with the planchette's movements instead of the other way around. Brandon watched their arms but he couldn't see their muscles flexing, the way you'd think would happen if you were trying to swoop a chunk of wood in an enormous figure eight.

Then the planchette moved back to the alphabet at the top of the board. It slid from letter to letter, moving so fast Brandon had to lean all the way over the board to see where it paused. It started at *F*, then moved to *I*, then *R*, then *E*.

"Fire," Brandon whispered. He shivered.

"Is there something you'd like to tell us?" Maria murmured into the still-swerving planchette. "Do you have a message for the living?"

The planchette started moving even faster as soon as the words had left Maria's lips. Brandon did his best to scribble down all the letters.

MARIA MARIA MARIA
USTED CONSEGUIRÁ LO QUE MÁS DESEA
MARIA

"Usted," Lily whispered, her eyes flashing as she followed the planchette's movement. "That looks Spanish. What does it mean, Ree? What's it saying?"

Brandon expected Maria to flinch, the way she always did when someone brought up the fact that she knew Spanish. Maria liked to pretend she was just as pasty white as Brandon and Lily, even though anyone who looked at her knew better.

Except—Maria had her eyes closed. It didn't look like she'd heard Lily at all.

How was Maria moving the planchette with her eyes closed?

"What's going on?" Brandon whispered to Lily.

Lily shook her head. Her eyes never left the board. Her long blond hair was falling out of its neat French braid. Brandon would've thought she'd whip out her bobby pins and fix it back up—Lily hated for anything to be out of place—but this was a different Lily from the one Brandon knew. This Lily was bending forward over the board, sweat clinging to her temples. Her eyes were fixed on the planchette, waiting for it to move again.

The pointer swung to the *C*.

"*C*," Brandon read, scribbling it down and looking back toward the board to make sure he didn't miss any more letters. But it was moving slower this time, looping around the board, until it finally spelled out:

CAWDOR KINGSLEY

"Whoa," Brandon muttered. "This thing must think it's talking to Delilah."

As soon as he'd said it, Brandon wished he could take it back. Maria's mouth was set in a straight, tight line. He'd hurt her feelings.

Then her arms jerked to the left so fast Brandon was worried she'd get hurt for real.

Lily moved too. It looked like the board was dragging her.

The planchette was pointing to the word "NO" in the far corner of the board. Then it moved back toward the center, only to jerk back again to the "NO." It moved there two more times. Then three.

NO. NO. NO. NO. NO.

"All right, we get it," Brandon said. "You said 'no,' right?"

The planchette was still moving. Back to the alphabet this time. More Spanish.

LO QUE ES SUYO ES TUYO

Brandon rubbed his forehead, trying to figure out what that could mean. He'd taken a year of Spanish in middle school before he transferred to Acheron and started French. The first sentence, the one with *"usted"* in it, had meant something like *You will have what you most desire.* And *"lo que es suyo es tuyo"* meant something like *That which is his is yours.* Well, it could be either "his" or "hers."

The planchette was still moving.

LO QUE ES SEGUNDO SERA PRIMERO

That was a little easier to translate—*That which is second will be first*—but it still didn't mean anything to Brandon.

"All righty, then," he muttered. "Thanks, spirits, for your ever-so-clear words of wisdom."

He waited for one of the girls to shush him, but neither seemed to have heard. Lily's eyes were fixed on the planchette, but they looked empty, vacant. Across from her, Maria's entire body trembled except for her hand. Her hand, resting on the planchette, was perfectly still.

This was all getting a little too intense for Brandon.

"Hey," he said, leaning over the board. The planchette started to move again, slowly this time, in plodding figure eights. "Hey, ghostie, hey, Casper, buddy, what about me? Why does Maria get all the love? I'm doing all this work writing down your fancy foreign poetry. Don't I get a fortune cookie of my own?"

The girls didn't bother to chastise Brandon this time either. He wondered if they could speak at all.

That idea scared him. He was about to suggest they stop playing when he heard a strange sound from above.

Brandon looked up.

He was the only one. The girls were both bent over the

planchette. It had come to a sudden stop in the center of the board.

The cats were still staring at something in the corner of the ceiling that Brandon couldn't see.

What he did see was the chandelier. Swinging on its cord, hard, as though someone invisible were pushing it. Or riding on it, pumping their legs, like a swing.

The planchette swerved so fast it almost skidded off the table. Brandon leaned over the board again. He didn't bother trying to write anything down this time. He couldn't possibly keep up. The board went to *H*, then *A*.

Lily and Maria both had their eyes closed now. The chandelier was rocking harder.

HABRA TRES PRESAGIOS

There will be three . . . something. Brandon had never seen that last word, *"presagios,"* before.

There wasn't time to dwell on it. The planchette was still flying over the letters. He didn't realize it had switched to English until it had already spelled out the same set of words twice.

THIS IS HOW IT ENDS
THIS IS HOW IT ENDS

"How *what* ends?" Brandon whispered.

The planchette jerked in the girls' hands and shifted back to the middle of the alphabet. Moving just as fast as before, it spelled out:

MEMENTO MORI

Brandon rubbed his forehead again. That wasn't Spanish, but he knew that phrase. He'd seen it before. It was Latin. He tried to remember what it meant. Something about—

A jagged piece of glass flew past Brandon's face, missing his eye by an inch. A split second later the chandelier crashed down onto the table, smashing the Ouija board into shards.

Brandon screamed. Pieces of glass whizzed around him and tinkled onto the floor by the hundreds, the thousands, smashing against the wood and shattering into jagged slivers.

Brandon waited to feel the first one slice into his skin. He burrowed his head into his arms to protect his face.

Then it was over.

The room was pitch-dark and silent. Brandon shook so hard he could barely breathe.

It took him half a minute to realize he wasn't hurt. The glass crunched thick under the soles of his sneakers when he dropped his feet to the floor.

Then he remembered the girls.

"Maria?" Brandon peered into the dark. A blurry shape was huddled in the chair where Maria had been. "Ree? Lily? Are you all right?"

One of the girls made a sound like a whimper.

"Hey." Brandon crept toward Maria, trying to avoid the biggest chunks of glass, afraid of what he'd find if he got too close. One of the cats brushed against his leg, its back arched, hissing. Somewhere far away, footsteps pounded down the hall. His vision was adjusting to the darkness. "Talk to me, Ree. Say something."

Maria was still sitting in her chair. Her eyes were closed. Brandon's heart leaped in his chest.

"Maria!" He grabbed her by the shoulders and shook her.

"What?" Maria blinked.

Brandon exhaled. He wanted to slap her for scaring him so badly.

Maria's eyes were empty, but she could sit up, so she must be all right. Brandon went to the other side of the table to check on Lily.

It was a miracle the table hadn't collapsed. The chandelier looked like it weighed about a thousand pounds.

Lily was on the floor, but she was sitting up too, rubbing at the dust in her eyes. "Did it work?" she said when Brandon reached her.

"I don't know what the hell it did," Brandon said. "But we are never, ever playing that game again."

Bang. Bang. Bang.

Brandon's heart sped back up. Then he realized this sound was *normal*, not whatever that bizarre knocking had been before. This time, someone—a human someone—was pounding on the door to the staff kitchen.

"Open up!" It was Ross, the first-floor dorm monitor. "Guys, open this door right now or this will be a lot worse for you!"

Wait. Wasn't that door unlocked? Didn't the cats come through it earlier? How did—

Never mind that. Brandon had bigger problems.

He stepped gingerly over the broken glass, cracked the door, and peeked through the gap. Ross pushed past him, slamming the door open wide and flicking on the overhead switch. Brandon blinked against the sudden light.

The shadows that had clung to the corners of the room were gone. All he could see were dust and cobwebs and some revolting fungus creeping along the edges of the rug.

This was it for Brandon. He'd been caught out after lights-out once already this year. Tonight would be strike two. And the empty wine bottle would mean an automatic phone call to their parents, which meant he could count on being grounded all summer long.

But Ross didn't care about any of that. He hadn't even noticed Brandon yet. His eyes were locked on Lily.

All the Acheron staff, even the twentysomething dorm monitors like Ross, who just worked here for the free housing, were obsessed with Lily. If the disabled girl got hurt on their watch, there'd be hell to pay.

Ross texted for backup and helped Lily to her feet. Brandon gathered up her crutches from where they'd fallen and passed them to Ross. Lily glared at both of them.

"See who all's out there and get rid of them, will you?" Ross told Brandon, gesturing toward the main door. He picked up the wine bottle from where it had rolled under the table and shook his head.

Brandon wondered how much this would cost to clean up. Not to mention the priceless antique that had been destroyed. *Antiques,* if you counted the Ouija board.

He tiptoed over the glass shards and pulled on the knob of the main door. It was unlocked, but now it seemed to be jammed. He had to throw his shoulder into the door to crack it open.

On the other side, a group of pajama-clad freshmen were gathered in the hallway. Felicia was at the very front. She was his friend Austin's kid sister, but lately Brandon had realized he liked Felicia a lot better than he liked her brother. Felicia brushed her tangled hair back from her face and smiled at Brandon, but she looked worried. That crash must've echoed through the whole building.

"Jeez, are you okay?" Felicia asked.

"Just an accident, guys," Brandon told her and the others. "Ross is here. He said for you all to go back to bed."

Felicia pouted. Brandon shrugged and whispered, "Sorry, Fee," trying to make sure she knew it wasn't personal. She gave him another small smile and left, pulling her friends with her. Brandon closed the door again—it moved easily this time—and turned back to the room. Maria was standing up, still blinking slowly.

"All right," Ross said. "It's a miracle none of you got hurt with all that glass flying, but since nobody needs to go to the health center you should just go back to your rooms. I'll call maintenance and write up the incident report tomorrow, and the dean will call your parents. How the heck did you pull the chandelier down, anyway?"

"We didn't pull it," Brandon said. "It fell."

"Uh-huh." Ross ran a hand through his thick brown hair and sighed. "Just go. Watch out for the broken glass. Lily, do you need help getting back?"

"Like I said, I'm *fine*," Lily snapped.

* * *

Maria could hear the others talking, but they were far away. It felt like she was alone at the bottom of a cave, listening to the faint echo of distant voices on the surface. By the end of the session, that was all she'd wanted. She'd pleaded silently, over and over, for the board, for everything, to go away, to leave her alone.

Now she'd gotten her wish. The thing in the corner was gone. The room was empty.

But the shards of the Ouija board on the table—something was nagging at her. Something important.

It wouldn't be until hours later, when she was struggling to fall asleep, that Maria would remember what it was.

The board had been destroyed before she could tell it goodbye.

2

NOTHING IS BUT WHAT IS NOT

"Ten!" Delilah whispered.

"Nine!" The dozen seniors squeezed into the tiny dorm room joined in. "Eight!"

Maria took another gulp as her friends cheered in hushed voices. She was the only girl who'd ever join the guys' absurd beer-chugging contest.

"Seven!" everyone chorused. Maria coughed. Lily resisted the urge to snatch the beer can out of her hand.

"Six! Five! Four!"

Maria fist-pumped. The movement made her tank top ride up. Just a fraction of an inch, but enough to get appreciative looks from the boys sitting at her feet. Lily wanted to kick them.

"Three!" Emily, leading the chant, took a dainty sip from her drink. Lily could've sworn she was intentionally slowing the countdown to trip Maria up. "Two! . . . One!"

Lily gazed from face to face. Every single person in this room—except Maria, of course—was useless.

Lily hated Acheron to the depths of her soul. She longed to tell all these losers to shut up and get out of her room before she shoved them out the door herself. She bit her lip and took another sip of seltzer instead.

"Zero!" the group chorused. Maria lowered her empty beer can and wiped her mouth. She laughed as Ryan took the can from her and crushed it in that way guys did when they were being stupid.

The grin on Maria's face almost looked real. She collapsed onto the bed next to Lily, fanning herself dramatically even though it was freezing in their room.

Lily raised her eyebrows at Maria—their usual look, the one that meant *People are watching us, so you can't sit that close*—and Maria slid down onto the floor next to Austin, still giggling.

"Congrats, Ree." Austin tipped his drink to Maria's beer can in a toast. A trickle of rum rolled down the sleeve of his black mesh shirt. Austin was the school's resident dealer, and for some reason he liked to pretend he was goth. "I can't believe they let you off with a warning. That chandelier's been up there since the Stone Age. You've got the magic touch, Princess."

Delilah, slumped on the floor next to him, giggled and held up her drink, the liquid glistening in the candlelight that shined across the room. Her own top was so tiny it wouldn't have had room to ride up. She was on her third Diet Coke of the night, and she was high on oxy. The combination of caffeine, fake sugar, and prescription painkillers had her at maximum intolerability.

"It was crazy," Maria told Austin. Lily could see her hiding her smile. "Anyway, they told our parents too."

"As long as they don't stop you from going to homecoming," Caitlin said. She'd climbed onto Maria's bed and wrapped herself around Ryan. Tamika, who'd been dating Ryan up until yesterday, glared at them from the other side of the room. "That's all that matters, right?"

Lily rolled her eyes. Caitlin, and all the other pathetic excuses for humans in this room, probably thought the dance really *was* all that mattered.

"What'd your parents say?" Emily asked.

Maria shrugged. Her parents hadn't said a word. Not to her, anyway.

Lily, Maria, and Brandon had been brought into Dean Cumberland's office that morning while the dean called their parents one by one. Lily's mother had been so relieved to hear Lily wasn't hurt, she barely even listened to the part about the drinking and the rule breaking. Brandon's father had announced over speakerphone that Brandon would be grounded all summer, and did Dean Cumberland think that was punishment enough or should he take away Brandon's computer and his phone, too?

But no one had answered at Maria's. Not at either of her parents' offices or on their cell phones. Finally the dean left a sternly worded message with Maria's mother's intern.

Maria had called her parents to explain. She'd left a voice

mail pleading for her mother to call her back. But Maria's phone didn't ring that day.

Instead a dorm monitor stopped by their room while Maria was out at soccer practice. She told Lily the dean had spoken to Maria's parents, and to tell Maria the girls didn't need to worry about last night—the chandelier would be easy enough to restore for next semester.

Lily had never met Maria's parents, but she knew enough about them, and about how Acheron was used to dealing with the genteel Southern families who were its livelihood, to know what that meant: the check was in the mail.

That didn't help with Brandon's two strikes, though. He was stuck staying in his room all night from now on. Unless he wanted to risk getting caught again. Three strikes on your record meant a minimum one-year suspension.

Sucked for him.

Lily hadn't been in the mood for a party after what had happened the night before. Neither had Maria. Still, though, Delilah had asked. She wanted to celebrate, she said, because Acheron had done so well on the Kingsley Prize finalist list that morning.

And when Delilah Dufrey asked for a favor, you didn't say no.

You wouldn't think it to look at her, slumped on the floor giggling at a joke everyone else had forgotten ten minutes ago, but Delilah could be terrifying when she wanted to be.

That afternoon Delilah had caught Lily and Maria in the cafeteria. She'd made a big show of fixing her lip gloss in her pocket mirror and said, "Don't you guys think it would be awesome if we hung out in your room tonight after lights-out? We've all been working so hard with the big game coming up. We deserve to take a break. I mean, we all saw how amazing the list was, right?"

There was no saying, *No, Delilah, I don't think that would be awesome at all, actually.* Not unless you wanted to lose every friend you had.

That was the kind of power Delilah wielded. Somehow, she'd appointed herself the queen of the senior class.

It wasn't as if Lily and Maria weren't popular. Maria was at almost the exact same spot as Delilah in the social hierarchy. Two boys had already asked her to homecoming, and even though she'd turned them both down, rumor had it another offer would come in before the week was out.

But "almost" didn't cut it. At Acheron, if Delilah Dufrey didn't like you, you might as well resign yourself to spending your high school career with the mousy-haired girls who gave themselves teddy bear tattoos with ballpoint pens.

It wasn't just that Delilah was hot, either. Though she was, of course. She was hotter than she had any right to be, with her long blond hair and her sparkling eyes and her pert little nose that was so perfectly shaped the freshmen took bets on whether she'd had a nose job.

Nope. There had never been a single thing wrong with Delilah Dufrey.

She'd been unanimously elected homecoming queen last year, and everyone already knew the same thing would happen this year too. She was first in their class, edging out Maria by one

one-hundredth of a point. She was senior class president and captain of the soccer team, the cross-country team, and the debate team. She was only vice president of the Gay-Straight Alliance, but that was because Mateo had founded the GSA back in their freshman year. And, of course, because Delilah wasn't gay. At least, not gay enough.

And as of today, Delilah was first in line for the Kingsley Prize.

The Cawdor Kingsley Foundation Prize went to five graduating seniors from Virginia private schools based on their grades, extracurriculars, and all the other usual stuff. Each of the five winners came from a different school, and Acheron had had a winner every year since the award was created. It came with a free ride to the college of your choice, plus two years of grad school. Winning it pretty much guaranteed you'd get into any college in the country.

At Acheron, winning the Kingsley Prize was just called "winning." You said the word and everyone knew exactly what you were talking about.

Cawdor Kingsley himself was dead now, but before that he'd been some rich "Southern gentleman" who'd made his fortune running manufacturing plants that had killed every fish, plant, and amoebic creature in half the rivers in the state. Like many a Southern gentleman before him, he'd been a proud member of his local White Citizens' Council, barely one step removed from the Klan. Now his great-grandkids were trying to redeem the family name by giving his money away to everyone they could think of.

The preliminary list of finalists had gone up early that morning, with Delilah's name right at number one. The list was just a formality, though. Everyone had already known the prize would go to Delilah. That was how it worked when you'd already won everything else there was to win. Most of the seniors hadn't even bothered to put their names in.

That was the reason Maria had spent the evening getting drunk and glassy-eyed. Or part of the reason, anyway.

Officially, there would be a second round of judging in a few weeks, because the prize committee was still accepting late applications. They wouldn't announce the declared winners until after Christmas.

Not that it mattered. Delilah was in first place now, and when the time came, Delilah would win. Then she'd get into her dream school, Princeton, and she wouldn't even have to pay for it. Winning made you the most important person at Acheron. The alumni threw you a huge party. You'd be on the front page of the school newspaper and the local paper, too. Best of all, your name got added to the official Kingsley plaque, the first thing the student ambassadors showed to every group of prospective parents who came through the campus.

Every senior knew Delilah was guaranteed to win this year's Kingsley Prize, just as they knew she was a shoo-in to win homecoming queen. Most of them knew about Delilah's oxy habit, too, but no one seemed to care.

It had been more than a year since Delilah first started sidling up to Lily in the cafeteria, asking if she'd gotten her prescription filled yet. Lily was supposed to take the pills for her legs, but she hardly ever did—anything stronger than an Advil made her feel out of control, which made her anxious and nauseous, and sometimes that was worse than the pain in the first place—so at first she started giving Delilah one pill at a time, when she asked. Slowly, that turned into two pills at a time. Then four. Now Lily just handed over the whole bottle at the start of each month, saving only a couple for her really bad days. Once last semester Maria had seen Delilah bent over the sink in the locker room, snorting up the crushed pills with a rolled-up dollar bill. Super-classy homecoming queen behavior.

"Hey." Mateo sank onto the bed next to Lily. He was sweaty, with dark hair curling over his forehead, but he smiled and held out a fresh can of seltzer. "Looks like you're all out. Want this one?"

"No, thanks." Lily tossed her empty can in the recycling and crossed her arms. It took more effort for her to go over to the cooler than it did for everyone else, but that didn't mean she wanted gestures of pity.

"No worries. I'm stopping for the night myself." Mateo set down his beer bottle and smiled again. He was showing off that slight Puerto Rican accent that made the other girls joke about trying to turn him straight. "So, are you excited about Stanford?"

Lily hid her surprise. No one ever asked her about Stanford. "Yeah, I guess."

Stanford had been the number one school—really, the only

school—on Lily's list for as long as she could remember. She'd been hearing about it since she was a kid. Her parents had met there. Every now and then she took down the old album and looked at the pictures of them laughing together over candy-colored drinks, playing Frisbee on manicured lawns, and making silly faces into a black-and-white photo booth, looking at each other with light in their eyes.

To see Lily's parents today, you'd never know they were the same people. Their faces were creased from years of worry, and the light in their eyes had been replaced by the dull glow of fatigue and resignation.

At Stanford, though, her parents had been happy.

Maybe at Stanford, Lily could see what it was like to feel that way. She just needed to make sure Maria wound up there, too.

Lily had told a few people at Acheron she was going to Stanford, but no one seriously thought she'd get in. No one remembered that Lily wrote poetry for the school literary magazine, or that she'd worked her ass off as class vice president ("President" Delilah was pretty much useless), or that her application essay on why the Americans with Disabilities Act had set the disability rights movement back thirty years had been called "sheer brilliance" by all three of Acheron's college counselors. No one cared that Lily was a fourth-generation legacy at Stanford, or that her grandfather's name was up on a sign over the entrance to the political affairs building.

When people at Acheron looked at Lily, they didn't see all the things she'd done. They only saw The Girl with the Crutches.

Lily had been in the popular group ever since she first transferred to Acheron in sixth grade, when her newness and her
crutches made her exciting and exotic. Except for Maria, though,
no one had ever bothered to talk to her about anything real. And
she'd heard what people around here said about her and Stanford.
That if she got in, it would be "affirmative action."

Lily had been in an accident when she was a kid, and even
after all the surgeries she still couldn't make it twenty feet without her crutches. Her legs hurt like hell most of the time. There
wasn't a single day when Lily didn't have to push past the pain
just to swing down the three steps that led to the school cafeteria.

Adults excused her from everything from gym class to field
trips with a condescending look. And these Acheron assholes
thought Lily had an *advantage.*

"I've got an idea!" Delilah said. "Let's play Truth or Dare!"

The room bubbled with excited murmurs.

"Oh, no. We can't! Not after last time!" Caitlin leaned over
and whispered something into Ryan's ear.

Tamika tossed her phone down onto the comforter. "I'll
start!"

The others leaned in from where they were perched on the
beds and rugs, each waiting to hear who Tamika would call on
first.

"Let's see . . ." Tamika always drew these things out so everyone would look at her as long as possible. "Kei. I dare you to tell
us what *really* happened when you and Emily went behind the
Rite Aid on the trip to Monticello."

Everyone howled as loudly as they dared. Kei and Emily flushed, but they were smiling broadly.

God, Lily hated room parties.

It was so hard to care about all this drama. Lily tried to keep track of her straight friends' romances—it was important to play along—but it got so exhausting. If Lily had her way, the whole school would consist of just her and Maria.

And if anyone should win the Kingsley Prize, Maria was the one.

But right now she was only in second place.

A lot of good second place did them. There was no chance of moving up with Delilah in the picture.

Maria might get into Stanford without the prize, but there was no way to know for sure. Winning was the only way to guarantee she and Lily could stay together next year. It was the reason Lily had bought the Ouija board in the first place. Maria had seemed so resigned to losing that Lily had to try *something* to snap her out of it, even if it meant pretending she believed in all the stuff Maria always said about spirits. Lily figured she could move the planchette, tell Maria she was destined to win, and maybe, just maybe, it would be enough to lift Maria over the top.

Lily would've tried anything by that point. She'd even broken the no-drinking resolution she'd been following ever since the end of freshman year just to get Maria into the old dining hall.

The worst part was, Maria *deserved* to win. Delilah most certainly did not.

The only reason Delilah was class president was because she'd thrown a weekend-long poster-making party on her parents' private island in the Outer Banks over Labor Day, right before the election. The entire class was invited. Lily had spent the first week of school slathering aloe on her sunburn, glaring at the hundreds of VOTE DUFREY posters that lined the halls, and listening to eighty-seven renditions of "how Delilah hooked up with the hot college guy from the minigolf place and Ryan caught the whole thing on video." Everyone agreed that Delilah was the biggest badass ever and she'd looked super cute in her purple lace bikini.

The rest of the world had to play by one set of rules, but Delilah Dufrey got to make up her own as she went along. It made Lily want to vomit.

By some miracle, Delilah only beat Maria in the election by three votes, so Maria was named class activity director. She got stuck running the student council bake sales. Delilah's only job, apparently, was to sit at the front of the council room and yawn her way through the agenda at meetings.

But that wasn't the end of Delilah's crimes. Maria should've been captain of the soccer team, too. She was a better player than Delilah, but unlike Delilah, *she* didn't hook up with the coach.

That was the most important difference between Maria and Delilah: Maria always followed the rules.

It was one of Lily's favorite things about her. It was Lily's least favorite thing, too.

If Maria hadn't thought she was following some unwritten code, she'd have turned Delilah in last year when she saw her kissing Coach Tartar in the equipment closet. She'd have taken a picture and sent it anonymously to the dean. Or she'd have pulled Delilah aside during a practice and quietly blackmailed her into dropping out of the election. She at least would've done something when she spotted Delilah snorting up pills in the locker room.

Instead she'd let her every chance to get rid of the witch go by without a word. No one except Maria and Lily—and probably Brandon, since Maria still told him everything—knew the whole truth.

And why? Maria still believed in nice girls finishing first. Someday, she seemed to think, someone was bound to tally up everything she'd done and give her a medal for being a good person. It made Lily want to scream until her lungs ached—because it meant they were still at Delilah's mercy.

It had been Delilah who'd picked Maria and Lily's room for the party tonight. Their room was everyone's favorite hangout spot. Sure, it was right next door to the old dining hall, but the room was also designated as "handicap-accessible," so it was the only room in the whole dorm that had its own bathroom. That way, if you needed some privacy, and you were wasted, you didn't have to go all the way down the hall and risk getting caught by a dorm monitor.

Their room also had a thick gray carpet none of the other rooms had, and that helped muffle the party sounds. Over the past year, that carpet had accumulated half a dozen spilled-beer stains. Lily had tried every carpet-cleaning spray she could find, but no matter how hard she scrubbed she hadn't been able to get rid of those spots.

Tonight, though, stains were the last thing on Lily's mind.

She needed to talk to Maria about what had happened.

Not about the chandelier, or the calls to their parents, or Brandon's two strikes. She wanted to talk about the part of the night she could barely remember.

What the Ouija board had said. What it meant.

Why Maria had acted so strange. As if she knew something the rest of them didn't.

Delilah was sitting on the floor with her back propped against Maria's bed, her eyes heavy-lidded and her head tilted onto Kei's shoulder. She rubbed his knee with one hand and twirled her ever-present tube of clear lip gloss with the other. She'd draped Lily's grandmother's quilt across her lap to keep out the chill.

Maria, who analyzed everything, had a lot of theories about why Delilah needed to do drugs to have fun. She thought Delilah had family pressure to live up to. A profound inability to find release. A deep, hidden reservoir of self-loathing.

Lily had a theory, too. It was that Delilah was an asshole.

And while there were a thousand reasons they hated Delilah, there was one thing that bothered them above all.

Delilah had been the first girl Lily ever kissed.

Kei finished hedging his way through the story about what happened with Emily behind the Rite Aid—it was awkward, since everyone knew Emily had hooked up with a guy from

Georgetown Prep later that night—and Delilah stood up. "My turn!"

"It's Kei's turn," Lily said. "Have you never played Truth or Dare before?"

Delilah ignored her. "Maria! Truth or dare?"

Maria sighed. She and Lily always picked dare.

Delilah lifted her chin triumphantly. "I dare you to give Ryan a lap dance."

The room filled with muted catcalls. Ryan grinned, blushed, and patted his lap. Caitlin and Tamika both glared at Maria, who was blushing too.

Lily wished Delilah were a bug she could step on. One quick squishing sound and she'd be out of their lives. Poof.

Maria was walking slowly toward Ryan when her foot caught on the edge of the carpet and she fell onto Mateo's outstretched legs.

"Whoa, there, whoa." Mateo laughed as he caught her. "I think Princess's had enough party for tonight."

Had Maria done that on purpose? Lily honestly couldn't tell. Maria was a very, very good actress.

"Oh, come on, she doesn't get out of her dare just because she's drunk," Delilah whined. "Everybody's drunk."

"How about if Maria does an alternative dare," Mateo said. "She can, like, name all fifty states in alphabetical order in under three minutes."

"That's the most boring dare ever." Delilah groaned.

Maria sat up. "Alabama, Alaska, Arizona . . ."

It was actually kind of funny, since Maria had just chugged a beer and kept hiccuping. She got tripped up on Delaware and Iowa, and everyone counted down at the end to make sure she really did it in three minutes. When she was done, she was flushed and giggly.

"Austin," she said. "Truth or dare?"

"Dare." Austin didn't hesitate.

"I dare you to tell us the scariest story you've ever heard."

"Whooo!" A bunch of people giggled.

Austin didn't laugh. "You don't want me to do that, Princess."

"What's the matter, Austin?" Tamika whispered. "You scared of ghosts?"

Austin still didn't laugh.

"I've got a scary story!" Delilah said. "This one time, I went running by the lake at night and —"

"Wait, wait, Maria just said to tell a scary story," Kei interrupted. "Not about something that happened to *you*."

"But it *was* scary!" Delilah said. "It was the scariest story ever!"

"You did not go out running by the lake at night," Tamika said. "No one goes out to the lake at night. Besides, the security guards would catch you."

"No, I totally did it," Delilah said. "It was a couple of years ago. All of a sudden it got really cold, like, out of nowhere, and then I heard someone else run past me. He totally brushed my sleeve. Which was weird, because I hadn't seen anyone else running. And when I turned to see who it was, there was no one there!"

"Dun-dun-DUN!" Kei whispered loudly. Everyone, even the boys, dissolved into giggles.

Lily closed her eyes and tried to imagine what it would be like if she really could get rid of everyone else and have the whole world to herself. Her and Maria.

If only there were a way . . .

3

HOURS DREADFUL AND THINGS STRANGE

For the life of him, Mateo couldn't figure out what the hell Maria was doing.

She was still sitting next to him from when she'd fallen, but she was scribbling on a notepad now. Off to one side, in the dark, where the others wouldn't see.

He could've asked her, but ever since he'd come to Acheron, Mateo had made it a policy not to ask the rich girls too many questions. They only got flustered and made something up, and at the end of it he was just as embarrassed as they were.

Now that he knew the truth about Maria, though, it was harder to hold back. Last week, Brandon had told him about her and Lily Boiten. They were "in loooove," Brandon had said, giggling. Maria thought she was probably bi, Brandon said, but Lily was all-the-way gay.

Mateo didn't believe it at first. Both those girls seemed way too uptight to like pussy. Now that he was paying attention, though, he was surprised he hadn't figured it out before.

There was the way Maria was staring at Lily, for one thing. As if she wanted to shove everyone else out the door so Maria could have her all to herself.

There was something about the way they were with each other, too. An easiness. They looked like they could have whole conversations without ever needing to talk out loud.

It made Mateo kind of jealous, honestly. Not of the part where the girls felt like they had to stay closeted—which was kind of weird, actually, since for him, being gay had only upped his stud factor at school. Maybe Maria felt like she had to keep quiet since her mom was a state senator?

No, the part that made him jealous was that he'd definitely never been "in loooove." He'd been hooking up with Brandon for a few weeks, but he didn't see it lasting through the semester. He liked the guy, sure, but there just wasn't that much *there*. It was more of a *we're the only two gay guys in this backwater school, so let's screw already* thing than a Romeo-and-Juliet one.

Or Romeo-and-Romeo. Whatever. Beer.

"Hey." Mateo nudged Maria's shoulder. Another dare was starting on the far side of the room. "You okay?"

"What? Oh. Yeah." Maria shrugged. "Thinking about the match."

Mateo smiled at her. She didn't smile back. Caitlin and Emily had started a contest to see who could touch their noses with their tongues. All the guys except Mateo were watching, rapt.

"Don't worry," he told Maria. "You ladies have been working your asses off in practice. You'll crush 'em."

The girls' soccer team was playing its league championship next week, and it was going to be a lot harder than the guys' game had been. Mateo's team had won easily, and a WVU scout even showed up to watch. Mateo had been checking the mail every day since, praying for a scholarship offer.

But the girls were gearing up to play Acheron's big rival, Birnam Academy. Birnam had won the Virginia state championship two years in a row, and all the girls on Acheron's team were freaking out about the game. Why? He couldn't really say. It wasn't like any of *them* would need scholarships to go to college.

Some people thought the Kingsley Prize committee cared about the team's record, but Mateo was pretty sure that theory was mostly bullshit. Just like the Kingsley Prize itself. He hadn't even bothered to put his name in for the thing. Delilah Dufrey had it in the bag.

Mateo liked Delilah. They'd been friends since Mateo first transferred to Acheron in ninth grade. He could've been the weird new brown kid at school—and the gay one, to boot—but Delilah had started hanging out with him right away. When he told her he wanted to start a Gay-Straight Alliance, she said she'd be vice president. Thanks to Delilah, joining the GSA became cool, and so did Mateo.

But if anyone had asked his opinion of the Kingsley thing, he'd have said that if some rich, dead dude wanted to give out a free ride to college, he should give it to someone who actually needed one. Not someone whose parents could afford the most expensive school on the planet four times over.

The championship game was a matter of pride for Maria and the others, though, and Mateo certainly understood about pride. Soccer was the whole reason he'd come here. Acheron had recruited him from Birnam back in middle school. Offered him a full scholarship in exchange for captaining the soccer team and upping Acheron's diversity quotient. Getting into college didn't feel half as sweet as listening to that crowd cheering your name.

Just then, the air conditioner stopped humming. The hall light went out. The room sank into dim candlelight.

Great. Another power failure. Acheron's electrical system was about as old as the house itself. Someone, somewhere, was probably microwaving popcorn.

The room fell silent. Even Delilah's giggling trailed off. Emily, who'd just been dared to dance like Beyoncé, stopped mid-hip-thrust. Mateo rummaged in his pocket for the matches they all carried and lit two extra candles on the bedside table. Across the room, Austin lit three more.

A sharp clang came from the far corner—the dark, empty corner near the boarded-over fireplace, on the wall the room shared with the old dining hall.

Caitlin squealed. Everyone turned to look in the direction of the clattering sound.

"Emily, was that you?" Mateo asked. Emily had been closest to that side of the room. "Are you okay?"

"Yeah." Emily shook her head. "I mean, no. Whatever that noise was, I didn't make it."

Maria walked unsteadily into the dark, empty corner and bent down. A photo frame lay facedown on the ground. She flipped it over. It was an old picture of her and Brandon from her beach house last summer, in a pink novelty frame that said "BFFs 4-EVA!" in block letters along the bottom. Brandon had the same picture up in his room.

The glass in the frame Maria held was cracked neatly in half, the fracture running right over Brandon's face.

Maria frowned and turned the frame over in her hands. Lily whispered from her perch on the bed, "Don't worry, Ree, it was a crappy picture of you anyway."

They all laughed, even Maria.

It was weird, her and Brandon being best friends. They seemed like total opposites.

Mateo had always liked Maria, of course. Everyone did. She was smart and cute and funny. She had dimples that flashed when she smiled, and she had a way of looking at you that made you feel like you were the most important person in the world. She was the school princess, only one step down from Queen Delilah herself. Which Delilah never let Maria, or anyone else, forget.

No matter how much they adored Maria, though, the popular crowd seemed to think Brandon was barely good enough to be allowed across their threshold. That was Acheron for you. The school used to be a farm run by slaves, now it was a factory for shallowness and broken souls.

And for Maria and Brandon, most of what they had in common wasn't stuff they talked about with everyone else. In fact, they seemed to spend most of their time together talking *about* everyone else.

Brandon had shown Mateo the list they used to keep in his old bio notebook. Freshman year, Brandon and Maria had made up nicknames for everyone in their class. Austin was "Pseudo-Vamp," because he dressed all in black even though his favorite song was "Love Story" by Taylor Swift. Caitlin was "Dumber Than a Dumb Blonde Joke." Delilah was "Her Most Insufferable Majesty." Mateo was "Gay or Eurotrash?" (which made Mateo laugh harder than it probably should've). At the very bottom of the list was a name that had been crossed through so many times it was barely legible. Lily's name. Before she and Maria got together they'd called her "Braided Just a Little Too Tight."

Brandon kept giggling as he pointed down the list. Mateo smiled too. The names weren't really that funny, but he was sure they'd seemed hilarious in ninth grade. He could picture the two of them lying side by side on Maria's bed, telling jokes at their friends' expense. Brandon had been doing it for the shits and giggles, but Mateo had a feeling Maria meant every word she wrote.

You wouldn't know it to look at her, standing there smiling at everyone like they were her favorite people in the world, but Maria knew exactly what she wanted. How much of her was real and how much was her playing at what she thought these people expected from her?

"Hey," Kei said. "I've got a scary story, actually."

"Oh, come on," Lily said. "Just because the lights went out that doesn't mean we have to pretend we're at a little kids' slumber party."

"What's the matter, Lily, you scared?" Mateo grinned at her. "It's just another blackout. What, you think La Llorona's gonna get you in the dark?"

Lily kept her lips in a tight line. Most girls cheered up when Mateo teased them, but Lily wasn't most girls.

When Mateo turned away, he saw Maria looking right at him. Her face was pale, her eyes narrow.

"What did you say?" she asked Mateo.

"What? About your roommate being a wuss?"

"No, the other part."

Maria looked drunk all of a sudden. *Really* drunk. Mateo felt bad for not noticing sooner.

"You sure you're okay?" Mateo asked her.

Maria must've imagined it. He couldn't have said La Llorona's name. No one knew about La Llorona except Maria.

And her old nanny, Altagracia. But Altagracia was dead.

"I'm okay," she told Mateo.

She was not at all okay. Tonight was not a normal night. "Okay, so here's my story," Kei said. "Back in the Civil War, there were a bunch of Union officers camped out here, using the house as their command base, and there was a mutiny, and—"

"Everybody knows that story," Tamika interrupted him.

"The ambassadors tell it to you on the tour."

Maria's eyes drifted in and out of focus as she gazed from face to face. Room parties always felt endless.

"Yeah, but did you know the security guards still hear them?" Kei said. "They said you can hear the soldiers marching out on the grounds at night. They say that one lieutenant—the one who was shot by his own soldiers—you can still hear screaming at midnight when the moon's full."

"Oh, that's so not true," Emily said.

"I've never heard any soldiers, and I've been going to this school since the fourth grade," Ryan said.

"Yeah, that's bull," Tamika said. "Like the one about the ghost of the old lady who's supposed to come sit on your chest and smother you at night. Or the rampaging Indian spirits who stalk little kids. I mean, come on."

"They're not Indians, they're Native Americans," Caitlin said. "And you'd be pissed too if your land got invaded and your whole tribe got slaughtered."

"Yes, please, tell me more about the evil things white folks have done," Tamika said.

"Has anybody ever seen the kids on the lake?" Caitlin asked.

A hush fell over the room.

Oh God. Had someone else seen the kids on the lake? Maria had been sure she was the only one.

"Have *you*?" Austin asked.

"Well, no," Caitlin said. "But you know the story, right?"

"Oh, sure," Ryan said. "I mean, they teach that story to all the ambassadors, too. But it's bullshit about there being stupid lake ghosts. Come on."

"Wait, what story?" Mateo asked.

"The little kids say the lake has ghosts," Ryan said. "The *true* part of the story is, back in the seventies, when the school grounds first got extended to include the lake, there were three kids who drowned all in one night."

Everyone was quiet for a moment. It was one thing to think about Civil War soldiers dying on their campus, but the seventies weren't *that* long ago.

"That's why no one's allowed to swim there," Kei added. "I heard there's, like, a whirlpool way out in the deep part that sucks you under."

"The little kids think there's a bogeyman who grabs you and drags you to the bottom," Ryan said. "I think the school made that up so people would be too scared to go swim there. Like the one about the football players."

"No, that one's true too," Mateo said. "I heard it before I came here. My parents told me they'd kill me if I ever went near the football field during a thunderstorm."

"That's an urban legend," Ryan said. "You can't really die just because you're on a football field and lightning hits the goalposts. Do you pay attention in physics at all?"

"But the one about the lake is totally true," Caitlin said. "There are pictures of the kids who died in an old yearbook. They were a guy and two girls and they were all in, like, a love triangle."

"A love triangle?" Austin said. "Spare me."

Maria had seen the kids on the lake. And there were four of them, not three. But she'd only told Lily and Brandon about that.

Brandon. Oh God, Brandon. She still had to figure out what to say to him about last night.

He'd pulled her into a side corridor that morning after class, breaking away from Felicia, the little freshman who always followed him around like a puppy.

"What the hell happened last night?" Brandon had whispered to Maria. "Did you have a psychotic break or something?"

"Of course not." Maria had shifted her backpack strap on her shoulder, her heart pounding. She should've come up with some reasonable-sounding explanation, but all she'd been able to do since the chandelier fell was replay the spirit's message in her head. The chiming voice she'd heard sing each line as the planchette spelled them out.

"So what was that?" Brandon asked. "How was that thing writing stuff *when you and Lily had your eyes closed?*"

"I don't . . ." Maria shook her head. "It doesn't matter. It was just a game."

"Just a game my ass. *You* took it seriously."

Maria kissed Brandon on the cheek, the way she did when she wanted to make him laugh. It didn't work this time.

He shrugged. "We can talk about this later, I guess."

Maria nodded and promised to meet him during dinner tomorrow at the corner table by the salad bar, where they could talk without being overheard.

She'd have to figure out some way out of it between now and then. There was no way she could tell Brandon the truth.

Maria wished she'd never told him about any of it. The mirror on her grandmother's porch—or the strange things that had happened when she was younger.

It was just that before Lily came along, Maria had never had anyone to talk to. Not anyone who actually understood her. Brandon was so good at listening.

It had been that way ever since he'd first come to Acheron. They'd put him at the bio table next to Maria's, and when he'd been too squeamish to slice open his fetal pig, Maria had snuck over and done all his incisions at lightning speed. Maria, it turned out, was something of a fetal-pig-dissection prodigy.

They sat together at lunch after that. Brandon gave Maria his yogurt as a thank-you present. He told her she had the prettiest eyes he'd seen since Enrique Iglesias's. Maria asked who Enrique Iglesias was. They'd been best friends ever since.

That was before she got to know Lily. Before she understood what it meant to *really* care about someone. To feel like you'd disappear into the air if that person wasn't always right beside you.

But it took years for Maria to understand that. In the meantime, she told Brandon about all of it. The voices that whispered outside her room at night when she was little, low enough that she couldn't make out the words. The time in kindergarten when she woke up in the middle of the night to see her Raggedy Ann doll laughing at her from the shelf over her bed.

About how sometimes, even in the middle of August, she'd

walk past a certain spot in a room and feel an icy chill, the room growing so cold she could see her breath. She'd know someone was watching her, but when she turned, she saw only her own shadow.

She'd told Brandon about the worst time, too. She'd been eight years old then. She was fast asleep when she felt a weight settling onto the edge of her bed. She opened her eyes, expecting to see her mother, but the room was empty, save for that icy chill. And the faint outline of a little boy with black eyes sitting on the foot of her bed.

The boy whispered her name.

Maria had screamed, and Altagracia had come running. Maria told her about the boy, and Altagracia searched her room from floor to ceiling. She didn't find anything, but Maria knew what she'd seen. What she'd felt.

That was when Altagracia first told her about La Llorona. She was a guardian angel, Altagracia said. She watched out for girls like Maria and protected them fiercely. She'd watched out for Altagracia, too, when she was a girl. As long as La Llorona was with her, and Maria hid her fear, she'd be safe from the dark spirits that walked the earth.

Maria had forgotten all about La Llorona, and Altagracia too. She'd thought about her old nanny only a handful of times since she'd come to Acheron.

Today, though, Maria hadn't been able to stop thinking about either of them. Ever since she'd listened to the audio from their Ouija session.

Most of the recording was Brandon giggling and shuffling papers around, but the knocking was there, too. It sounded ten times louder on the playback than it had last night.

As soon as the knocking ended, the humming began.

On the recording, Maria recognized the tune the voice had been humming in her ear. Something about it was a little off, but it sounded like "Estoy Contigo." The song Altagracia used to whistle under her breath as she baked.

"Estoy Contigo." In English, it meant "I Am with You."

Maria couldn't quite make sense of it all. There had to be an explanation. Some key answer that connected all the pieces.

Altagracia had died the summer before Maria's first year at Acheron. She could've become a spirit, Maria supposed, and followed Maria away to school. To protect her from the dark spirits, like La Llorona.

That all felt so far away now, sitting on the floor of her dorm room, surrounded by the people who made up Maria's new world. The Truth or Dare game had gotten off track. Caitlin and Ryan were kissing on Maria's bed. Austin and Mateo were telling dumb jokes. Delilah was wearing that idiotic look she always got when she was high and playing with her stupid plastic lip gloss tube.

Maria peered down at her notepad. She should really double-check the math, but she was sure she'd gotten it right.

That afternoon she'd gotten back her French extra-credit paper, an essay on the paradox of free will in *L'Étranger*. That paper counted as an extra test grade, and she'd gotten an A-plus. When she factored that in to her overall grade, it canceled out the quiz from the week she'd had bronchitis and brought her semester average up to a solid A.

That made Maria's GPA *exactly* the same as Delilah's. As of today, they were tied for first in their class. If graduation were held right now, they'd be co-valedictorians.

"Lo que es segundo sera primero," the Ouija board had said.

That which is second shall be first. Maria had only been behind Delilah in the class rankings by a tiny fraction of a point. Numbers three and four in their class, Lily and Mateo, were far behind them, out of the running.

The spirit in the board had been right.

Valedictorian. Maria could feel it. Standing up on that stage, clutching the podium with her fists, every set of eyes in the room on her. They'd all know she'd earned it. If she could talk her history teacher into letting her do one more extra-credit project, she could surge ahead in the class rankings when Delilah wasn't even looking.

But it was only November. Between now and graduation there would be more papers. More tests. More chances for Delilah to cheat and screw her way back into first place.

And even if things stayed the way they were, being tied for first in the class wasn't enough to push her over the edge for the Kingsley Prize.

Being valedictorian wouldn't make her soccer captain. Or class president. Or even homecoming queen. Not as long as Delilah Dufrey still reigned.

"It's all such bullshit," Maria muttered.

"Sorry, what?" Mateo turned back to her, raising his eyebrows.

"Nothing."

She leaned back against the bed. It was a fight just to keep her eyes open. Until she spotted Lily smiling their private half smile at her.

Lily was the only person here who actually mattered. The one Maria could honestly say was her equal. No, *not* her equal; Lily was better than Maria in every way that mattered.

Lily drew her eyes away from Maria after a long minute. She was in the same spot on the edge of her bed where she'd been since the party began, talking to Tamika about how hot their French teacher, Monsieur Seyton, was supposed to be. Tamika was shooting angry looks at Caitlin and Ryan at the same time.

"Hey, I have a story," Maria said suddenly.

Everyone turned to look at her. "What, another ghost story?" Mateo said.

"Yeah." Maria wasn't sure what had made her want to talk about this. Now that she'd started, though, she couldn't stop. "There was a huge fire here back in the sixteen hundreds. Everyone on the whole plantation died. The family that lived here, their slaves, even their animals. First, though, they all had to go into this dark tunnel underground. Everyone was packed so tight they couldn't move. That's where they died. It was pitch-black, and the smoke was so thick no one could see anything except the fire. All you could hear was screaming. Thousands and thousands of screams."

The room was silent for a long moment. On Lily's side of the room, the candle flames danced in the darkness.

"Did you make that up?" Caitlin finally said.

Maria shook her head, though she couldn't remember where she'd heard that story. She hadn't realized she'd known it until just now.

Huh. Something didn't feel right.

She took another long drink. Half a can, gone. Still, her alcohol haze was fading as quickly as it had come on.

Lily looked at her pointedly. Telling her to act normal. She was right. Maria blinked fast, trying to shake off this feeling.

"This is dumb," Austin said. "Enough stupid stories. I dare two girls to make out with each other."

Everyone laughed, louder than they should have.

"Which two?" Emily asked, giggling.

"Any two!" Austin looked hopefully up toward the bed where Lily and Tamika were sitting.

Maria and Lily locked eyes again. This was the only thing they still disagreed on.

Maria had wanted to tell everyone the truth from the beginning. From the earliest days—those first kisses at the end of long nights of talking; the startling discovery that yes, she really did like girls, too, and this girl in particular—Maria didn't see the point of keeping it a secret.

Maria didn't want her parents to know yet, obviously. Her mother was a state senator, and Maria didn't think she'd take the news well, at least not until she quit politics. But no one bothered keeping secrets at Acheron. It was basically impossible when you lived on top of everyone you knew.

Besides, this was good news, wasn't it? Weren't you supposed to share good news with your friends?

Lily didn't think so. After their fourth straight night of fooling around after lights-out, Maria mentioned that she'd told Brandon, and Lily freaked. She was positive word would somehow get back to her *very* conservative parents. She thought the guys at school would tease them and the girls would be grossed out. She was afraid Mateo would make them join the GSA and sit around every night talking about boring gay political stuff. She even worried it would hurt Maria's mom's reelection campaign.

Maria didn't think it would be so bad if their friends knew. No one outside of school would have to find out. But she'd agreed to keep the secret since it was so important to Lily.

After all, it wasn't as if Lily was being this way just to upset her. She knew how much Maria wanted to tell everyone the truth. There had been more than one night already this year when Maria had held Lily while she cried. Lily always said she wished she could come out, but she wasn't ready. Maybe next year.

Maybe in a few years.

Maria promised never to rush her. She never wanted Lily to do anything she wasn't comfortable with.

Now they'd been together almost a year, and Maria was more in love with Lily than ever. She'd do whatever it took to keep the two of them together, here at Acheron and next year at Stanford.

But she still hadn't gotten used to the constant lying.

Maria tossed her empty beer can into the paper garbage bag

Ryan would smuggle out later and reached for a fresh one. Mateo, ever the gentleman, popped the tab for her and said, "You sure you want to keep going? You look kind of out of it."

"I'm fine." Maria took a long drink of the cool yellow liquid and stood up. The room swayed. Ryan and Caitlin were on Maria's bed, limbs squirming together like some water creature in one of Brandon's manga books.

Maria shook her head. "I'm going to the bathroom."

"You need help?" Mateo tried to catch her arm. "You going to puke?"

Maria ignored him and caught Lily's eye. Lily stood up to follow her, and Maria's rapid heartbeat began to slow.

They'd figure all this out. Together.

4

LEAVE ALL THE REST TO ME

Lily watched Maria make her way shakily toward the bathroom. This might be the only chance the two of them got to talk all night.

Lily reached for the dresser to steady herself so she wouldn't have to deal with her crutches and hopped toward the bathroom on her right leg. Delilah reached out to help, giggling. "Give me your hand!" Delilah squealed.

Lily slapped her away. Delilah and the others laughed.

Lily smiled. They could think it was a joke if they wanted.

"Princess is totally going to hurl, man," Austin told the others. "At least she's got her roommate to hold her hair back."

Good. Lily followed Maria into the bathroom and turned on the water in the sink and the shower full blast. Hot water—it was already cold enough in that tiny room. The others would think Lily had the water running so they didn't have to hear Maria throwing up, and Lily and Maria could talk without having to worry about the sound carrying. Lily shut the bathroom door, turning the lock. The heavy brass bolt looked like it had been rotting in the deep brown wood for the last three hundred years.

Maria sat on the edge of the bathtub next to the door. Lily lowered herself next to her, trying not to grimace as her muscles clenched.

She was tired of everyone's stupid stories. The obnoxious blind girl Lily roomed with before Maria used to talk about ghosts, too. She even dreamed about them. She'd wake up panting in the middle of the night. Once Lily had to hobble over to her bed and shake her until she woke up. She'd been gasping so much Lily was afraid she was going to stop breathing.

Lily had been having nightmares all her life. People didn't need to make such a big deal about them. She never had.

She leaned into Maria's shoulder and rubbed her hands together. Their room was always cold, and the bathroom was especially freezing. "Hey."

"Hey." Maria looped her arm around Lily's back absently.

"Swell party."

"Tell me about it." Maria took another swallow of beer.

Lily took the can out of her hand and put it on the sink. "How many of those have you had?"

Maria shrugged. Lily smiled uneasily.

It had been Lily who'd suggested the two of them become

roommates. That was the summer before last year, when her old roommate finally graduated. There were no other disabled students left at Acheron, so Lily could've had a single room, but she asked Maria to move in. They were only casual friends back then, because Maria was a jock with a string of popular ex-boyfriends and Lily was neither of those things. Even so, something about Maria had always struck Lily.

It wasn't just that Maria was gorgeous. It was more the way she looked at Lily. Like she was *really* looking at her. Really listening to what she had to say.

Maria was the only one in their class who looked at Lily like she saw a girl who happened to be holding crutches. Not a pair of crutches that happened to be holding up a girl.

Lily waited a full minute to see if Maria would start talking, but she didn't say a word. Instead she played absently with the tail of Lily's braid and stared straight ahead, as though mesmerized by the mildew forming in the cracks under the sink.

It was eerily reminiscent of how she'd looked the night before. Staring into that empty corner of the ceiling, like there was something up there only she could see.

"Can we talk about last night?" Lily finally said. "Please?"

Maria shrugged again.

"I barely even remember what happened," Lily said. "Was that real? Because I know I didn't move that thing myself. And I don't speak Spanish."

Maria slowly turned to face her. "What difference does it make?"

Lily laughed without humor. "It said something to you, didn't it?"

"So?"

"So? What did it mean?"

"I don't know."

"Please don't lie to me, Ree."

"I'm not lying."

Lily took Maria's hand and squeezed it. Maria squeezed back.

Maria had a thing about holding hands. She could do it for hours and never get tired. Sometimes she even liked it better than kissing. When you were holding hands, she said, you knew it wasn't about sex. It was about liking somebody and wanting them to know it.

Last year Maria had been in charge of a fund-raising drive for the student council. They were supposed to raise $5,000 for a women's shelter in Lennox. Maria started calling Acheron alumni and made their goal with her very first call, to a lawyer in New York who said she was delighted to hear Acheron was finally trying to do some good in the community. The lawyer wrote a $5,000 check then and there, and everyone celebrated the end of the fund raiser.

But then Maria raised their goal to $10,000. She made more phone calls. She organized parent receptions and car washes. The council members grumbled about how much work they had to do, but no one worked harder than Maria, even though it was the middle of soccer season. They raised $12,000 for the shelter in the end—and the girls' soccer team lost the league championship qualifier to Birnam. Maria said the fund raiser didn't have anything to do with it, but Lily suspected that if the team had won that game, Maria would've looked a lot better to the Kingsley committee.

Maria was sweet, no question. Sometimes, though, that sweetness got in the way of her getting what she deserved.

"I looked up the Spanish," Lily told her. "It said you were going to get whatever you wished for most."

Maria shook her head.

"It did," Lily said. "Didn't it?"

"Something like that."

"Then come on, Ree!" Lily squeezed her hand. "You should be happy! Whoever it was—Jesus or Satan or my great-grandpa James—it said you're winning. We'll get to be together next year!"

Maria shook her head again. "You know how much I want that, but none of this means anything. It's done."

"It's not done until they announce the actual *winners*. That won't be until after Christmas break. It's barely even November. We've got time to change things."

"But it's too late to—"

"Don't you want to come to the same school as me?" Lily shook her head. She loved Maria, but she could be so frustrating sometimes. So willing to accept things the way they were. When Lily always saw the way things *could* be. "Don't you want to win, Ree? Isn't that what you've wanted your whole life?"

That wasn't fair to say, and Lily knew it. Of course Maria wanted to win.

The Kingsley Prize was half the reason Maria's parents had sent her to Acheron instead of one of the day schools near their house in McLean. Everyone knew an Acheron senior always got a spot on the list, and it would look good for Maria's mother if her daughter won the most prestigious scholarship in the state.

Lily hated to picture Maria at some boring, lesser college, like Cornell or UVA. She'd be wasted someplace like that. Someplace where she wouldn't be challenged.

Someplace where she might meet someone she liked more than Lily.

But it wouldn't be that way. Lily wasn't going to let it.

"At least try, that's all I'm asking," she begged Maria. "Don't make me go all the way to California without you just because you didn't want to try."

"I tried." Maria stared down at the floor. "I'll try again. I'll keep trying. Maybe if they'd made me soccer captain I'd have had a chance, but—"

"Wait." Lily frowned, thinking. "The Kingsley Prize. Homecoming. Soccer. Maybe there's a way to do all of that."

Maria's heart pounded. The air in the bathroom was starting to feel way too much like the old dining hall had the night before.

That strange sensation hovered at the edges of her consciousness. The feeling that she and Lily weren't the only two people here.

"Hang on." Lily pulled her phone out of her pocket. Maria watched over her shoulder. She was texting Brandon. Asking him when the athletics department had scheduled the fall round of drug testing.

"What are you doing?" Maria said. "What difference does that make?"

"It's just an idea."

Lily's phone buzzed right away. Apparently, Brandon was still awake, hanging out alone in his room while his friends were all down here. It made Maria sad to think about.

According to his text, the testing was scheduled for Wednesday. If they told anyone where they got the info, Brandon would get suspended for sure, and—

Lily shut off the screen.

"Wednesday," Maria said.

Lily and Maria gazed at each other. Suddenly Lily's plan became clear.

Maria had always regretted not turning Delilah in. She'd be soccer captain right now if she'd told on Delilah and Coach Tartar. She might even have been in the top spot on the list this morning.

Was this . . . her second chance?

"If Delilah comes up positive on the drug test—"

"Then she's off the team, and on probation too," Lily finished. "Maybe even suspended."

Last year two seniors had tested positive for pot a month before graduation. They'd gotten suspended for three weeks. They both had to take incompletes for the year and make up the credits over the summer.

"It'll go on her permanent record," Lily said. "The prize committee will find out. It would go on her college applications too."

"And that means—"

Maria's heart was still pounding. But with excitement this time.

Delilah was high *right now.* Right on the other side of that door. How perfect would it be if she got herself kicked off the team, kicked out of first place in the senior class, kicked off the list of Kingsley finalists?

Lily was right. It should have been Maria the whole time. All of it should have been hers. With Delilah out of the way, Maria could have everything she'd ever wanted.

This was too good to be true.

Wait.

"Hang on," Maria said. "Today's Saturday. How long does oxy stay in your system?"

Lily picked up her phone again and Googled. It wasn't easy to find the answer. They had to go to a bunch of different sites, and they all seemed to say different things. Most said you'd test positive for oxy about three or four days after your last dose.

"Three or four days," Lily said.

"Three or four days."

"So if she took the stuff tonight—"

Maria counted. "Wednesday is four days away. It might work."

"It's five days away, counting today. "

"So we're screwed." Maria leaned over the edge of the tub

and put her head between her knees. It was all over before it had even begun.

"Unless she does it again right before the test," Lily said slowly.

That sensation was prickling along Maria's neck again. The feeling of being watched.

"She won't." Maria kept her head down, her eyes fixed on the floor. "We have practice every day this week. She never parties the night before a practice."

"She might if *you* asked her to. Hasn't she been pestering you to go with her into town?"

"Ugh, yes."

Delilah loved going into the decrepit little town next to campus. In Lennox, the teenagers wore "Jesus Saves" T-shirts, the storefronts had been boarded up for the past decade, and a redneck with a bottle tucked into a brown paper bag sat on every other stoop. Going into town and goofing off while the townies watched with hatred in their eyes had always been one of Delilah's favorite activities, especially when she could do it with Maria.

Lately Delilah had been getting sentimental about school ending. She kept talking about how she was going to miss her friends *so much*. Even though, as far as Maria could tell, Delilah didn't have any real friends.

That, Maria thought, was why she did oxy. Because it made her feel like she loved everyone.

Maria was pretty sure Delilah didn't know how to love

anyone at all, except maybe herself. She'd feel sorry for her . . . if she didn't hate her so much.

"Tell her you'll go out Tuesday night," Lily said. "To that sketchy bar by the Kroger. They never card. I'm out of oxy until next month, so I'll get some from Austin. Once Delilah sees you have it she won't be able to say no."

"Yes, she will. The night before a practice when the league championship is three days away? She will."

"Well, if she does, then when she goes to the bathroom you put it in her drink."

Maria's head jerked up. "I what?"

Lily's face was so calm it was scary. "You're not doing anything to her she doesn't do to herself every weekend already."

Maria closed her eyes so she wouldn't have to see that look on Lily's face anymore.

This was crazy. It was beyond crazy—it was *insane*. Resenting your friend was one thing. Drugging her was something else.

"But—no," Maria said. "I just can't."

Lily said something else, but Maria didn't hear her.

There were rules. Laws. The world was set up a certain way.

Maria's mother was a politician. All her life, Maria had been trained to be the model daughter. Speak when spoken to, keep your hair combed, and don't break the rules. Or, if you do break the rules, don't let anyone catch you.

The problem was, Maria never really *understood* the rules. She didn't get why everyone cared about them so much. She just knew that if she acted like she did, most of the time she got what she wanted. If she studied long enough, she got an A. If she practiced hard enough, she won the game. If she worked hard to raise money for charity, her name moved up the ranks for the Kingsley Prize.

And most of the rules were pretty simple. You didn't kick puppies. You didn't say mean things to little kids.

You didn't put things in people's drinks.

"I can't do that." Maria spoke each word slowly, carefully. "I can't just drug someone."

"She's drugging herself right now! If the test were tomorrow, the same thing would've happened, and you would've been fine with that."

Maria's head was spinning. She didn't know if it was the beer, or Lily's words, or that strange, otherworldly humming in her ear.

She wasn't supposed to think this way.

But what Lily was saying made sense. Too much sense to ignore.

This might be the last chance she got. The only time she could beat Delilah.

Lily was right. She always was.

They weren't doing anything to Delilah she wasn't already doing to herself.

"Besides," Lily went on, "this is what the *spirits* said would happen anyway, right?"

It was hard for Lily to stake her whole life on something an old piece of wood off eBay told her. But if that was what it took to make Maria take this seriously . . .

Maria was staring at the floor again. Lily laid a soft hand on her cheek and turned Maria to face her.

Lily swallowed, but she didn't let her face change. She couldn't let Maria see her uncertainty.

She couldn't let herself feel bad about this, either. Guilt was a weak, useless feeling. Guilt got in the way.

Delilah didn't go around feeling guilty for the things she'd done. She just enjoyed what she'd gotten from them.

"Look," Lily said. "When you show it to her, she'll probably take it. You won't have to do anything except have a drink and pretend to be nice to her. Everything will work itself out from there."

Maria stared into Lily's eyes. Lily held her gaze.

She'd never been able to look away from Lily's eyes for long.

Maria didn't say anything for a long time.

Finally, she said, "I love you."

"I love you too."

Maria leaned her head on Lily's shoulder. She kissed her, right at the place where her T-shirt collar met bare skin. Lily made a contented sound.

"Think about what it's going to be like, Maria." Lily's voice was slow and rhythmic. Maria loved it when she said her name that way. "Not having to worry about *her* getting in our way. Then next year we'll never have to see her again. It'll be just the two of us, in California, away from all these awful people. We can do whatever we want."

"Just the two of us," Maria echoed.

She pictured it. Sitting on the lawn of their college campus, holding Lily's hand, where anyone could see.

Next year they could finally really live.

If they could just skip the part between now and then, Maria would be perfectly, deliriously happy.

She lifted her head and kissed Lily's lips.

Usually Maria was careful when they kissed. She knew Lily's legs hurt more than she let on. If Maria got carried away, if she was too reckless, she might wind up hurting her somehow.

Tonight Maria forgot about being careful. They both did. Maria loved Lily so much in that moment she wanted to fuse them together until they never had to be apart again.

Their kisses were hard and fast, the mist from the shower clinging to their hair and making their skin slippery. This was the kind of kissing that didn't stay in one place. The kind where lips and tongues and voices and breath all got mixed up.

They kissed so long they forgot what they'd been thinking. They kissed so long they forgot how to think altogether. Every word they'd spoken vanished into the steam from the shower. Nothing mattered but this feeling.

Maria loved kissing Lily more than anything. More even than the feeling of winning.

Sometimes Maria would find herself sitting in Advanced Calc at ten in the morning thinking about this feeling. About the way their bodies fit together. The sensation of Lily's skin against her own. The way it felt when it was dark, and they were alone, and all the layers that separated them in the light—the rules and the lying and the loneliness—were gone. When it was just the two of them, connected in a way Maria had never known was possible before.

She pressed her lips into the curve of Lily's neck, the soft place just above her collarbone, and Lily giggled, a soft giggle reserved just for moments like this. Usually, Maria was anxious to tell the world about what she had with Lily, but sometimes she was glad to have these moments all to herself.

Maria slid her arm around Lily's waist, under her shirt, and had her bra unhooked before either of them remembered half the senior class was just on the other side of the door. Then, for a frantic minute, even though they remembered, they didn't care.

Things might have gone further if something hadn't slammed into the wood behind them. Both girls leaped up, remembering the knocking from last night. Lily was scrambling to fix her shirt when Ryan whispered loudly through the door, "Hey, Princess, you done hurling yet? Or can you take a break while I piss?"

Maria turned off the faucets. "You asswipe," she hissed back. Laughter echoed from the other room.

Without the rush of water, the room seemed empty. Whatever feeling she'd had before, of something in the room with them, it was gone now.

But Maria remembered.

She remembered everything. What they'd said. What she'd agreed to do.

First, though, she had to go back out there and smile at everyone. Fake her way through the rest of the night and another three days. Pretend to still be normal.

When she was pretty sure she never had been.

ACT 2

in lightning

5

CAN THE DEVIL SPEAK TRUE

"Thrice to thine and thrice to mine,
And thrice again to make up nine."

A bunch of kids from the lower school were playing jump rope on the back lawn of the main house. They had a whole line of double Dutch stations set up, each counting down to see who could jump the longest without tripping. Brandon was in a hurry—he had to catch Maria before she disappeared again—but he still had to go all the way around the twenty-plus kids. The prepubescent crowd at Acheron took their jump rope competitions very, very seriously, and their rhymes always got stuck in Brandon's head.

"Thrice to the flame in blanket dark,
And thrice again to grieve her heart."

Brandon tried to cut between two sets of jumpers, but the girl swinging the nearest set of ropes gave him some major stink-eye without breaking her chant. She couldn't have been older than ten, but she was scary enough that Brandon backed off and went the long way around toward the top of the hill, where the house sat perched and looming, its white faux-marble columns gleaming despite the setting sun. On the hill beside it, the tiny family cemetery from the house's plantation days rose up, the weathered tombstones shining bright.

"For a charm that's strong and true,
Give what I ask. I'll do, I'll do, I'll do."

Brandon quickened his step as he came around the last group of kids and up the hill. The chanting went on, but soon he was out of earshot.

He'd spent most of dinner helping Felicia study for her ambassador test—she was applying to be one of the student ambassadors who gave campus tours, hoping it would up her chances for the Kingsley Prize when she was a senior—but all night he'd kept one eye on the door, looking for Maria. She'd promised to meet him there. But the cafeteria closing time had come and gone, and she still hadn't shown up.

Brandon had to find her. It had been three days since the

séance, or whatever you called it, and Maria had been avoiding him. The only times he'd seen her were in class, where she was always so raptly focused on note taking he couldn't catch her eye, and that time he'd tried to talk to her in the hall. She'd acted just as weird then as she was acting now.

He reached the big house and strode across the shiny white portico, through the open back door, and straight down the hall to Maria's room. When he knocked, though, there was no answer. He checked his phone. Nothing. This was the third time she'd promised to meet up, then ditched him without so much as a text to explain.

Brandon ran a frustrated hand through his hair and took the stairs up to the fourth floor. Maybe one of the other seniors had seen her.

As he climbed off the landing, though, he saw a familiar black ponytail bouncing toward the end of the hall ahead of him. Was that seriously her? She never came up here anymore.

"Maria?" he called. "Maria! Hey, Ree, hang on a sec."

Maria stopped but didn't turn around.

"Hey!" Brandon jogged the length of the hall to catch up with her. Why didn't she look back? She had to know it was him. "Where've you been? We were supposed to meet at dinner, remember?"

Maria tilted her head. For a minute Brandon could've sworn she didn't recognize him. She'd been acting so strange lately.

Then Maria's face broke into her usual smile. "Crap. Hi. I'm sorry. Lily and I spaced out and missed dinner, I guess."

"Wait, you mean you didn't eat at all?" That wasn't like Maria. Not during soccer season. She was the only girl Brandon knew who routinely went back for third helpings of the cafeteria's eggplant casserole.

Maria didn't answer. Her smile was still in place, but her eyes darted around the hall.

She was keeping a secret from him.

That wasn't like her either. Brandon and Maria always told each other everything.

"Something's wrong, isn't it?" Brandon lowered his voice and stepped closer to Maria. The fourth floor of the dorm was pretty empty—most people were still at dinner, or hanging out on the front steps during these last precious hours before lights-out—but there were a couple of people milling around at the far end of the hallway. "Are you still freaked from the other night? I kind of am. I even had a dream about it. Do you think it meant—"

Maria cut him off. "There's nothing to be freaked about."

Brandon didn't see how that was possible. In his dream, he'd remembered where he'd heard the Latin phrase the board had spelled out, *"Memento mori."* He'd learned it in history class sophomore year. It was an old saying that inspired a lot of art back in the days when "art" consisted mainly of paintings featuring dancing skeletons and creepy-looking guys holding their pet skulls.

In English, *"Memento mori"* meant "Remember you must die."

Maria was Brandon's best friend. He knew her better than

anyone. And he was positive that for Maria, that night with the Ouija board hadn't just been about what the planchette spelled out. Maria had seen something in the room with them. Or at least she thought she had.

Brandon had never totally believed all the stories Maria told him about when she was a kid. He'd believed *her*, of course—she'd never lie to him—but he'd always figured there had to be some sort of rational explanation for the stuff she thought she'd seen.

There hadn't been anything rational about that chandelier crashing down onto their heads, though.

"Well, what do you think it was?" he said. "Some kind of crazy trick Lily planned? Because you can tell her it worked. She officially sent me into full-on paranoia. How could she even get up there to reach that chandelier?"

Maria looked up and down the hall again, her face blank.

She wasn't even listening. This conversation was getting him nowhere.

"Who did you come up here to see?" he said.

The whole high school lived in this dorm, with the classes separated by floor. The first floor was for the freshmen, the fourth floor was for the seniors, and the juniors and sophomores were in between. All the seniors lived on the fourth floor except Maria and Lily.

(Acheron liked to advertise that it had a "progressive" attitude toward housing, meaning boys and girls were "trusted" to live on the same floor and not get up to anything. Which was only one of the biggest pieces of bullshit used to advertise their school.)

Maria used to visit her friends' rooms all the time, but that had been the pre-Lily version of Maria. Now it was rare to see her up here more than every other week or so. When she did come, she usually went straight to Brandon's room and straight back down the stairs when she left.

"What? Oh. No one." Maria finally met his eyes. Then she looked away just as fast. "Delilah."

"Delilah?" Brandon raised his eyebrows. Maria avoided Delilah the way he used to avoid his piano teacher when he hadn't practiced that week. "What for?"

"Nothing." Maria shrugged. "I don't know. We're going out. It's nothing."

"You're going out with Delilah?" Now Brandon really was worried. "What's going on? It's okay, you can tell me. I won't tell Lily."

Maria looked tired. "It's seriously nothing. Oh, by the way, don't tell anyone we're going out. I can't get in trouble again, not with the championship game coming up."

Brandon frowned. Something was definitely wrong here, but he didn't know how to help if Maria wouldn't tell him what it was. "Look, can we talk seriously for a second?"

Maria didn't even blink. "Brandon, promise you won't tell anyone we're going out?"

"Of course. But, Ree, are you sure you're all right? Because —"

"Let's talk tomorrow, okay? I'm already late."

She brushed past him toward Delilah's room without waiting

for him to answer. Brandon stared after her.

This wasn't the Maria he knew. This Maria scared him.

She disappeared into Delilah's room before he could say anything more. A minute later he heard laughter coming from behind the door.

Maria and Delilah? Laughing together? This was even worse than he'd thought.

Brandon was knocking on Mateo's door before he even knew why. Mateo grinned when he opened it.

"What's up?"

"Girls are weird," Brandon told him.

"You just figured that out?" Mateo pushed the door open wide so Brandon could come in. His roommate, Sean, was out. The room was strewn with sports equipment—cleats and jerseys on Mateo's side of the room, sweatbands and basketball socks on Sean's. There was also a lacrosse stick and a stapled packet of papers labeled "Student Ambassador Guide to Acheron Academy," but those were Felicia's. She was always leaving her stuff in her friends' rooms, and Mateo was too nice to call her out on it.

Mateo closed his laptop and Brandon filled him in on what had just happened, leaving out a few salient details. He didn't tell Mateo the girls were going off campus, since he'd promised Maria. He didn't mention the séance, either. He didn't want to scare away his brand-new boyfriend with the news that he may have hallucinated a supernatural creature.

"I don't even see why Maria would want to hang out with her in the first place," Brandon finished. "Delilah's such a fake."

"You think so?" Mateo frowned. He was sitting in his desk chair, which Brandon didn't like, because it only left the bed for him to sit on, and he worried that sitting on the bed alone made him look pathetic. Or desperate. He wasn't sure which.

"Yeah," Brandon said. "She's, like, Maria's most hated person ever."

"I always liked Delilah." Mateo shrugged. "Sure, she's kind of fake sometimes, but so's everyone here, right? Maria's just as bad."

"No, she isn't." Brandon tugged on the hem of his sweater, annoyed. "And she's my best friend."

Mateo's face softened immediately. "Sorry. I didn't mean it like that. I just don't think Delilah's any worse than anybody else. Plus she's fun to hang out with. Remember when we went to Kings Dominion for junior skip day and she made us all spend the first two hours in the lazy river? Most awesomely relaxing day ever."

"Yeah, well, Delilah just likes bossing people around."

Mateo raised his eyebrows. "Maybe Maria should think a little more about relaxing."

"That's not the point." This conversation wasn't going the way Brandon had expected. "I'm just saying, the way Ree was acting tonight, it wasn't like her. There's something weird going on. She might need help."

"Yeah. You're pissed 'cause she's hanging out with someone else and she didn't invite you to tag along."

"That's not it at all."

Well, maybe it was. A little.

Mateo got up from his chair and sat next to Brandon.

"You're right," Mateo said. "Girls are weird."

"Yeah."

"Yeah."

They kissed. Brandon felt less pathetic now.

Still, he couldn't forget that scary look on Maria's face when she pushed past him in the hall. What if something was seriously wrong? She'd been acting really weird ever since the séance. What if she'd seen something that night that really upset her? What if she didn't want to tell anyone because she was afraid they wouldn't believe her?

And what would any of that have to do with Delilah?

Brandon pulled away after a couple of minutes. "I'm just going to go check on her. Really quick."

Mateo smiled. "By all means."

"I'll come straight back."

"Take your time." Mateo was still smiling when Brandon left.

Brandon knocked on Delilah's door, but there was no answer. So he went down three flights to Maria's room and knocked again, covering his mouth as he yawned. He'd been up late Monday writing a paper on *Julius Caesar*, and he'd barely slept since then.

There was no answer at Maria's room, and no light under the door. Brandon was turning to go when the door cracked open and a voice whispered, "Did it work?"

"Did what work?" Brandon said.

"Oh." The door opened wider and the light flicked on. Lily blinked against it. "Hi."

"Hi. Um. Sorry." Now that Brandon could see into the room, it was clear Lily was alone. "I didn't mean to wake you up."

"You didn't. Everything is fine. I was just studying. How are you?" Lily smiled brightly.

Brandon couldn't remember the last time Lily had smiled at him when Maria wasn't there to see. He'd already run into her once that afternoon, in Austin's room, and Lily's expression had been just as dull and gloomy then as always.

"I'm okay," Brandon said. "I just wanted to see if Maria was here."

"No. She's at the bio lab. She got special permission to work there after hours on her senior thesis project."

Uh-oh. Had Maria lied to Lily? Things were even worse than he'd thought.

"Bio lab," he repeated. "Are you sure?"

"Of course I'm sure." Lily smiled that bright smile again.

"All right, well . . ." If Maria was keeping a secret from Lily, he wouldn't give her away. "When she gets back, could you tell her I want to talk to her? She can text me anytime. Even if it's late."

"Will do." Lily just kept on smiling. Brandon didn't trust that smile.

He said good-bye and started back toward the stairs. As soon as he heard Lily close the door behind him he turned toward the front door instead.

The lights in the hall flickered, then went out. A collective groan went up from behind the closed dorm room doors, but Brandon wasn't worried about the power.

Something was happening tonight, and it was connected somehow to the Ouija board. Brandon didn't know how he knew that, but he was certain of it.

Maria needed his help.

The least he could do was wait up for her. If she was so freaked out she was keeping secrets even from Lily, she needed one person she could rely on. He texted Mateo to say he wasn't coming back upstairs after all and went out onto the front steps.

It was still hot out, but the sunlight was fading. There was no sign of Delilah or Maria, but a dozen other seniors were outside, sitting on the steps with books open on their laps and phones in their hands, talking and texting while they feigned studying. They all waved at Brandon, but no one motioned for him to join them.

It didn't matter. Brandon turned on his phone and clicked over to the book he was reading, *The Talented Mr. Ripley*.

He'd wait here at least until lights-out. Then he'd hide somewhere if he had to. Brandon didn't want to think about how much trouble he'd get in if he got caught outside after curfew, but either way, this was more important.

Maria needed him.

6

THE ATTEMPT AND NOT THE DEED CONFOUND US

"Hola, guapa. ¿Qué hay?"

For the fourth time that night, Maria ignored the guys shouting at her from the back of the bar.

Delilah ignored them too and kept fiddling with her lip gloss case. She was just glad they weren't shouting at *her*.

Maybe Spanish girls were used to that. Random sketchy-looking guys with tattoos and accents yelling at you wherever you went.

Delilah always got mixed up about where Maria was from. She knew her house was in northern Virginia, but she'd seen Maria's parents every year when they came to drop her off at school, and they both looked a lot whiter than Maria did. She'd heard Maria was adopted, from Mexico or Brazil or one of those places, but Delilah had never asked her about that. Adopted kids could be funny about that stuff.

She was glad Maria had wanted to come out tonight, though. It felt like they'd lost touch since Delilah got made team captain this year. She wished Maria hadn't taken that so hard. Delilah had thought about asking their coach, Jake, to make them co-captains again, but her dad said Princeton would take a captain over a co-captain any day of the week.

Tonight felt almost like old times, though. Maria had knocked on Delilah's door after dinner and asked if she wanted to sneak off campus to Porter's, the townie bar where you always felt like you'd picked up an STD just from sliding onto a barstool. No one minded, though, since they made their drinks with three parts gin, half a part tonic.

It was hot outside, too hot for Virginia in November, so the girls were dressed in summer clothes. There had been a lot of giggling and peering around corners to make sure the security guard didn't see them as they crept across the manicured campus lawn, silently slapping at the mosquitoes that danced under their skirt hems. They'd run past the lake in their flip-flops, cutting through the honeysuckle bushes that lined the northern edge to squeeze through the gap in the fence, sweat and humidity clinging to their hair and eyelashes. Safely on the other side, they'd kept running all the way to the bar, bright-eyed with anticipation of an old-fashioned girls' night out. They laughed as they passed the old buildings that had been abandoned years ago—the big, boarded-up movie theater, the vacant drugstore with the colony of feral cats in its parking lot, the Dollar General where old men sat on the stoop drinking out of paper bags.

Delilah shouldn't really have been drinking tonight. She had a self-imposed rule about partying before a practice. This year they had a shot at the league championship, maybe even the state. She didn't want to show up at her first Princeton team practice coming off a season where she hadn't tried her very best.

Delilah tried her very best at everything. If she ever stopped trying, she figured, she might as well be dead.

Tonight, though, she was making an exception to her no-partying rule, because that was what good friends did. Maria had acted like the two of them going out tonight was really important. She must have been stressed about something, because as soon as they sat down at the bar Maria had ordered a Corona and downed it in three gulps.

When she was ready, Delilah hoped Maria would tell her what was wrong. Delilah liked to be helpful. In the meantime, she wasn't about to let Maria show her up on the drinking front. They were always just a little bit competitive, the two of them. So Delilah had ordered a Red Bull and vodka, then winced her way through half of it. She finally had to put it down before it burned her throat. Then she made a big show of leaning over the bar's ancient window-unit air conditioner and trying to suck in the cool, stale air. Maria only laughed and ordered another round for both of them.

All night, Maria had been laughing a little too hard and drinking a little too much. When she wasn't laughing, she was staring into space and fiddling with something in her purse.

Delilah hoped Maria wasn't pissed about the Kingsley Prize. It wasn't like she could've actually been *surprised*. Delilah had a higher GPA, higher SAT scores, and better extracurriculars.

Besides, she was Delilah Dufrey. Everyone on that prize committee knew her name.

Maybe it was something else. Maria had been acting strange for a long time. Since last year, really. Ever since she'd moved in with Lily.

Delilah was sort of jealous, to tell the truth, of how those two had become best friends overnight. In her whole life, there had never been anyone Delilah liked as much as Maria and Lily seemed to like each other. Even her ex-boyfriends never got that close. There was something about the way Maria and Lily seemed to read each other's mind that made Delilah feel wistful.

On the other hand, something about Lily had always struck Delilah as . . . off.

Even that one time. At the pool party at Tamika's house at the end of freshman year.

Everyone else had gone in to watch TV, and Delilah and Lily had been the only two left outside. They were lying on lawn chairs in their bikinis, sipping screwdrivers through straws and giggling about nothing in particular. After a while, Delilah leaned her head on Lily's shoulder, and Lily turned toward her. Their eyes met. They stopped giggling. They kissed.

Delilah didn't remember who started it, but it was probably her. Delilah tended to be the one who started these things. Usually with guys, but it worked out the same either way. Her therapist said she did stuff like that because she was trying to "reclaim affection she felt lacking in her immediate family environment." Blah, blah, blah.

She'd felt guilty after the party, though. The next day, she'd seen the sappy look on Lily's face when she swung into French III on her crutches and she'd realized that for Lily, that kiss hadn't been some fun little experiment. It had been the start of something else altogether.

Delilah tried to avoid Lily after that, but when you went to a school as tiny as Acheron, avoiding wasn't really an option. She figured disabled people were probably shy, so she wouldn't have to worry about Lily bringing up what had happened. She was wrong.

A week after that day by the pool, Lily followed Delilah to the hall bathroom during a room party. That was right after Austin had gotten his brother's ID, so both girls were pretty drunk. They'd gone into a stall and kissed again, because apparently Delilah still hadn't learned her lesson. After a minute she came to her senses and told Lily what she should've told her the first time—that she was flattered, but she wasn't gay.

Lily stared at her like she was speaking Gaelic. She stammered out some half apology in that crazy Southern accent of hers. Then slowly, slowly, she backed out of the stall and crutched her way out of the room.

Ever since that night Delilah had always been nervous around Lily. When they met up so Lily could hand over her extra pain meds, there was something eerie about the way she looked at Delilah. As if she held a gigantic grudge. Lately, Maria had started giving Delilah those same weird looks.

Sometimes Delilah wondered if Lily had told her what happened, but she doubted it. Delilah certainly never told anyone when embarrassing things happened to *her*. What was the point?

"I have to pee." Maria hopped off her stool and looped her purse strap over her shoulder.

"Oh, me too." Delilah suddenly felt the drinks she'd had. She uncapped her lip gloss and applied a quick fresh coat. "I'll go when you come back."

"All right." Maria wasn't even looking at Delilah. She was still hunting around for something in her purse.

Maria stumbled toward the bathroom at the back of the bar, ignoring the taunts from the tattooed guys as she passed them. Her phone was in her hand, the number pressed, before she'd even locked the door to the single-stall women's room behind her.

Lily answered on the first ring. "Did she take it yet?"

"I haven't tried." Maria's voice was ragged. "Listen. I don't think I can do this. I'm going to just come home."

"You're *what*?"

Lily dropped the notecards she'd been highlighting and hurled her pen to the floor.

To get the capsules she'd had to flirt with Austin, *Austin*, the perpetually stoned goth loser of the senior class. He'd been playing some video game with Brandon, but Brandon had stepped outside as soon as Lily knocked on the door. When she'd finally worked up the nerve to ask, Austin pretended not to know what she was talking about. She'd had to practically beg him. To stick her chest in his face so he'd remember she didn't just have crutches, she had boobs, too. Only then had he agreed to give her anything.

She certainly hadn't done all that just to have Maria punk out on her at the last minute.

"I can't," Maria said. "Look, she'll probably test positive from the other night anyway. We don't need to do this."

Lily spoke through gritted teeth. "We don't *need* to? Or you don't *want* to?"

Maria sighed. "It's only—come on, she was my friend, once, a long time ago, and . . . I don't know. She keeps acting like everything is so great, and—and, I just can't."

Lily's breath hitched in her throat. Maria kept going before she could say anything.

"It isn't right," Maria said. "You aren't supposed to do this stuff. I mean, sure, all the people at this school are huge jerks, but we're talking a whole different level here. Everybody wants to win, but you don't just turn around and destroy somebody's entire life to get there. If I do this to her, what's to stop someone else from turning around and doing it to us?"

"You're being hysterical." Lily had to fight to get the words out. They were supposed to be past all this by now. "No one will know we had anything to do with it."

Maria kept going as if she hadn't even heard. "If I do this, it'll never be over, not really. Every day, from now until forever, I'll wake up and know what I did."

Maria made a choking sound.

"I'm sorry, Lily," she whispered. "I just can't."

"You're *sorry*?"

Lily closed her eyes and took smooth, deep breaths. She'd been a champion swimmer before the accident, and she'd learned how to keep a level head during meets, even when it didn't look like she had a chance in hell of winning.

Maria was just being Maria. She was a born goody-goody.

But there was another side to her. The one Lily had seen Saturday night in the bathroom. The one who knew what she really wanted.

All Lily had to do was wake up *that* Maria.

It wasn't even hard. All she had to do was say exactly what she was thinking. Including the things she wouldn't normally say out loud.

Lily opened her eyes and took another smooth, deep breath.

"How exactly did you think this was going to work?" Lily said.

Maria cringed at her sharp tone. Lily was talking fast. Like what she was saying was so obvious she didn't even need to think about it.

"Did you think the ghosts in the Ouija board would magically get rid of her for you?" Lily said. "Or maybe we should try sprinkling some fairy dust and see if that will do the trick?

Christ, Maria, were you lying about wanting to come to Stanford in the first place? Are you secretly glad you're going to lose, so you can be rid of me next year? Do you want to just go off and do your own thing at some crappy little state school?"

"Stop it." Maria wanted to cry, but the tears wouldn't come. They never did. Maria couldn't remember the last time she'd cried. "You know that's not true."

"Then suck it up. You promised you'd do this. Were you lying then too?"

"No, I—" When had Maria promised? She didn't remember promising. Lily wouldn't say that if she hadn't, though.

"Do you even want to be with me?"

"Yes!" Maria sputtered. "You know I do. I—"

"Were you lying when you said you loved me?"

"Of course not!"

It was happening. It had already started happening, even before Maria dialed Lily's number.

All night long, Maria had been building up a wall inside her.

She'd been going over all the reasons this was a bad idea. Telling herself she wouldn't do it. She couldn't. It went against her very nature.

That wall was breaking into pieces now.

It didn't matter what Maria tried to tell herself. Lily was right.

Maria knew how this worked. What the board had said. She knew what she had to do.

The world had rules, but those rules weren't made for people like Maria and Lily.

"Then go out there and do it," Lily was saying. "Tell her you've got some of my pain meds, then bring her back to the bathroom to take it. You can pretend to have some too. She won't know the difference. When she's high all she can see are the damn stars."

"She'll know I didn't really do it." Maria wasn't sure if she was arguing with Lily or herself. "If she tests positive and I don't, she'll know—"

"So what? What's she going to do about it?"

Maria shrugged into the phone.

She didn't really care. The details didn't matter. It would still be the worst thing Maria had ever done.

On the other end of the phone, Lily was silent. Maria couldn't even hear her breathe.

When she finally spoke, her voice was so low Maria had to strain to hear her.

"Do I need to remind you what Delilah did to me?" Lily whispered. "How badly she screwed me up? How she made me feel ugly and worthless and perverted? How miserable I was after that until you came along?"

Maria swallowed. Her phone buzzed with a text, the way it had been doing all night. She hit the Dismiss button and swallowed again.

"She's a waste of space," Lily said. "She doesn't deserve your pity."

Maria had never physically hurt anyone in her life. She'd always figured it would only make things worse in a world that already sucked most of the time. Sometimes, though, when she thought about what Delilah had done to Lily, she got obsessed with the idea of how good it would feel to punch her in the face.

Delilah hadn't earned what she had. She'd won class president because she cheated. She'd gotten captain because she'd slept with the coach. She didn't study as hard as Maria, but somehow she always got perfect grades anyway.

She was probably sleeping with all the teachers. The men and the women both.

Delilah wouldn't be in first place on that stupid list if it hadn't been for all those things. Maria had *worked*. She'd earned everything she had.

Delilah got high every weekend they didn't have a game. If Princeton knew that, surely they wouldn't let her in. If the prize committee knew . . .

But they didn't. Delilah had never gotten caught.

What was the difference, really? If Delilah broke the rules to get what she wanted, why shouldn't Maria?

That was what made up her mind.

She opened her purse. Austin had been all out of the usual pills, so he'd given Lily two little red-and-yellow capsules. Same trip, different form. Lily had explained it all to Maria. The oxy pills had already been crushed up, and the powder was inside the capsules. All Maria had to do was open the capsules and pour the powder out on the counter so Delilah could snort it. Or, if Delilah said no, she'd just open a capsule over Delilah's drink and dump the powder in really fast when the bartender wasn't looking. But hopefully it wouldn't come to that.

"All right." Maria swallowed again. "All right. I love you."

"Love you too. Come straight back when you're done. I'll wait up."

A bell jingled out front. Maria said good-bye and turned off her phone, ignoring a bunch of texts from Brandon, then tucked it back into her purse.

To make extra sure she couldn't back down, Maria showed the capsules to Delilah as soon as she got back to the bar. "Want some?" she whispered. "It's oxy."

Delilah's eyes widened. "Since when do you do oxy?"

Maria shrugged. "I've always wanted to try it. It's supposed to be awesome."

Delilah seemed to accept this explanation. She peered down at the capsules. "I thought oxy only came in pills."

"It's inside the capsules, already crushed up." Maria hoped she sounded like she knew what she was talking about. "It's a new kind."

Delilah sighed. "Let's try it this weekend. Practice is tomorrow, and . . ."

Maria closed her eyes. She must've looked as devastated as she felt, because Delilah quickly added, "After the game! Definitely. We can hang out somewhere, just the two of us. You don't want your first time to be on a school night, do you?"

Maria slid the capsules back into the front pocket of her purse. She should've known it would happen this way. "All right."

"Awesome. It's a date. Now I have to pee or else I'm going to pop." Delilah stood up. "See you in a sec."

Maria watched her go. Her hands shook, but she didn't hesitate. As soon as Delilah was safely in the bathroom, Maria grabbed her drink and pulled out a capsule. She tugged on the ends, but the capsule didn't come apart. She put Delilah's drink between her knees to hold it steady while she pulled, holding it directly over the glass so all the powder would go inside.

Finally, the two ends of the capsule came apart. But instead of powder, there was clear liquid inside, spilling out into Delilah's drink.

That was weird. Maria lifted up the glass and squinted at it. She didn't see any residue.

"Hi! You got my drink?" Delilah was at her side so fast it was as though she'd teleported there. She grabbed the glass out of Maria's hand and took a drink before Maria could stop her. "What, did you want a taste? Is it good?"

Maria shook her head. She couldn't speak.

She could take the drink away from Delilah. Make up a story about a bug flying into it or something.

But then Delilah took another sip. Then another.

Soon the glass was almost half-empty, and Delilah was still looking at Maria with a smile.

It was over. She'd done it.

There was no going back from here.

7

PRESENT FEARS ARE LESS THAN HORRIBLE IMAGININGS

A thousand feelings raced through Maria as Delilah finished her drink.

Terror. Regret. Anxiety.

Eagerness.

She was sure Delilah would figure out what Maria had done.

She didn't.

Delilah was making fun of a sophomore on the soccer team whose underwear always showed through her shorts. Maria forced a giggle. Her heart was racing so fast she was afraid she might actually die of panic, right here, in the dive bar next to the Kroger. Delilah just laughed as if nothing were wrong.

She'd gotten away with it.

Lily was right, of course. Everything was working exactly as they'd planned. By this time tomorrow, they wouldn't have to worry about Delilah ever again.

Maria closed her eyes and waited for the satisfaction to wash over her. Nothing happened.

An hour passed. The girls sat at the bar, talking, laughing, ordering more drinks.

Maria couldn't remember how this usually worked, but she was pretty sure Delilah should be high by now. Maybe Austin had given them defective drugs.

Maria started to relax. Maybe this was all working out for the best. She'd done what she'd promised Lily, and nothing had happened.

Maybe this was a sign. Maybe the universe had given Maria a second chance.

Then Delilah started to change.

At first it was barely noticeable. Delilah just smiled a lot, and giggled at nothing.

The stuff must've worked after all. Delilah always smiled a lot when she was high on oxy.

But then something wasn't right.

Delilah kept staring into the desk lamp at the far end of the bar. Maria couldn't remember her ever just staring like that before.

"Wow," Delilah said. "Wow. Wow. Wow. Maria, I don't know what's up, but I feel so good right now. Do you feel it? So good. Wow."

Maria didn't answer her. Her heart was racing again.

Fifteen minutes later, Delilah was still saying the same

things, but louder. Loud enough that people were starting to look at them. Not a lot of people—there weren't many in the bar to begin with, just the bartender, a gray-haired couple in a booth off to the side, and the tattooed guys in the back—but all of them were watching Delilah.

"Wow." Delilah stuck a shaky hand in front of Maria's face. "Look at me, Maria. I'm all tingly."

"Uh-huh." Maria looked over her shoulder.

"Wow," Delilah said. "Wow, Maria. Would you look at that? Just look. Look how pretty it is."

Maria looked. Delilah was staring down at the ring of condensation her just-finished drink had left on the polished wooden bar. Maria didn't see what was so pretty.

"We should probably get back to campus before it gets too late," Maria said.

Maybe she shouldn't have dumped the whole capsule into the drink. Would it show on the drug test if she'd given her too much? Would they figure out what had happened somehow?

Maria slid off her stool and reached for Delilah's arm. "Come on, let's go."

Delilah didn't move. She was leaning down, looking at the counter. Her face was sweaty.

"Okay, yes, it's pretty," Maria said. "Come on now. Hop on down."

Maria tugged on her arm, but Delilah still didn't move. Maria turned around, wondering what she was supposed to do now, and backed into something solid.

It was one of the tattooed guys. He was looking at Delilah.

"¿Qué le pasa a tu amiga?" the guy said. Spanish for "What's the matter with your friend?"

"Nothing's wrong with her," Maria answered in English. She didn't have time for this.

"What's she on?" the guy said.

"She isn't on anything."

The guy shrugged. "She's sure acting like she's on something. You need help?"

"No." Maria certainly didn't need help from anyone who'd greeted her with "Hola, guapa."

The guy shrugged again and went back to his friend.

Maria pulled harder on Delilah's arm, but Delilah had leaned so far over the counter her nose was almost touching it.

"Hey," Maria said, suddenly inspired. "Hey, you know what? There's something really pretty back at the dorm. Come down and I'll show you."

Delilah ignored her again.

"All right, fine." Maria was done playing nice. She hitched her hands under Delilah's armpits and threw all her upper-body strength into hauling her off the stool.

It worked. Delilah landed shakily on her feet, still twisting her head back to look at the counter. "But—"

"I promise, there's even prettier stuff outside. Let's go." Maria tossed a few twenties onto the bar without bothering to count them and put her arm around Delilah's waist, pulling her toward the door.

When they finally got out onto the empty street, the unnatural fall heat slammed into them. In the light of the single street-lamp over their heads and the hazy glow coming from inside the bar, Maria could see how dilated Delilah's pupils were. Her entire body was trembling. This wasn't how Delilah usually acted after a line of oxy.

Maria's heart sped up again. What was in those capsules?

"All right," Maria said. Delilah had gone limp, her entire body sagging against her, her sweat making her slippery where she clung to Maria. She dropped her purse. Maria grabbed it, wound the strap back over Delilah's arm, and heaved her up as well as she could. For a second she thought about going back into the bar and asking the tattooed guys for help, but the fewer witnesses the better. "Let's go."

Delilah nuzzled her face into Maria's ponytail. "Your hair is so soft. It's so pretty. You're so pretty, Maria. It's not fair."

"Uh-huh." Maria took a step forward, but it was hard with Delilah dragging her back.

"I can see every single hair," Delilah said. "They're like little tiny snakes. I can see every single molecule. I can feel every molecule of the air, Maria. Can you feel it?"

"Yep." Maria didn't want to listen to Delilah talking about snakes in her hair. She unwound Delilah's arm and pushed her face away. "Look, I need you to walk. We've got to go."

"Okay." Delilah was all smiles now. "Where are we going?"

"Back to campus."

"Yay!" Delilah skipped ahead. Suddenly she had more energy

than she'd had all night. Well, at least she wasn't staring at Maria's hair anymore.

She waited until Delilah turned around, then took the red-and-yellow ends of the empty pill capsule, plus the unopened capsule she hadn't used, out of the front pocket of her purse, sliding them neatly into the lining of Delilah's purse instead.

Tomorrow. Maria repeated the word in her mind like a mantra. This would all be worth it tomorrow.

Ahead of her, Delilah stopped in her tracks, her eyes fixed on something in front of them. Maria put a hand on her back to push her forward. Delilah fell into step with her, but her stare didn't break.

"Do you see it?" Delilah whispered.

"See what?"

"The air. There are cords in the air. Ropes. Tying the air all together. We have to cut them, Maria. We have to save the air."

"Uh-huh." Maria was getting anxious again, but Delilah was moving. That was what mattered.

"We have to, Maria. We have to save the air, or else we'll die. We'll choke. The cords will crawl down our throats and wrap around our lungs and we'll be dead, dead, dead."

"Right," Maria said. "Just keep walking."

"Unless we're already dead. Do you feel dead, Maria?"

"Will you shut up, please?"

"I feel kind of dead. Maria, you used to always look so happy, but now your eyes, they look dead."

They were almost back to campus. Maria wouldn't have to

put up with this much longer. When the test results came back she wouldn't have to put up with Delilah at all.

"Do you have a knife, Maria?" Delilah said. "Does someone have a knife?"

"Nope, no knife."

"Okay. Wait. Maria. Maria, the air, it's important."

Maria didn't like how Delilah kept saying her name. It reminded her of the Ouija board. "Super important," she echoed.

"Also, Maria, can I ask you?"

"What now?" Maria snapped.

"How did you get that scar?"

Maria shook her head. "I don't have any scars."

"It's dark, dark red. Like a flower. A flower made of fire. It's all over you. You're beautiful, Maria."

"God, shut *up*."

Maria shoved Delilah through the gap in the fence. Delilah went, stumbling. She was standing frozen on the other side in the middle of a honeysuckle bush when Maria climbed through.

Delilah was staring at the reflection of the moon off the glassy black surface of the lake. Fog poured off the water, the way it always did.

"Do you see them, Maria?" Delilah said. Maria pulled her out of the bush. The way Delilah was acting they were liable to get caught, even if the security guards didn't watch the perimeter very closely at this time of night.

"Come on," Maria said. "We've got to get inside."

"I can see them," Delilah said. "The kids on the lake. I can see their *souls*, Maria."

Maria stopped pulling.

She'd only been at Acheron a few days when she'd seen the kids on the lake. It had been a month after Altagracia died. Maria had gone out for a walk in the afternoon and looked into the mist coming off the lake, and she'd seen them there.

Four shapes. Three teenagers and one skinny little girl in a long dress.

They were hovering a foot over the lake's glassy surface. Half-transparent, half in shadows. Outlined in light. Four sets of shiny black eyes.

Maria had tried to tell herself it was La Llorona looking out for her. But La Llorona was one spirit, not four.

Maria tried not to look at the lake now, but it was too vast to avoid completely. The "Staff and Students Shall Not Enter the Lake at Any Time" sign on the far edge. The ribbons of mist in the air above the water. The way the moonlight glistened too brightly on the surface.

She didn't see any figures, not this time. Delilah was still staring, though, her jaw agape.

Back when Acheron was a real plantation, the lake had been toward the back of the main complex. Hardly anything was left now of the original plantation—just the house, the cemetery up on the hill beside it, and a tiny, boarded-up clapboard church that was supposed to be somewhere in the woods.

The main campus buildings, the "state-of-the-art facilities" the school's brochures bragged about, were all on the other side of the house. They weren't state-of-the-art enough to keep the rest of the place from feeling ancient, though. The plantation dated back to before the American Revolution. There were stories about a secret passage under the church the Siward family had used to escape from Indian attacks. During their campus tours, the student ambassadors always said in spooky voices that archaeologists used to poke around in the woods and the cellars, looking for more information on the plantation's history, but the expeditions stopped when the archaeologists started disappearing.

Those stories seemed a million miles away, but now that she was standing here with a girl who was out of her mind, seeing things that might or might not have been there in the dark, the stories felt like they were closing in on Maria—Acheron's stories, and her own. The boy with the black eyes at the edge of her bed. The faraway shapes in her grandmother's mirror.

She told herself to ignore it. She got a grip on Delilah's shoulders, turned her around, and pushed her toward the house, where the nighttime spotlights made the already unnaturally white walls gleam even whiter. Delilah stumbled, but she twisted her head to look back at the lake while Maria shoved her on.

"They're dead," Delilah said. "All of them. Did you see? That girl, I think she was trying to tell me something, but I couldn't hear."

Maria shivered again. She wished Delilah's hallucinations weren't quite so specific.

"Do you ever get afraid, Maria?" Delilah went on. "About the future? About being away from all this? It's so perfect here. I don't want to ever leave."

"Sure." Maria kept pushing. Ahead, the spotlights went out, plunging the house into darkness. The power had gone again.

"We should stay here forever," Delilah said.

Delilah kept twisting her head around as Maria pulled her the rest of the way to the house. When they finally reached the door to the service entrance, the one that never latched all the way, Maria was so relieved she could've kissed the painted white bricks. Now they just had to get down the hall and up to Delilah's room on the fourth floor.

"You have to be quiet, all right?" Maria whispered.

Delilah didn't react. She hadn't said anything since they'd left the lake.

Maria glanced at the corner of the building, the window of her own first-floor room. The curtain was pushed back. A face peered out at them.

Lily. She was smiling.

Maria smiled back. Then her smile faded as Delilah pulled away from her.

"No," Delilah said, too loud. "No. Can't go inside. It's poison. The air in there, it's bad. If we go in there we'll die. It'll strangle us and we'll die, Maria!"

"Shut up." Maria looked around, but there was still no sign of the guards. "When you're in your own bed you'll feel better."

"No!" Delilah shoved away from Maria, her head darting fast from side to side. She grabbed at her throat as if she were choking. Her sharp nails dug into Maria's pale skin, leaving deep red scratches that didn't fade when Maria yanked her wrists back.

"Stop it! Just come on." Maria put her arm around Delilah's waist again and hauled her to the entryway. She braced herself against the door. "The air isn't going to strangle anybody. Trust me. You'll see when we get there."

She nudged the door open and shoved Delilah ahead of her. Once they were inside Delilah was bound to stop talking about poison.

Sure enough, Delilah didn't say another word. Instead she clamped her hand over her nose and mouth, her eyes bulging out. Well, at least she was being quiet.

As Maria pulled Delilah down the hall, she heard it again. The humming. The same song as the other night: "Estoy Contigo." *I am with you.*

This time it was coming from the stairs above them. Maria looked up, but the stairs at Acheron were tall and steep. You could never see very far up, especially at night when the power was out.

"Do you hear that?" Maria whispered to Delilah, even though she knew it was useless. Delilah couldn't hear anything outside her own head right now.

The humming was still there, though. And Maria knew what it meant.

Altagracia was here.

Maria hadn't gone to her funeral. Her parents had said she was too young.

Was that why she was here now? Was Altagracia angry because Maria hadn't mourned her?

Maria had to stop thinking this way. Delilah's craziness was making her crazy too.

She pulled Delilah onto the stairs and dragged her up two steep flights. Delilah fought her the whole way. The stairs were dark, lit only by clusters of candles the students left at each landing whenever the lights failed. Maria moved as slowly as she dared, worried Delilah would accidentally catch her clothes on fire.

"Do you see that, Maria?" Delilah whispered when there was only one flight left. She'd unclasped her hands from her face, but her eyes were still bulging. "Do you see her?"

"Her?"

Maria looked up, startled. Altagracia couldn't *actually* be here. Could she?

No. Maria looked and looked, but there was no one on the stairs but the two of them.

Maria's eyes were big, black holes.

Delilah was sure, if she squinted, she'd see straight through them to the back of Maria's head. She reached out to touch Maria's eyes, to see if her fingers went straight through the emptiness, but Maria pushed her hand away.

Delilah whimpered. She was trying, trying, trying not to breathe, but it was so hard. With Maria's eyes looking at her like shiny black stones, and the woman in the blue dress on the stairs above them carrying the candle.

Delilah could hear the woman's heavy skirts rustling. If she looked at the woman, she'd have shiny black stones for eyes too.

But she couldn't look at Maria, or at the woman in blue. Because she was forgetting. She was forgetting not to breathe.

No! That was dangerous. If she breathed, if she took in even one molecule of this air, this dirty, poisoned air, she'd—

No. No no no no no. Delilah had to get outside, where the air was clean. Where it was safe. The air in here was all wrong.

This air belonged to someone else. Some*thing* else. Something dead.

They were almost on the fourth floor. Almost to her room. The woman in blue was ahead of them. The woman paused at the open dormer window at the top of the stairs, holding her candle up to the window frame. Her dress flowed down all the way to the floor, where the fabric was black and ragged with burn marks. She pointed toward the window, gesturing for Delilah to look out.

Outside the air would be clean. The woman in blue was showing her the way. She was a guardian angel.

Delilah understood now. This woman had been sent here to help her. To lead her where it would be safe.

That was why Maria couldn't see her. Because Maria was dangerous.

Maria wanted Delilah to suffocate. Maria wanted her to die.

Delilah had to get away from her. Away from this poison air. She had to get outside where it was clean. Where the woman in blue was pointing with her candle. She had to—

"No!" someone screamed, but it didn't matter. All that mattered was that, oh God, finally, *finally*, Delilah could breathe. She could open her lungs and take a big gulp of the cool, clean air rushing past her; the woman in blue was gone but that didn't matter either because she was safe now; here the air was clean, pure; it was—

The air stopped rushing. Something crunched.

Delilah didn't think anymore after that.

8

SLEEP NO MORE

Maria was screaming.

Lily could hear her four floors down. Screaming like Lily had never heard anyone scream before.

Lily sat up on the bed and shoved her hair out of her eyes. She cursed her crutches, cursed the three flights of stairs between her and Maria, cursed—

Something thumped outside. Loud. Like a boulder had hit the grass.

Lily yanked the curtain aside. Not something. Some*one*. There was someone outside on the ground.

Lily was up and out the door in an instant, swinging faster down the candlelit hall on her crutches than she could ever remember moving.

It couldn't be. Unless Delilah had gotten mad and pushed her?

Delilah was bad but not *that* bad—and anyway Maria would've fought back, she—

Oh God. Oh God oh God oh God.

Lily shoved the front door open, telling herself it didn't make sense, she must've been hearing things, it was probably just an owl or something, it couldn't have been—

A girl was lying on the grass, one arm and one leg bent under her. Lily's scream caught in her throat.

She moved across the lawn as fast as she could, telling herself, *It isn't, it isn't, it isn't*—

And it wasn't.

It wasn't Maria.

It was Delilah.

But not really. This broken thing lying in the dirt, a piece of bone jutting out of her shin, blood pooled on all sides of her—it couldn't be Delilah.

Lily bent down over the grass and vomited. Then she stood up, wiped her mouth with the back of her hand, and brushed her wet hair out of her face. She went over to Delilah, tossing her crutches on the way and ignoring the pain as she limped on her bad leg.

Delilah's head was twisted to one side, her purse still strapped to her arm. Her eyes were wide-open, her pupils huge. Lily waved a hand in front of her face. Delilah didn't blink.

Lily trembled but didn't hesitate to press two fingers to her neck. Blood pumped under Delilah's skin.

Lily closed her eyes, exhaled, and crossed herself. Crickets chirped in the trees.

She looked up at the fourth-floor dormer window. Maria was leaning out of it, looking down at them with her hand clasped over her mouth. Lily signaled for Maria to come downstairs, holding a finger to her lips. Maria's scream had been bad enough. They had to stay absolutely silent now.

Maria backed away from the open window. Lily could see her arm shaking even from four stories down.

An image entered Lily's mind.

Maria and Delilah, struggling at the window. Delilah, pushing. Maria, pushing back. Pushing just a little too far.

No.

Lily didn't have any idea what had happened.

She didn't want to know. It didn't matter now.

Lily had a job to do. This had to look like an accident.

Or a suicide attempt. Should she try to make it look like Delilah had jumped headfirst? Lily could pick her up by her hair and smash her head against the ground. Or she could look for a rock and crush her skull with that. Skulls were supposed to be really soft, weren't they?

No. There wasn't time. They'd be discovered any second now. Had Maria planted the capsules on Delilah the way they'd planned? Lily bent down again, the pain seizing its way up both legs as she slid her hand into front pocket of Delilah's denim skirt. Delilah's body was warm through her clothes.

Lily kept her head tilted to the side so she wouldn't have to look at Delilah's face. At those scarily vacant eyes.

Her fingers closed around something smooth and hard in

Delilah's left pocket, and Lily smiled with relief before she pulled out a lip gloss in a red plastic case.

Wait. Lily had seen Delilah play with this lip gloss case a thousand times. It was supposed to be clear. But it was red, now, because it was slick with blood.

Lily's hand spasmed. She dropped the case, and it rolled onto the ground. Dirt and dust coated the sticky surface.

Lily cursed and bent down again to pick it up, cringing at the pain. She wiped the plastic tube on the grass, trying to scrub off the blood and dirt. It didn't work. It was caked on too thickly.

She held the case up in front of her face, studying it. The red stain was thickest at the base. It matched the biggest bloodstain on Delilah's skirt. A red-brown patch at the top of her left leg. When Lily had first gotten here, the spot had been about the size of Lily's palm. Now it was as big as her arm, from her wrist to her elbow.

Delilah was dying right in front of her. Soon her eyes would go black and her pulse would flutter and fade and it would all be because of what she and Maria had done.

That was when Lily heard something behind her.

A tiny sound. Far away. But not far enough.

A footstep, squelching in the muddy grass.

Lily whipped around. Excuses flashed through her mind. Explanations no one would believe. Lies her tongue was bound to trip over.

No one was there.

She was sure she'd heard it. She turned to gaze out over the yard, then scanned the horizon.

She still didn't see anyone. The grounds were deserted.

Nothing was moving. No one was making a sound except her and the crickets.

Lily couldn't afford to lose it. Not tonight.

She turned her eyes back to the lip gloss case. Her hand was shaking so much it was hard to focus on it.

What should she do? Put it back in Delilah's pocket? It had fingerprints on it now, from where Lily had touched it.

Oh, no. Oh *God*. Lily's hands were covered in Delilah's blood.

Lily flung out her hands, half expecting them to come loose from her body, separate from the rest of her.

She tried to wipe her hands on the grass. Then she took a tissue out of the pocket of her pajamas and scrubbed at her fingers.

The blood only spread farther. As if it were blooming out of her own skin.

Cursing again, Lily stuck the tissue and the lip gloss in the waistband of her pants, grabbed her crutches, and made her way back to the side entrance of the building. She pushed the door open with her shoulders and swung down the dark hall to the main first-floor bathroom. In the flickering candlelight of the tiny room Lily flung the lip gloss into the toilet and flushed it away, turning the handle with her foot even though it hurt like hell. Then she hopped to the sink and turned on the water.

Blood smeared the handle of the faucet. Silver from the metal surface gleamed through the thick red goop.

Lily shoved her arms under the stream of water, rubbing at her skin until it turned raw and red.

The power came back on with a jolt. Lily clapped a wet hand over her mouth to suppress another scream.

The light stabbed at her eyes like hot needles. She lifted her hands to block it out. Blood and water dotted her cheeks and lips and forehead.

The door swung open behind her.

She tried to think. How to explain, how to —

But it was Maria.

"Oh my God. There you are. Oh my God." Maria collapsed onto the floor at Lily's feet. She leaned her head against Lily's good leg, the one that was mostly fine from the knee down.

Lily forced herself to keep breathing.

"What the hell happened?" Lily turned the water on higher, so they wouldn't be heard, and splashed water on her face and neck.

"She jumped out the window." Maria's words came in short, stuttered bursts, like it hurt to breathe. "There was something wrong with that pill you gave me. She was acting really weird. She—oh my God, she's dead, she—"

Of course. It had to have been something like that. That image, of Maria pushing her—it was nothing.

Maria wouldn't do something like that. She couldn't.

"She's not dead." Lily dried her hands and face. She pulled the tissue out of her waistband and dunked it under the water, too, then dropped it in the trash can under a wad of paper towels.

She looked for stains on her pajamas, on her crutches, but she didn't see anything.

She was clean. Clean enough to do what she had to do next, anyway. To find a dorm monitor and tell them someone outside needed help.

If she did that.

They could just leave her there. Wait and see. It might be better for them if—

No.

"She's unconscious and bleeding, but she has a pulse," Lily said.

"She does?" Maria looked up at Lily, still clinging to her leg. It hurt. "You checked?"

"I checked."

"Oh, thank God." There were tears in Maria's eyes. "I was so scared, so scared, so—"

"I know. I heard you scream." Lily paused. "You shouldn't have done that."

Maria sat back on her heels. Her eyes crinkled around her tears. "I didn't scream."

"You did. I heard you."

Maria shook her head. "I didn't. I knew if I screamed, they'd all come running. I put my hand over my mouth so I couldn't."

Come to think of it, why *hadn't* anyone else come running outside? Or gone up to the fourth floor to see what had happened?

The building was as silent as ever. There were no sounds of feet on the stairs. No dorm monitors shining flashlights into dark corners.

Had Lily just imagined the sound of screaming? Like she'd imagined the footstep outside?

Never mind. They didn't have time to worry about things like that.

"Go back to our room." Lily wiped her hands again. "Get in bed. I'll go tell a dorm monitor."

"Tell them what?"

"That I saw something fall out the window. If they get her to the hospital fast she might still live."

Maria stood up. "Might?"

Lily shook her head.

Maria pressed her face into her hands. "There was something wrong with that stuff. It wasn't oxy."

"It was Ecstasy." Lily turned off the faucet.

"It was—what?"

Lily sighed. "It turned out Austin didn't have any oxy on him, but he had a few capsules of liquid X he got from some guy in town, so I said I'd take that instead."

Lily didn't meet Maria's eyes. Even though it wasn't *completely* a lie.

Oxy would've been too big of a risk. They only had one chance, and they needed something they could be sure would show up on the drug screen.

Lily had needed to drop a lot of vague hints to get Austin to tell her exactly what he had on hand, which, as it turned out, was mostly weed and prescription stuff. Once he showed her those two little capsules, though, Lily knew it was their only choice. X would show up on a test for sure, and it would be easy for Maria to put it in Delilah's drink when she wasn't looking.

And obviously, putting it in her drink was the only way. Delilah would never take something this close to the championship game unless they made her.

Maria was still sitting on the floor, but she released her grip on Lily's leg and stared up into her face. It was impossible to tell what she was thinking.

"You . . ." Maria swallowed. "You didn't tell me."

"I didn't think it mattered, and there wasn't time anyway." Lily sighed. "I didn't think it would make her go crazy."

Maria shook her head slowly. "I didn't know. It's—I didn't mean for this to happen. We didn't mean to—"

"It doesn't matter what we *meant* to do." Lily put her wet hand on Maria's cheek and turned her to face Lily, just as she'd done three nights before. "If anyone finds out what we did tonight, that's the end of it. Of everything. We have to play this right. Go get in bed and stay there until I come and get you. You have to trust me now."

Maria stared at Lily. Their eyes locked.

Then Maria nodded. And she did as she was told.

9

A THING MOST STRANGE AND CERTAIN

A whirring sound woke him up. The power was back on.

Thank Christ. Mateo could barely breathe. The heat on the fourth floor was nearly unbearable without electricity.

He tried to roll over and go back to sleep, but his roommate, Sean, chose that moment to let out an enormous snore. Mateo groaned and grabbed his phone off the desk. It was after midnight. He had a new text from Brandon.

Sorry. I'm waiting up for Maria.

Of course. God forbid his boyfriend take priority.

Mateo couldn't work up the nerve to be annoyed, though. He thought back to the kiss they'd shared that night and smiled. Lately, every kiss with Brandon was better than the one before it. Maybe they were getting to be more like Romeo and Romeo than he'd thought.

Mateo reached down to pull his blankets back up, but they weren't there. He must've kicked them off while he'd slept. He stood up and stumbled toward the end of the bed, rubbing the sleep out of his eyes.

A flash of white caught his eye out the window. There was something on the grass, past the front steps. Probably trash one of the rich kids had left on their way in for lights-out.

Mateo was still rubbing his eye as he stepped closer to the window and saw that it wasn't trash. It was a person.

He knew because he could see their head cocked at a scary, scary-ass angle.

"Hey!" he shouted.

Sean rolled over, blinking at him. "What, man?"

"Hey!" Mateo shouted again. He unlocked the window and shoved it up, the ancient wood squeaking in protest as the glass slid in the frame. "Somebody!"

"Jesus, what's going on?" Sean was sitting up.

"Hey!" Mateo leaned out the window. "Get up! Get up!"

He didn't know if he was shouting at the immobile person on the grass or at the rest of the house. He didn't know if he was awake or dreaming. This would be a terrible, terrible dream.

"Somebody!" he shouted again.

There were voices in the hall. Footsteps. Running. Knocking, on his door. Someone else was shouting, "What is it? What's going on?"

That was when Mateo knew for sure he was awake. He yanked open the door. It was Caitlin, who lived in the room next to his, wearing a long white nightgown and loose, flowing blond hair that made her look like something out of an old, spooky movie.

"Go get a dorm monitor," Mateo told her. His heart felt like it was going to explode in his chest. Somebody had to do something. Somebody had to fix this. "Now! Go!"

"What is it?" Caitlin's nightgown sagged off her shoulders. It made Mateo think of the body in the grass. No, the *person* in the grass.

He closed his eyes. Frustrated tears pricked at them. He couldn't believe Caitlin was still standing here, waiting. Why did no one else understand what the hell was happening? "Go! Go find a dorm monitor. Tell them there's someone outside who's hurt."

Caitlin nodded, her eyes wide. She turned and ran through the crowd that had gathered by Mateo's door.

"What is it?" Ryan and some of the other guys came into the room, squeezing past Mateo toward the open window. "What's going on?"

Mateo just pointed. He couldn't speak anymore. His throat ached.

Behind him, Sean was on his phone, calling 911. Mateo should've thought of that.

He had to get out of this room.

He pushed through the crowd and took off for the steps. People were gathered around the dormer window at the top of the stairs, too, but he didn't pause to look out. He took the steps two at a time, nearly tripping, but he didn't care.

By the time he got to the front door there were already a dozen people gathered on the curving staircase that led to the front lawn. A bunch of his friends were outside. He saw Austin and Felicia, and Kei, and Maria, and Emily, and Brandon.

Brandon.

Mateo ran straight over and hugged him. He didn't know why, but it seemed really important to hug Brandon at that moment.

"What happened? Who is it?" Mateo could hear sirens in the distance.

Brandon shook his head. His face was red, and his eyes were super bright, like he'd been crying. "They're—it's—they're saying it's Delilah."

"Delilah?" Mateo's throat was closing up. "What happened?"

"I don't know." Brandon pointed out to the grass. For the first time since he'd gotten outside, Mateo turned to look. The sirens were getting closer.

A few people—Ross, Maria, and Emily—stood bent over the figure on the ground. Below them Mateo could see a foot in a pale pink flip-flop.

He sat down. Or maybe he fell. There was no way to be sure. One second he was standing up, the next he was sitting heavily on the last of the stone steps that led to the front doors.

"Are you okay?" Brandon was sitting next to him. Mateo wasn't sure when that had happened either.

"What happened to her?" Mateo tried to see if there was a

rock or something Delilah could've tripped over, but all he saw was smooth grass. What would she have been doing walking on the lawn in the middle of the night anyway?

The sirens were so loud he couldn't hear Brandon's answer. A fire truck tore down the driveway. It steered right onto the grass and pulled up to where the crowd was gathered. The groundskeepers were going to be angry later.

An ambulance pulled up next, and the EMTs jogged out. They looked so small. Mateo didn't see how they could fix this. He'd only seen her from the window, but he was certain Delilah was dead.

The EMTs made everyone move back to the steps. Brandon took Mateo's hand. Maria sat down on the other side of Brandon, and Lily sat next to her. Mateo hadn't realized Lily was out there.

"Do you think she's all right?" Brandon said.

"She's alive, at least," Maria said.

Mateo leaned around Brandon so he could see Maria. "Could you tell?"

"Yeah. She had a pulse." Maria was breathing very fast.

"What the hell happened?" Mateo looked around at his friends. They all looked just as confused as he did. Well, except for Lily. Lily had the same blank expression she always had.

"Someone said she fell out a window," Brandon said quietly.

Mateo jerked his head up in shock. "A *window*?"

"That's what I heard. They think that's the only way she could've gotten so banged up."

Mateo shook his head. Delilah was an athlete. She wasn't

clumsy. She wasn't suicidal, either. Unless . . .

"Was she on something?" He whispered it, meaning for just Brandon to hear, but Maria heard too.

"I think she was," Maria whispered. "But don't worry. I took care of it."

Wait. What?

Mateo leaned over to look at Maria again. Brandon and Lily were looking at her, too. Lily's forehead creased.

"What do you mean, you took care of it?" Lily said.

"I went in her purse and found what she had on her when Ross was on the phone."

"Wait, when?" Brandon said. "Just now?"

Maria nodded. Her face was earnest. Like she didn't understand why they were surprised.

"You should give it to the EMTs," Mateo said. "Maybe they can use it to figure out how to help her."

"I can't," Maria said. "I took it inside and flushed it."

"You did *what*?" Lily said.

"Why the hell would you do that?" Mateo gestured to the crew working on Delilah. They were putting one of those braces on her neck that you always saw on car crash victims. Two police cars had pulled up, and the officers were talking to the dorm monitors. "Why didn't you just let these guys do their thing?"

Maria opened her mouth, then closed it. Mateo hoped she realized how profoundly stupid a thing she'd done.

"I was afraid if they found drugs on her she'd get in trouble," Maria said. "I figured she probably had something in her purse, and she did. I was only trying to help."

Mateo shook his head. He couldn't deal with this right now.

"Why did she even have her purse with her?" he said. "It's the middle of the night. Did you see what she was wearing? Was she in pajamas or . . . ?"

That was when Mateo looked at Maria. She was wearing a skirt and cardigan.

She was dressed to go out.

Thunder crackled above them. The rain started in thick, scattered drops. Then the sky, which had been clear seconds ago, opened up, dumping buckets of water onto the lawn.

They all jumped up. The entrance to the front hall was too narrow for everyone to fit through at once, and soon Mateo was soaked. He looked back over his shoulder as the paramedics loaded Delilah onto a stretcher. One of them was holding up a plastic sheet to protect her from the rain. A new burst of thunder overhead was so loud, one of the girls cried out.

Mateo reached the shelter of the doorway, but instead of going inside he turned around to watch. As soon as the stretcher was loaded inside, the paramedics slammed the doors and the ambulance peeled out over the grass, water spewing up behind its tires.

A few EMTs had stayed behind to clean things up. With Delilah gone, no one seemed to be in a particular hurry anymore. Mateo jogged out onto the grass, ignoring the water that poured over his head. The first paramedic he reached was a young guy, probably not much older than Mateo.

"Is she going to be okay?" Mateo said.

The guy looked at Mateo and raised his voice to be heard over the pounding rain. "She a friend of yours?"

"Yeah."

"Well, we don't know, really," the guy said. "She must've fallen from pretty high up. She lost a lot of blood."

"Did she break any bones? What about her head, did she hurt it?"

"She'll need an X-ray, but probably several broken bones, yeah. Listen, you should get back inside. Someone from the hospital will call the school and let you know how she is."

"Is she going to live?" The words were out before Mateo could stop them.

The paramedic wiped the water out of his face. "Look, you should talk to one of your teachers or something. They'll know more than I do once the hospital calls."

Mateo nodded. He went to stuff his hands in the pockets of his jeans when he realized he wasn't wearing jeans. He'd run outside in his T-shirt and boxers. Christ.

He turned and followed the others inside. The dorm monitors were telling people that if they wanted to hear the news about Delilah when the hospital called, they should wait in the second-floor common room. Mateo went upstairs to get dressed, then joined the others.

They waited four hours.

Mateo couldn't sit still. He paced across the common room. He climbed the stairs, up and back down again and again. He wandered out the door, through the front lawn. The groundskeepers were already out, cleaning up the spot where Delilah had lain. Leave it to Acheron to start sweeping up the mess before dawn even broke.

Mateo nodded at two of the groundskeepers he knew, Peter and Daniel, and they nodded back, their lips tight. Sometimes when he saw these guys out on campus Mateo would stop and talk to them—the groundskeepers and the cafeteria workers were the only people here he could count on to speak Spanish—but he couldn't imagine doing that tonight. He went back to the common room.

Nearly everyone else had gone back to their rooms or fallen asleep in the stiff-backed chairs by the time Ross and the cop came in. Ross looked awful, his shirt still wet from the rain and his eyes red, a paper coffee cup clutched tight in his hand. He went over to a girl who was crying and gave her a hug. The cop sat down and wrote something on a clipboard. Ross turned to the room and said, as though he was already tired of saying it, that Delilah was still alive, she was in surgery, and she'd tested positive for drugs.

Everyone gasped. Mateo rolled his eyes. Like everyone didn't know Delilah liked to party.

Then the cop told them what drug the test had found. LSD. LSD?

Delilah did oxy. Everyone knew that. They knew it as well as they knew their own names.

What the hell was Delilah doing? Dropping acid by herself

and jumping out of windows?

That wasn't like her. Not with a championship game three days away.

Or was it? Delilah had been high more and more often lately, Mateo had noticed. A couple of weeks ago he'd asked her if she was okay. She'd laughed him off, and he'd let it go.

He should've kept asking.

Where had she gotten LSD, anyway? Mateo's eyes roamed the room for Austin, the only person at Acheron who might have something stronger than pot on hand. But Austin wasn't there. A lot of people had gone upstairs already. Brandon was one of them—not because he was tired but because he couldn't deal with sitting in this room any longer. Mateo texted him with the news about Delilah and looked around to see who else was still awake.

Caitlin and Tamika were sleeping in the corner. Ryan was staring at his phone, bleary-eyed. Maria and Lily seemed to be alert, though. They were slumped against each other in the far corner of the room, but their eyes were open.

They both looked terrible. Lily's dirty-blond hair had fallen into her face, and she hadn't even bothered brushing it back. She kept fidgeting with her hands, sliding them in and out of her pockets, her fingers twitching. Maria looked even worse, with her sweaty hair and ashen face covered in tear streaks. She'd changed clothes, Mateo noticed. Instead of the skirt and sweater from earlier, she was wearing sweatpants thrown on over pajamas, like the other girls.

Mateo got up, his joints stiff from sitting hunched over for so long, and went over to the empty chair next to Maria. Both girls turned to look at him without much interest.

"So, that's weird," Mateo said. "LSD?"

"Yeah, weird," Maria said.

"Any idea where she got it?" he said. "I thought Austin didn't usually sell hard stuff."

"He doesn't." Maria lowered her voice to a whisper, even though everyone else was too far away to hear. "She could've gotten it from anyone. A townie, probably."

"She went and bought acid from a townie and dropped it on a random Tuesday right before the league championship?"

"I don't know, okay?" Maria's eyes crinkled. "I wish it wasn't true. I wish none of it had ever happened."

"Hey, we all do, right?" Mateo said.

Lily patted Maria's hand and made a soothing noise. That was the most overt display of affection Mateo had ever seen pass between them.

"She was acting kind of strange." Maria stared down at a stack of old yearbooks on the coffee table. "Talking about the future. About being scared, and stuff."

"She was?" Mateo sat up straight. "What did she say? When did you talk to her, tonight?"

"I don't remember what she said exactly." Maria dabbed at her eyes. "Will you stop asking questions? You're making me feel worse."

"Sorry," Mateo said. "This whole thing just doesn't make

sense. I mean—it sucks so much."

"Yeah, it does." Maria's eyes were red.

Mateo watched her for another minute, then got up. "I'm going to go see if the cop knows anything."

"He won't," Lily said.

How did she know that?

Mateo hesitated and looked down at Lily. She looked right back at him, with that same vacant expression. Sometimes Lily creeped him out.

"I'm just going to check." He left before Lily's eyes could bore into him any deeper.

The cop was sitting in the chair just outside the glass-walled administration office. Ross was inside on the phone. Mateo sat in the empty seat next to the cop and tried to remember how his father always said to deal with police officers. The trick was to be extremely polite and say as few words as possible. They were less likely to notice your accent that way.

"Thanks for helping our friend, sir," Mateo said.

The cop didn't look up from his clipboard. "Sure thing."

"So, uh . . ." Mateo didn't know what to ask. He just wanted to know something more than the few words Ross had told them. "Are you guys, like, looking for clues and stuff?"

The cop looked up then. "Clues?"

"Yeah. You know. Fingerprints. Crushed blades of grass. DNA evidence. In case of, like, foul play." As Mateo spoke, though, he thought about Peter and Daniel and the crew outside, cleaning up the lawn.

The cop wiped his upper lip with his sleeve. "Well, I'm not really at liberty to say."

"Oh. Okay." Mateo felt like an idiot, just like he had with the paramedic. At least this time he had clothes on.

"But I'll tell you, kid," the cop went on, turning back toward his clipboard, "this stuff, it isn't like it is on TV. Usually, in real life, when a girl does LSD and jumps out a window, that's the only clue you need."

"Oh."

The cop stood up. "Hey, listen. I'm sorry about your friend."

"Thanks," Mateo said.

The cop brushed off his pants and went into the office to talk to Ross.

Lightning struck outside the window behind him. It was so bright and loud Mateo held up a hand to shield his eyes.

This was pointless. He didn't need to be here. Delilah wasn't coming back tonight. He should be with Brandon.

Mateo started up the stairs.

Brandon had been desperate to get out of that waiting room. Mateo and Maria and his roommate, Jamie, and everyone else were still down there, but Brandon couldn't take it any longer.

He hated seeing his friends that way. He hated everything about this.

He wasn't quite sure what "this" was, exactly. He only knew he could've done something to stop what had happened, and he hadn't.

He'd waited on the front steps for hours, scanning the horizon for any sign of Maria and Lily, until it was too dark to see anything. Then he'd kept waiting after that. When it was two minutes until lights-out and everyone else was filing inside, he'd stayed where he was, sending Maria text after text. Then Tony, the campus security guard, came over. All it took was one stern look before Brandon was walking inside after everybody else.

Thinking about his two strikes. Thinking about getting in trouble with his dad.

He should've said to hell with all that. He should've snuck off campus and gone looking for them. He could've found them before they—

Before they what, exactly? Where the hell had Maria and Delilah gone? And if they'd gone out together, how had Delilah wound up jumping out a window and Maria wound up sitting miserably in the common room?

There must've been something he could've done tonight. Before tonight, even.

He could've been nicer to Delilah. He could've tried to help her before she moved on from oxy to acid to whatever else if she hadn't jumped out that window and gotten caught.

Of course, she would've gotten caught even if she hadn't jumped out the window. Tomorrow was the surprise drug test. Brandon had spent the afternoon working in the athletics office, pretending to laugh at the assistant coaches' dirty jokes while he printed out the consent forms and set up the equipment for the testing company.

Had Delilah known about the test somehow? Lily and Maria had promised not to tell anyone, but what if they had? Was Delilah sending out a cry for help, like they'd been warned about in eighth-grade health class?

Or maybe it wasn't really about the drugs. Maybe the drugs had just given Delilah permission to do something she'd wanted to do anyway.

If that was it, well . . . Brandon could understand that.

Middle school had been awful. In seventh grade, every day when he woke up—when he realized it was another day, that he'd have to see *those* kids again, put his head down and pretend he couldn't hear them *again*, put every bit of energy he had into not crying *again*—it felt like a weight on his chest that only got heavier every time. Seventh grade was when his panic attacks started getting worse. That only gave the people at school another reason to laugh at him.

There was a big church in his hometown that had a bell tower. His mom used to drive by it on their way to the Walmart. Sometimes Brandon would look up at that tower and wonder what it would feel like. Maybe it would feel like freedom. Anything would feel freer than having to face school every single day.

Things had gotten better since he'd come to Acheron. It had been years since he'd last thought about that bell tower. About what it would feel like to fly.

Everything was different when you didn't have to be alone.

But Delilah hadn't been alone. She was constantly surrounded by people.

Maybe she'd been just as alone anyway, and no one had noticed.

A sudden knock on the door made him jump. It sounded too much like the knocking they'd heard that night in the old dining room.

That was stupid. Brandon shook it off and opened the door. Sure enough, there was nothing sinister on the other side. Instead, there was Mateo.

Despite everything—the fear and the anxiety and the guilt and all the other stuff he didn't have words for—Brandon smiled. Mateo smiled back.

He closed the door behind him.

Maria barely noticed the roll of thunder that rocked the building as she sank deeper into the seat next to Lily. She'd give anything to collapse at Lily's feet again and have Lily tell her what to do next.

But she couldn't do that. She had a part to play. She had to sit here and act like she wasn't screaming inside.

If only she could hit Rewind. Go back to that moment, sitting at the bar, with the capsule in her hand. The capsule of who the hell knew what. Oxy? Ecstasy? LSD? She'd lost track.

If only she could tuck it back in her purse. Go on with her night. Pretend to laugh at Delilah's jokes. Take her home, go to bed, and wake up tomorrow, ready for another day in Delilah's shadow.

It would be better than this. Anything would be.

Nothing was ever going to be right again. Every day, for the rest of her life, she'd remember what she'd done.

She hadn't seen Delilah since she'd disappeared out the window. It had happened so fast. All she'd gotten was a glimpse of Delilah's blond hair ducking out of sight. Then she'd seen Delilah's shoe come off, falling out the window a second after she did.

Maria looked again at the police officers. Another one had come in a minute ago, a woman. She was typing something on her phone. The other one was accepting a fresh cup of coffee from Ross. Neither of them seemed likely to haul Maria off to jail anytime soon.

But the doctors and the detectives were bound to figure out someone had slipped the drug to Delilah. They'd find out who Delilah had gone out with that night, and it would all be over.

It was only supposed to be oxy.

Lily lied to her. Why did Lily lie to her?

Ross came out of the office. He went up to the policewoman and muttered something to her. She shook her head.

"What does that mean?" Maria whispered. "Does that mean Delilah's—"

"Shh." Lily tilted her head toward the office. Maria got the idea and leaned in too, trying to hear.

The woman beckoned to the other officer to join them. The three of them spoke in hushed tones. Maria could only hear a few snatches of conversation. "Parents on their way . . . outcome is uncertain . . . criminal charges."

At that last one, Maria and Lily locked eyes. Lily was biting her lip. It was the first time all night Maria had seen her look nervous.

Finally Ross came to stand in the middle of the room.

"Hey, folks," he said to the silent group. Everyone sat up. The people who were asleep were nudged awake, rubbing their eyes.

"We're probably not going to know anything more tonight." Ross looked around into each student's face. He had such kind eyes. "I know you all care about Delilah, but you might as well go on back to your rooms."

Caitlin raised her hand, the same hesitant way she did in class. Instinctively, Maria turned to Lily—they always rolled their eyes at each other when Caitlin did things like that—but Lily was still watching Ross. Her face had gone back to the same immobile expression she'd had ever since Maria had found her washing her hands in the bathroom.

"Has she woken up?" Caitlin asked.

Ross shook his head. "She's still in surgery. Even if she comes out of the coma, she won't be awake for several hours at the earliest."

God. Maria had sent someone into a *coma*.

"I don't want to go yet," Tamika said. She was crying. Crying because of what Maria had done. "Can't we wait until you know something more?"

The cops shrugged and turned to Ross. The three of them muttered together again.

Rain pounded against the windows. That sound usually

made Maria sleepy. After tonight, she couldn't imagine ever sleeping again.

She kept her eyes on the cops. A pair of handcuffs was tucked into the man's back waistband. When they found out what she'd done, would she be led away in those? Stuck in a cell with gang members and prostitutes? God, what would her mother say?

"How long do you think we have to stay down here?" Maria whispered to Lily.

"Shh." Lily's eyes darted around the room, but no one was watching them. "We stay as long as everyone else stays."

"They make me nervous. Those cops."

"Yeah, well, stop looking at them. You're acting suspicious."

"What if Delilah wakes up and tells them what happened? We have to do something. I just can't think of what. I can't think at all."

Maria's mind was swimming. Thoughts looped around each other in useless circles.

She wanted to move backward, not forward. But she couldn't do that. She could only cover up what she'd done.

Was she really supposed to just pretend she was the same person she'd been this morning?

Next to her, Lily shifted in her seat.

"Maybe she won't wake up," Lily muttered.

"Won't wake up? What, *ever*?" Maria pictured Delilah staying in that coma forever. A vegetable, even when they were all old and wrinkled.

Lily sighed. "She's already as good as gone."

No. It couldn't be true.

A sixty-year coma was the worst thing Maria could imagine. Surely Lily wasn't saying . . .

"If Mateo hadn't seen her out the window . . ." Lily muttered, her voice even softer than before. She stared out the window at the pounding rain. She looked like she'd forgotten Maria was there. ". . . it could've been morning before they found her."

Maria shook her head. "You said you were going to tell someone. A dorm monitor. You were going to go tell someone when I went back to the room."

Lily didn't respond.

Maria shook her head again. "If they didn't find her until morning, by then she'd have been . . ."

Maria grabbed Lily's chin and pulled her around to face her.

She saw it there. The dark, empty look in Lily's deep blue eyes.

Lily was saying exactly what Maria thought she was. And she was right.

Delilah wasn't going to spend sixty years in a coma. She was either going to wake up—or she was going to die. But it would be better for them if she died.

And it would be best of all if she did it soon.

ACT 3

in
rain

10

I FEAR YOU PLAYED MOST FOULLY FOR iT

Brandon was dreaming.

He knew it was a dream. He'd been having this dream for three years. But knowing it was a dream didn't stop it from scaring him to tears every time.

Tonight, though, was the worst the dream had ever been. Tonight, he couldn't wake up.

"Stop it!" Brandon shouted. He didn't know if he was shouting out loud or only in his dream. He hoped it was out loud. Maybe then he'd wake up. "Leave me alone!"

The man in his dream—his name was Rafael Martinez. Brandon hadn't known his name when it happened in real life, but in the dream he always did. It was the only thing that kept Brandon sane. *I know who he is—so this can't be real.*

Rafael lifted the knife. Brandon couldn't remember if the real knife had gleamed as brightly as the dream knife always did. Surely men like Rafael didn't go home and polish their knives every night. He'd probably just carried a cheap pocketknife. Nothing that had any right to be so scary. Except that anything's scary when someone's holding it in front of your stomach like they're about to slice out your entrails.

"Give it over, faggot," dream Rafael said, just like the real Rafael had.

Brandon wished his dream self were cleverer than the real Brandon had been that day. He wished he could come back to Rafael with a witty retort.

It didn't matter. The dream always played out the same way. He could only say and do the things he'd said and done when it had really happened.

Rafael, though, changed from dream to dream. He got worse every time.

The real Rafael hadn't been much taller than Brandon, and he'd had darting, nervous eyes and tobacco-stained fingers. The dream Rafael was ten feet tall, with long, sharp teeth that glinted when he spoke and huge hands that curved up like claws.

So dream Brandon cried, just like the real Brandon had that day. And as soon as the first tear leaked from his eye, the panic came on.

The panic attacks had started in kindergarten, when his parents used to fight a lot. Out of nowhere, Brandon would suddenly get terrified, and then he couldn't breathe, and then the earth would fall out from under his feet. It felt like he was dying. After his dad moved out, the attacks started to fade. He hadn't had one for six months before that day with Rafael, and he hadn't had any more since he'd left for Acheron. But every time he had this dream, he could feel the attack coming on just as clearly as it had that afternoon.

He couldn't breathe. Couldn't speak. Couldn't move. The knife Rafael thrust toward his face was hazy in his blurred vision. He was certain he was going to die.

Brandon had to try three times to pull his arms out of the straps of his backpack and hand it to the man with the knife. There wasn't even anything valuable inside—only his textbooks, his costume from the school play, and his wallet with a couple of dollars and his student ID—but Rafael never looked inside. Instead he swung the backpack over his shoulder and held the knife up in front of Brandon's face.

Just long enough for the panic to fade. For Brandon to think he really *was* about to die. To wonder how much it would hurt.

Then Rafael turned and ran, the soles of his sneakers pounding against the pavement. He looked back over his shoulder to make sure Brandon had stayed put. That was the last time Brandon saw his face.

It was getting dark. A streetlight came on. Rafael's eyes gleamed in the reflected light.

The dream should've been over.

It wasn't. Brandon knew how this part went. He knew Rafael would be back.

When Brandon used to have this dream, the cycle would simply repeat itself until he woke up. Rafael would come back and draw the knife. Brandon would cry. He'd panic. Rafael would threaten him, and then he'd take the backpack and run away, his eyes glinting. Again. And again.

Ever since they'd used the Ouija board, the end of the dream had changed. Now, when Rafael came back, it wasn't the same all-powerful man with the gleaming knife and eyes. It was the real Rafael. The dead one.

That day, after Brandon had told his mother what happened and she'd called 911, a couple of cops had gone out to look at the spot where it had happened. They'd said there wasn't much point checking it out, though. Sidewalk muggings didn't usually leave much evidence behind.

They were wrong. The cops found Rafael a block from where Brandon last saw him. It was the blood that had led them there. He'd been dragged under a bush, but the sidewalk next to him was drenched in red. He'd died of it—of blood loss—after a dozen or so knife wounds.

"Probably gang-related," the cop had told Mrs. Stuart while Brandon watched from the couch, still wrapped in the blanket his mother had folded over his shoulders when he'd first come home. "Whoever it was, they took the backpack. Must've thought it was drugs."

In the three years that had passed, Brandon had never been able to decide whether he was glad he knew what had happened to Rafael. At least he didn't have to worry about ever seeing him again. Still, he'd always know he'd contributed to the death of another human being.

Now that he'd had this dream every night since that damn Ouija board, though, he knew the answer. He wished he didn't know Rafael was dead.

Anything would be better than being visited in his dreams by this creature. This boy, not much older than him, who was covered in blood that ran from gaping holes in his flesh. Rafael still gripped the tattered remains of Brandon's backpack in his shriveled, bony fingers. He grinned at Brandon with those same long teeth, but the whites of his eyes were streaked with yellow.

"Leave me alone," dream Brandon told the creature. This time it came out as a moan.

Usually, the dream went on this way for hours. Tonight, though, Rafael faded away. Brandon wasn't on the street anymore. He was in his bed, in his dorm room, in the dark. He was awake.

And there was something in the corner.

Brandon tried to sit up. He couldn't move. Couldn't even lift his head.

The shadow was moving toward him.

Brandon tried to squint, but his eyes were as frozen as the rest of him. All he could see was darkness.

A weight settled onto the edge of his bed. The mattress sank under it, tilting Brandon forward.

He could see it now. Her. An old woman with black hair, dark skin, and black veins running up her arms. A long veil covered her face.

It—she—was moving closer to him. Gliding.

She climbed onto his chest.

A great weight pressed on him. He couldn't breathe.

He was panicking again.

Brandon tried to push the woman off him. He couldn't lift his arms.

He tried to take a gulp of air. Nothing came.

There was nothing he could do. He couldn't breathe. Couldn't speak.

He was going to die after all.

The woman above him laughed, a deep, throaty sound. She murmured something he couldn't hear in a language he didn't know.

Brandon tried to heave his chest. To see the thing's face. To breathe in, to fight—

He was paralyzed where he lay.

The old woman lifted her veil, and she wasn't old at all. Not anymore. She was young and beautiful.

She was Maria.

The scream died in Brandon's throat.

"Hey! Dude!" The voice came from so far away Brandon didn't think it was real at first. "Hey, wake up!"

Something squeezed his hand. Brandon jerked away, out of the thing's grip.

He could move again.

He jumped up, pulled away, tried to make his legs work so he could run. It—that thing—whatever it was, it couldn't have him.

"No!" he cried.

He was breathing.

Oh, thank God, he was *breathing*.

The thing that looked like Maria was gone.

Brandon rolled onto his side, taking in the dull glow of the desk lamp, the still-unfamiliar sheets, the empty bed on the other side of the room under the vintage poster of Carrie Fisher in a gold bikini.

This wasn't even his room. It was Mateo's.

He'd imagined the whole thing.

"Hey." Mateo was shaking his shoulder. "You all right? Were you having a nightmare?"

"Uh." Brandon sat up and hugged his knees. "I guess."

"The same one again?"

"Kind of." Brandon wished he hadn't told Mateo about that. The dreams had been embarrassing even before zombie Rafael had shown up.

Mateo put down the battery-powered lamp he'd been holding over Brandon. "It's a rough night all around." He rubbed Brandon's shoulders. It would've felt nice if only Brandon could stop trembling. "I had a bad dream too. Hey, did I ever tell you about La Llorona?"

Brandon couldn't remember, but he shook his head anyway. He liked listening to Mateo talk. Ever since Delilah's accident they'd been hanging out a lot more. Brandon figured it was because they'd been so freaked out by the accident, but when he mentioned it to Maria, she gave him this speech about how it meant they were "conflicted about their own mortality."

"It's stupid to be scared of La Llorona, but I always have been," Mateo said. "She's like the Puerto Rican equivalent of the monster under your bed. Your parents tell you about her so you'll be scared and behave."

"My parents told me there was no monster under the bed." Brandon's breathing was slowing down. He leaned back against the cheap dorm headboard, tipping his head onto Mateo's shoulder. "Just like there was no Tooth Fairy and no Easter Bunny."

"Wow. Your parents win the no-fun award," Mateo said.

Brandon laughed. Laughing felt good. He snuggled his face into Mateo's chest.

It was only a dream.

Everyone had crappy things happen to them, but that was life. You moved on. You dealt. You forgot about the crappy stuff and kept on living. You didn't have any other choice, right?

Mateo was still talking about La Llorona. Brandon looked down into those deep brown eyes. Sometimes he couldn't quite believe he got to sleep in the same bed as a guy who had eyes like that.

"One time I looked it up and it turns out La Llorona's actually supposed to be Mexican," Mateo said. "Every Hispanic kid in the world is scared shitless of her, though. She's the ghost of some lady who lost it and drowned her kids in the river. Now she comes back looking for them. Only she's forgotten what her kids look like, so she'll snatch any kid she sees and say, *'Aquí están mis hijos.'* It means 'Here are my children.'"

"She sounds dumb." Brandon yawned, but he was wide-awake. Thunder rolled outside the window. There had been a storm almost every night since Delilah's accident, nine days ago. Tomorrow it was supposed to be chilly and rainy, but yesterday had been hot and humid, more like August than November. Brandon had gotten stuck hauling extra water coolers out to the cross-country team. The guys always unscrewed the lids and dumped the water over their heads while the rest of the team cheered, and Brandon had to go back to the building for more water.

"Well, La Llorona might be dumb, but she still scared the bejesus out of me," Mateo said. "For all of second grade I wouldn't go out alone after dark 'cause I was afraid she'd come get me. She's supposed to be super tall and wear a long white dress and a white veil. Whenever I looked out my window and saw a white curtain flapping in a house down the street, I'd think it was her. I'd run and get in bed and pull the sheet up over my head."

Mateo ducked under the sheet and wiggled his fingers like a Halloween ghost. He was trying to make Brandon laugh. Distract him.

It didn't work. What Mateo had said about the veil reminded him way too much of his dream. Of the thing that looked like Maria.

"You were such a wussy kid," Brandon said.

"I still am a wuss, I guess. I just dreamed about her tonight," Mateo said. "There was this pale, skinny lady with dark hair and a veil in the bed instead of you. She turned around and looked right at me. Right at my face. Only I couldn't see hers because of the veil. She grabbed my shoulder and squeezed super tight with these long, bony fingers and she said, *'Aquí está mi hijo.'*"

Brandon bit his lip. "What happened after that?"

"I woke up. You were shaking like crazy. The whole bed was rocking. It's lucky Sean's sleeping over at Steph's room or he'd have gotten the wrong idea."

Brandon tried to laugh. The sound wouldn't come.

"Do you think it's because of the accident?" Brandon asked. "The bad dreams, I mean?"

"Yes," Mateo said. "If it *was* an accident."

Brandon sat up straight and moved to the middle of the bed so he could meet Mateo's eyes. Mateo looked right back at him, his face calm.

Had he been wondering too?

"You think she jumped on purpose?" Brandon was sure only *he* had thought about that. Whether Delilah might have planned it. "They said there were enough drugs in her system to make her think she could fly to the moon."

"I don't know what I think," Mateo said. "I've been trying to figure it out ever since that night. Something just doesn't seem right. I know Delilah. She wouldn't just up and do a bunch of drugs the night before a practice. Especially something she hadn't done before, like acid. Winning was too important to her."

Brandon frowned. Maybe Mateo had a point. He knew Delilah better than Brandon did.

"Delilah *did* do acid, though," Brandon said. "I mean, the hospital said so. Do you think they got the test wrong?"

"I don't know. Maybe." Mateo looked down.

There was a new note in Mateo's voice. One that made Brandon nervous. "What is it?"

Mateo hesitated before he answered. "There's only one other possibility I can think of, but it's crazy."

"What?"

"That someone pushed her."

"What? No way. Everyone at this school loves Delilah." What Mateo was saying was impossible. Even if what Brandon had just said wasn't strictly true, either.

"I know," Mateo said. "That's why it's so crazy."

Brandon still hadn't told anyone—not even Mateo—about Maria and Delilah going out that night. He'd promised Maria he wouldn't. But the thought kept creeping back into his mind.

There was something else that had been bothering him, too. The day of Delilah's accident, a few hours before he'd run into Maria in the hall, Brandon had gone to Austin's room to play the game he'd just downloaded, some fantasy thing called Toil and Trouble, where you had to make potions to confuse your enemies. They'd been throwing animated newt eyes and frog toes and stuff into their really disgusting animated cauldrons for half an hour—and then Lily showed up.

Lily *never* came to the fourth floor. The main house didn't have an elevator, and climbing three flights of stairs was a big deal for her. But there she was in Austin's open doorway, the pain clear on her face even through her smile.

She'd asked Brandon to give them a moment alone, and she'd

shut the door behind him. There was only one reason anyone wanted to be alone with Austin.

Except Lily didn't do drugs. She didn't smoke, either. The only time Brandon had even seen her drink was the night of the séance.

Brandon didn't really care if Lily was trying to buy drugs, but he cared about what happened to Maria. And as far as he could tell, pretty much everything Lily ever did had something to do with Maria.

So was it a coincidence? Could Lily have decided to start using the same day Delilah jumped out a window?

Maybe. But it didn't seem likely.

Plus, there was this—Maria still hadn't told anyone she'd been out with Delilah that night.

She should've by now, shouldn't she? The police, or the dean, or the doctors?

She might have information. Something they could use. Something that could help wake Delilah up. Sure, it was a long shot, but they were talking about a girl's life.

And why the hell had she gone looking in Delilah's purse for drugs before the paramedics got there—and then *flushed them down the toilet*?

None of it made any sense.

Brandon had barely had a chance to talk to Maria since that night. People were constantly buzzing over her, asking her questions, deferring to her the way they used to defer to Delilah. She'd even taken over Delilah's seat in the cafeteria, in the first chair at the table where all the popular seniors ate.

When she wasn't surrounded by her followers, she was with Lily. That was even worse.

Brandon had given Lily a wide berth since Delilah's accident. There was a new look in her eyes that scared him almost as much as the woman in his dream had. He couldn't shake the feeling that either Maria or Lily, or maybe even both of them, knew something more than they were saying.

"It's weird, isn't it?" Brandon said. "How Maria flushed the pills."

"Yeah." Mateo shook his head and turned to stare at the ceiling. "You always said she didn't like Delilah, right?"

Brandon didn't reply.

"That's a big risk to take for someone you don't even like," Mateo went on.

Brandon sighed. "I don't know what you're insinuating, but she's my best friend, all right?"

"Okay, okay," Mateo said. "But we should tell Ross, or the dean. *Someone* should know. Someone who can actually do something about it."

"There's nothing to do about it. You told me what that cop said."

"Yeah, but if Maria did something suspicious, someone should—"

Brandon sat up. "You think she pushed Delilah *out a window*?"

Mateo rubbed his eyes. "Sorry. I didn't mean that. I just—I wish she'd told the cops about the pills."

"Maybe she would if I asked her to," Brandon said slowly.

It made sense. Maria was probably afraid of getting in trouble over the drugs, but if Brandon talked some sense into her, Maria would do the right thing.

Or at least they could get it all out in the open. Maria could explain, and it would all make sense. Then he'd know—and Mateo would know—that they didn't have anything to worry about.

If she couldn't explain it, then, well, maybe he *did* need to worry.

"I'll ask her," Brandon decided. "Tomorrow."

Mateo sat up too. "For real?"

"For real."

Mateo grinned at him. Brandon grinned back. Maybe this really would be that easy.

"Are you working tomorrow?" Brandon asked. Mateo's work-study job was in the college counselors' office.

"Yeah," Mateo said. "Four to six. Then I've got to write this thing for the Lambda Literary contest and my French essay for my thesis advisor. I have to start my Kingsley application too. Tomorrow's kind of going to suck."

Brandon raised his eyebrows. "You're applying? For the *Kingsley* Prize?"

"Yeah. I decided to put my name in. The deadline's not until the end of the week. What the hell, right? If Delilah's not getting it, it's anybody's game."

Brandon's head swam. "How do you know Delilah's not getting it?"

"I'm guessing if they think she's a druggie who OD'd on campus, they won't pick her. Hey! You should put your name in too. It would be nice if the scholarship went to somebody who could actually *use* a scholarship."

"You don't need to win," Brandon said. "You're getting an athletic scholarship to WVU already."

Mateo grinned. "I think I'd rather go to UVA, though. They have a great architecture program."

Brandon pictured Mateo working in an architect office, wearing an awesome suit and drawing up blueprints for some fancy skyscraper. He'd be great at it. Mateo was great at everything he tried.

"I'm not going to bother," Brandon said. "It's too much work, and I won't get it anyway."

"You could." Mateo kissed him on the shoulder. It tickled. Brandon couldn't help smiling. "You're pretty awesome, you know."

Brandon changed the subject again. "Want to come running in the morning?"

"Out by the lake?"

"Yeah."

"No, thanks," Mateo said. "The lake creeps me out. The way it's always fogging up out there."

"Yeah, I know, but I'm trying to go every morning this week. I want to lose fifteen pounds before homecoming."

Mateo's lip quirked. "How far away is homecoming, again? A week?"

Brandon sighed. "I'm doomed already."

"You don't need to lose weight," Mateo assured him.

"Thanks."

Mateo leaned over and kissed him.

Brandon closed his eyes, trying to sink into the kiss. He was still jittery from the dream. And from Mateo's theory.

He'd ask Maria tomorrow. She'd tell him what happened, explain why she didn't know anything, and he'd believe her.

It would all be over soon.

Lily's computer froze up again.

She cursed at the screen. Not that it helped. The arrow was frozen over the Search button. Lily had tried four times now to look up the same thing, and every time the computer froze at the exact same moment, as if someone were playing a mean, boring joke on her.

She powered the computer off and closed the screen. Might as well let it rest for a few minutes. It wasn't as if she'd be going to bed anytime soon. She'd barely slept more than a couple of hours a night since Delilah had fallen. Neither of them had.

Well. That wasn't completely true. She wasn't sure how much Maria had been sleeping. She only knew Maria hadn't been spending more than a few hours a night in their dorm room. Lily had no clue what she was doing the rest of the time.

Earlier tonight, she'd tried to find out. She'd caught Maria's hand before she could leave, and she'd held on when Maria tried to break away.

"Stay here tonight." Lily tried to make it sound like a command instead of the desperate plea it was. "We can talk, or whatever."

"I can't," Maria said. "I have to go clear my head."

"Clear your head how? Where do you go every night?"

"Nowhere. For a walk."

"Where? Outside?"

"Yeah."

"What about the security guards? How do you walk around at night without getting caught?"

Maria shrugged. "They don't see me."

That didn't make any sense to Lily, but she had other things to worry about. "Stay here tonight. Talk to me. We hardly ever spend time together anymore."

"We're together constantly."

That was true, sort of. All day long, Lily didn't leave Maria's side if she could help it. She was afraid of what Maria might say if Lily wasn't there to keep her quiet.

Lying didn't come naturally to Maria. Neither did keeping secrets.

And they couldn't afford to let something slip. Not now, when everything was going so much better than they could've hoped.

The league championship had been postponed, but it was only a few days away now. Even if Delilah woke up she'd be in no shape to play. Maria had been made team captain—"acting" captain, the coach said, but close enough—and she was running the team through drill after drill, even when the rain pounded on them or the heat left them drenched in sweat. Some of the girls muttered that she was a tyrant, but Lily knew Maria was only making sure the team was at its best. They'd lost one of their key players, but they weren't going to lose the championship. Not as long as Maria had breath in her body.

Lily had gotten a promotion too, from student body vice president to "acting" president. So far she'd run one student council meeting. It consisted mainly of planning which days they were going to take turns sending flowers to Delilah in the hospital. No one seemed to care that Delilah couldn't even see them.

Sometime in the next few weeks, the school would post the updated list of Kingsley finalists from the second round of judging. Then everyone would know for sure that Maria had taken Delilah's place. With so much uncertainty lingering, though, it was hard to be happy about the good things that had come.

Was this all Lily's fault?

No. She hadn't known what would happen. Austin was the one who'd given her the acid instead of the liquid X he'd promised.

After Maria left the room earlier that night, Lily had started looking for clues. She kept thinking back to that night with the Ouija board. She'd tried to search for Ouija boards and prophecies, and that phrase the board had said to Brandon: *"Memento mori."*

But with the way her screen kept freezing up, it was useless. She might as well try to get some work done. Lily turned the computer back on and pulled up the preliminary paper she was working on for her senior thesis.

She started typing a new paragraph. *Charlotte Perkins Gilman's story is a clear demonstration of the repression suffered by women at the hands of their husbands, doctors, and other patriarchal figures in the late nineteenth century. . . .*

Lily's eyelids were getting heavy. Maybe tonight she'd be able to get some sleep after all. She should at least finish this page, though. She shouldn't get behind. They couldn't have people thinking something might be wrong.

In addition, Gilman offers a harsh critique of medical treatments of women in this time, including false diagnoses of a now-debunked disorder called "female hysteria," which was used to imprison women who dared to defy the conventions of male-dominated society. . . .

This wasn't working. She was too tired. Lily's eyes closed, then snapped back open a second later. She should just go to bed. Lily reached up to close the computer.

Wait. Something was wrong.

The paragraph she'd just typed was gone. In its place was a new line she didn't remember typing. The font was red, and the letters were in caps.

MAKE THICK MY BLOOD.

What? What was *that*?

At first Lily thought that line about the blood was all there was, but then she saw the scroll bar. There was more, farther down. She scrolled—she must've hit the Enter key a bunch of times while she was typing (why couldn't she remember that?)— and saw the next line.

IT WILL MAKE US MAD.

Lily shivered. Then she felt stupid.

What was this? Since when did she type nonsense in her sleep?

She couldn't risk losing control. If someone had seen her they'd have thought she was crazy. What would happen to her and Maria if people thought there was something wrong with them?

Lily had to keep up her strength. Act as normal as possible. For her and Maria both.

She certainly couldn't count on Maria to do it on her own.

11

BLOOD WILL HAVE BLOOD

Brandon waited all day to catch her alone.

It wasn't easy. Since Delilah's accident, Maria had become more popular than ever. Caitlin and Emily stuck to her side like conjoined triplets all through morning classes. He almost had a chance at lunch, but a girl from their physics class caught up with Maria in the salad line and started talking her ear off before Brandon could make it past the dessert station. He tried to grab the seat next to Maria's in sixth-period history, but by the time he got there Ryan had already slid into it and was making her laugh with some story about lacrosse tryouts.

It was strange, the way Maria laughed now. It wasn't the way Brandon remembered her laugh at all. She didn't even smile anymore. She just stretched her mouth open.

Maria got up halfway through history. Acheron liked to

tout how "progressive" it was—for a private Southern board-
ing school—so it didn't have official rules about hall passes and
things like that, but the teachers still got annoyed if you left
during a lecture. Even so, Mr. Forres nodded and smiled at Maria
when she left the room, as though he weren't in the middle of
explaining the Wars of Scottish Independence.

Two minutes later, when Brandon did the same thing, Mr.
Forres glared at him, but Brandon kept going. This couldn't wait
any longer.

He caught up with Maria as she was leaving the girls' bathroom. She looked up at him and started to smile her fake smile,
but he wasn't having it.

"Just tell me," he said.

"Tell you what?" Maria tilted her head and raised her eyebrows.

He didn't want to play this game. They were supposed to be
friends. Best friends. Best friends didn't try to trick each other.

Brandon took Maria's hand and laced his fingers through
hers. Usually that brought her back to earth, but this time, she
just kept fake-smiling.

He couldn't talk to her here, in the middle of the humanities
hall. He had to get her somewhere she could drop the act.

There were only a few minutes left before the period ended
and students spilled out of the classrooms on either side of them.
Brandon's eyes skittered up and down the passageway. The only
option was the row of language labs at the end of the corridor.
The tiny rooms were barely big enough for one person to turn

around in, let alone two, but he didn't have time to be picky. Brandon led Maria by her hand down the hall, pushed open the door to the nearest lab and ducked his head in to make sure it was empty. He ignored Maria's awful fake laughter as he pulled her in after him.

"What, do you want to make out?" Maria giggled. The desk and headphone set took up most of the space in the room, so Maria had to stand right up against him. "You could've just asked."

"This is serious," Brandon said. Maria's fake smile was still in place, but there was a dark look in her eyes.

"Serious, huh?" She giggled again. "What, do you want to talk coordinated outfits for homecoming? I'd love to see you in a cornflower-blue cummerbund."

"I'm not interested in homecoming, Ree."

"Oh, but you have to come to homecoming! Don't make me face all these Acheron robots without you. Promise you'll come!"

"Sure, whatever. I promise. Just be quiet for a second and let me say something."

Maria raised her chin. The challenge was in her eyes. She was daring him not to say it.

He took a deep breath and said it anyway. "I need to know why you haven't told anyone."

"Told who what?" Maria's eyes were wide and calm. She was giving him one last chance.

For a second he was tempted. He could just let this go. Switch back to the way things had been between him and Maria before. Or as close as he could get to that.

But he'd promised Mateo, and besides, there was no way to know for sure whether what Maria had seen that night was important. Not until she'd told the doctors every last detail. If there was any chance she might know something, anything, that could help Delilah, it was a chance worth taking.

Brandon took a deep breath.

"You should tell someone you were out with Delilah that night," he said. "You should tell them about the drugs you flushed, too. The doctors, or the cops, or the dean, or someone."

"What difference would that make?" Maria blinked up at him again. "They know what happened to her."

"You still have to tell them. There might be something you haven't thought of that could help the doctors figure out how to help her."

Maria's smile was gone. The only look left on her face was pity.

"You really think she's going to wake up?" Maria sighed. "I know we're all hoping for a miracle—it's only natural—but, look, she hit her head. She's probably got pretty serious brain damage, and—"

"Stop it." Brandon wanted to shake her. Instead he shoved his hands in his pockets. "Be normal, okay? It's me. You can stop putting on this act. Tell me the truth."

"There's nothing to tell. I'm not acting, Brandon."

She ran a hand through her long, dark hair. It was combed into smooth, perfect waves that always took half an hour and three palmfuls of hair product to get right. Maria used to only bother styling her hair when she was going to a dance or giving a presentation. Ever since the accident, though, Maria's hair had been perfect every day.

"Why did you let her do acid?" He could hear the desperation in his voice. "I know she's not your favorite person, but why didn't you stop her? And why did you let her go upstairs by herself when you must've known there was something really, really wrong with her? Do you really hate her that much? Come on, Ree, just *tell* me."

Maria leaned in toward him. In the tight space, the motion was enough to put her face an inch from his. He heard her take in a long, slow breath.

"Why don't you ask me what you really want to ask me?" she said.

Brandon clutched his hands into fists. "I did ask you."

"No, you didn't. Go ahead. Ask me if I pushed her."

"No." Brandon tried to back up, but his head collided with the wall. Stars sprang up in front of his eyes. "That's not what I said."

"But it's what you thought, isn't it? That I hate Delilah so much I'd want to *murder* her?"

"I didn't think that!"

"Then why all this drama? Come on, you said you wanted me to be honest, right? So you be honest too. Ask me."

There were tears in Brandon's eyes. "Did you?"

Maria leaned back. She pressed her middle finger between her eyes, the way she did when she felt a headache coming on. "No.

I didn't push anyone out a stupid window, and I can't believe my best friend actually just asked me if I did. Look, I don't know the first thing about what happened to Delilah, all right?"

A tear slid down Brandon's nose. He scrubbed it away with the back of his hand. Maria was looking him straight in the eyes. She looked so much like she had in his dream last night.

Brandon hadn't really thought she'd done anything wrong. Not until this moment. Not until she'd lied to his face.

"So she snuck away and did LSD when you weren't watching." He didn't bother to hide his desperation now. This was the only theory that didn't make him want to puke. "If it was something like that, you should still tell. You wouldn't get in serious trouble. They'd probably thank you."

"Yeah, I bet they'd give me, like, a medal." Maria's sarcasm was thick.

"I'm serious. Even if you do get in trouble, it's worth it."

"That wasn't how it happened." Maria was talking fast. "It wasn't—she didn't sneak away. She didn't even mean to do it."

"Then what *did* happen?"

Maria bit her lip, and her chin quivered. For a second Brandon thought she was about to start crying too. She drew in a deep breath.

Then her face smoothed out. She exhaled. When she spoke, her voice was steady.

"Someone slipped it in our drinks," she said. "I think it was this gang of Latino guys hanging out at the back of the bar. We both got up to go to the bathroom, and when we came back I thought my drink smelled funny. I ordered a new one, but Delilah kept drinking hers. The next thing I knew she was falling all over the place."

Brandon was so surprised he almost hit his head again. This wasn't the story he'd been expecting.

"What about the drugs in her purse?" he said. "Why'd you flush them?"

Maria looked to Brandon's right. He glanced over his shoulder, paranoid, but they were as alone as ever in their tiny windowless room. Maria toyed with the cross necklace at her throat before she met his eyes again.

"Look, when I saw her lying on the ground, I panicked," she said. "I didn't know what she'd taken, but all I could think was that she might have oxy on her, and she wouldn't want to get caught with it. So I felt around in her purse and found some pills, and I grabbed them. I didn't check to see what they were. They could've been Tylenol for all I know."

Brandon scrubbed his hand over his eyes. "If you thought some guys drugged you, why didn't you call the police while you were still at the bar?"

"I thought it was roofies and she just needed to sleep it off. I didn't want either of us to get in trouble for sneaking out."

"Jesus." Brandon couldn't keep up with all the thoughts racing through his head. Maria was making sense, but at the same time, she wasn't. "If you thought your drink smelled funny, why didn't you tell her?"

"I did. She said I was being paranoid."

Brandon wished he could believe all this. "So what happened?"

"I brought her home and took her to her room, and I went downstairs. Next thing I know, Lily's waking me up, telling me something happened and I've got to come outside. I swear, Brandon, if I'd known what she was going to do, I'd have stopped her."

Brandon believed that last part, even if he wasn't sure what to think about the rest. Maria was staring down at her feet, her eyes dark.

"Then why didn't you tell someone afterward?" he said. "This is serious. They're talking about criminal charges. Taking her off the Kingsley list. If she didn't do the drugs on purpose, it could make a big difference for her when she wakes up."

Maria bit her lip again.

"Oh." He looked away. "You want her out of the prize running."

"I wasn't thinking about that." Maria's lip trembled, but this time Brandon didn't believe her.

"It's better for you this way," he said. "If everyone thinks Delilah's just some big druggie."

"She *is* a big druggie."

"She could've *died*. She still could!"

Maria just stared at him. Brandon stared back.

This wasn't the Maria he knew. There was something seriously wrong with *this* Maria.

"You have to tell them." He wanted to shake her. Make her understand. "They have to find the guy who did it. What if he does it to someone else?"

Maria opened her mouth, then closed it. She turned toward the wall and shut her eyes.

For a moment he thought he'd gotten through to her. Then, slowly, she shook her head.

She was the best friend he'd ever had, but he couldn't let her get away with thinking this was okay.

"If you don't tell someone, I will," he said. Maria's head jerked up. "By this time tomorrow. That's long enough to find a way to tell them that won't get you in trouble."

"Are you . . . *blackmailing* me?" Maria's voice was high-pitched and incredulous. Brandon prayed no one was out in the hall yet. They'd have heard her for sure.

"I don't know. Maybe? If I have to?" Brandon shifted in his sneakers. He couldn't remember when he'd done something that felt worse than this. "Do you seriously not understand how important this is?"

"It's *my* problem. If you think it's so important, then let me figure out how to deal with it."

"No. Because I think deep down you want to tell someone anyway." A new idea dawned on him. "Lily. Was she the one who wanted to keep it a secret?"

"Don't be ridiculous." But Maria looked away again.

"This time tomorrow," Brandon repeated.

"If you say so." Maria pushed the door open and walked out, keeping her face turned away from him the whole time. The last he saw of her was her purse bouncing against her back as she turned the corner.

Well, the story would get out one way or another. By this time tomorrow, someone would have told.

Brandon bowed his head and prayed it wouldn't have to be him.

It wasn't the same anymore.

Maria had always thought *love* meant caring about someone so much you were ready to explode with it. Wanting to be with them even when you couldn't stand the thought of having anyone else near you.

Maria loved Lily. She always would.

Ever since Delilah had fallen, though, it had been hard to feel anything except that constant, unrelenting terror. Even familiar things, *good* things, seemed strange, wrong. Maria and Lily had barely touched at all since Delilah.

But tonight they'd been on Lily's bed, kissing, ever since lights-out. Earlier, when Maria had been gathering up her things to go out—she'd needed to walk, to think, to figure out what to do about Brandon—Lily had grabbed her wrist and said, "Stay. Please. Stay with me." Maria had closed her eyes, and before she could argue she'd been lying next to Lily, lips tangling. For a moment, a long, beautiful moment, the world had almost seemed normal again.

Maria knew how to do this. She knew how to wrap her arms around Lily's back and hold her tight, to kiss her all over like kissing was the only thing that mattered.

But it wasn't like it had been before. Not really.

She kept thinking about being with Lily that last night, in

the bathroom during the party. She wished she could go back to that moment. The energy. The wanting. She wished she could have another chance to decide.

When she broke away from the kiss, Lily wrapped her hand around the back of Maria's neck. Maria pulled away.

"What is it?" Lily whispered. "Did I do something?"

Maria didn't answer.

Lily reached up and slowly unfastened the top button on Maria's shirt. Maria pushed her hand away.

"Please," Lily whispered. "Tell me what you're thinking."

Maria rolled over to face the wall. She hadn't told Lily about Brandon's threat. She had to figure it out for herself first.

There had to be a way to fix this.

Delilah still hadn't woken up. Her parents were renting a suite in Lennox's only bed-and-breakfast and taking turns sitting in her hospital room. Trying to hold it together, the dorm monitors had told them.

The longer Delilah was in a coma, the less likely she was to remember how she got there. That was Lily's theory. Maria wasn't putting much faith in it, though. She had a feeling it was based on something Lily had seen on one of those crime shows on TV.

They couldn't get caught. It was Maria's first thought every morning and her last thought every night. *They couldn't get caught.*

It ran through her head all day while she kept up the act. Pretended she was just worried for Delilah, like everyone else. That she prayed every night for Delilah to get better and come back to the soccer team.

Not that it mattered.

Not now that she had Brandon Stuart, boy detective, to worry about.

He'd almost caught her, there in the language lab. She'd let herself get too comfortable with him. She'd almost slipped back into that easy truth telling that used to come so naturally with him. Before she knew it, she'd muttered something about how it hadn't been Delilah's idea to take the drugs. She'd quickly made up some story about gangs and roofies, but she could tell he didn't totally buy it.

God. The look on his face.

She couldn't bear to see him look at her that way. Never again.

She had to do something. But she was tired. She was so, so tired.

"Do you think anyone suspects?" Lily whispered.

Maria rolled back over to face her. She'd thought Lily would have fallen asleep by now, but her eyes were open wide.

"Do you?" Maria said instead of answering.

Lily drew in a breath. "There's only one person I think might."

Maria didn't respond. Maybe if she didn't say anything more, Lily wouldn't bring it up.

She wasn't that lucky. Lily was too smart for her own good.

"I know you don't want to hear this, but I'm worried about Brandon," Lily said. "He saw me in Austin's room. He'd be an idiot not to suspect."

Maria still didn't answer her.

"The question," Lily said, "is what are we going to do about it."

Maria wasn't sure how she felt about that "we."

"We have to find a way to throw him off track, at least," Lily said. "We can't sit around waiting for him to tell someone."

"He wouldn't do that," Maria said. "He'd talk to me first. I'm his best friend."

That was true, at least. He had come to talk to her first. Right before he'd given her an ultimatum.

Lily rolled her eyes. "We aren't kids anymore, Ree. You can't just figure you're safe because you're the school princess and he's your little gay BFF."

That bothered Maria, Lily talking about Brandon that way. It bothered her more that Lily was right.

"We'll think of something. Don't worry." Lily slipped her hand into Maria's, interlacing their fingers. Maria used to love how that felt, but tonight Lily's hand was cold and clammy. The pile of blankets Maria had thrown over them wasn't doing much to keep out the room's ever-present chill. "Anyway, it's all set. The prize committee will post the list of second-round finalists any day now, and you'll be in first place. It'll feel wonderful."

Lily didn't sound like she felt wonderful right now.

"Yeah," Maria said.

"We'll get to be together next year. It'll be everything we ever wanted. Finally."

"Finally," Maria echoed.

Getting made soccer captain hadn't been as satisfying as

she'd thought it would be. She wondered if it was the same for Lily. When Dean Cumberland had first told her she was *acting* student body president, Lily had smiled, but it wasn't the kind of smile she smiled when she was alone with Maria. It was the kind she saved for video chats with her parents back home.

Delilah was going to wake up. Maybe. Someday. With every day that passed in the meantime, though, their new reality felt that much more real.

Yet it didn't feel safe. It didn't feel certain.

None of it felt like Maria had thought it would. And she didn't see how it could possibly last.

That first night after Delilah fell, Maria had lain in bed, wishing, hoping, praying she could go back and undo it all. That she could pour that capsule out into the toilet instead of dribbling it into Delilah's drink.

She didn't wish that anymore.

But if Brandon told someone, the police would investigate. They'd figure out what had really happened. Everything would be ruined.

Maria squeezed Lily's cold hand one last time, unlaced their fingers, and climbed out of bed. Lily watched her go without saying anything more. Maria went into the bathroom and closed the door, not bothering to turn on the light. She needed to think this through with a clear head.

She couldn't let Lily get involved. Lily was too unpredictable. Besides, she might get hurt, and Maria couldn't let that happen. She needed her now more than ever.

Lily was right about Brandon, though.

Maria would have to handle him herself. After it was over, Lily would be glad she'd taken care of it.

Maria turned on the shower, the ancient pipes creaking as the hot water pumped through the silent building. Middle-of-the-night showers were a luxury reserved for Maria and Lily with their exclusive private bathroom.

Steam poured out into the room as Maria pulled off her clothes and drew back the transparent shower curtain. She stepped into the stall, letting the hot water pour over her back, and waited for clarity to come to her.

It didn't come. But the room started getting colder.

The water was still piping hot, but the chill struck her skin everywhere the water didn't. The steam was so thick she could barely see through the curtain. Maria cursed herself for not turning on the overhead light. The faint glow coming from under the door wasn't enough for her to even make out the mirror over the sink. All Maria could see in that space was a dark, round blur.

Wait.

Maria squinted at the shape. She drew back the shower curtain.

There was a thin, dark face in the mirror.

The scream formed in Maria's throat and bubbled up, but the only sound she let out was a tiny gasp.

She crossed her arms over her chest and buried her face in her hands. She dug her nails into her scalp. The pain was a needed distraction.

She had to stay calm. She couldn't shout. Couldn't run out the door, screaming and naked, into the school hallway.

You couldn't lose control when you were dealing with a spirit.

Maria counted in her head until she caught her breath. She opened her eyes slowly.

The face was fading. Then it was gone.

Had it ever really been there?

Maria shut her eyes again and rubbed them with the heels of her hands. When she looked back up, the face was still gone, but there was something strange in the mirror.

There were lines in the steam. As if someone had drawn on it with their finger.

Maria stared down at her hands. They were wet and wrinkled from the shower. She was sure she hadn't touched the mirror.

When she turned her gaze back up, the lines were clearer than before. They almost looked like writing, but they weren't in any order that made any sense.

Then she looked again, and she understood.

MUY BIEN.

It *was* writing. But it was backward, and in Spanish.

Altagracia?

Maria turned off the water, her hands trembling and slipping on the cold faucet. She grabbed her towel and wrapped it around her. Her wavy, tangled wet hair dripped onto her bare shoulders.

She stepped out of the shower stall, the tile floor freezing under her bare feet, and scrambled onto the bath mat. Her breath hung in the air.

She should've known. Spirits always sucked the warmth out of a space.

"Hello?" Maria whispered. She turned on the sink faucets so Lily wouldn't hear. The water that blasted out of them was hot. More steam poured out into the room.

Altagracia would help her. She'd always helped Maria when she was alive.

"Altagracia?" she whispered. "Is that you?"

The writing in the mirror faded. New lines began to appear. Maria shivered again.

ME PREOCUPO POR TI, MARÍA.

It took her a minute to decipher the backward letters.

I'm worried for you, Maria.

She shivered again.

If it was Altagracia's spirit, how could she have gotten here? Altagracia had died a hundred miles from Acheron.

Then Maria remembered. The Ouija board had spoken to her in Spanish too. And the chandelier had crushed the board before they could close the session. If they'd raised Altagracia's spirit during their séance, she'd now be free to come and go as she pleased.

"Yo también estoy preocupada," Maria said into the mirror. Her teeth chattered from the cold, but she answered in Spanish, the way Altagracia had always insisted, on Maria's parents' orders.

I'm worried too.

The letters in the mirror faded again. Just as quickly, a new set began to appear.

It was worse than the feel of the planchette sliding under her hands. That night, Maria could've stopped the session if she'd wanted to. Now she could only watch the letters form.

Maria's shoulders stood tense. Shivers rocked her body.

She wished Altagracia would speak to her. She needed to hear her voice again.

"Altagracia?" Maria whispered, softer than before. "It *is* you, isn't it?"

The new row of letters faded in.

¿CUÁL ES TU DESEO, MARÍA?

What is your wish, Maria?

Her wish.

Did Maria really have to say it out loud?

"I'm worried about Brandon," she said slowly. "About what he said he'd do to me."

The letters on the mirror faded until there was nothing but steam.

Maria exhaled. It was over. She'd told Altagracia what was bothering her, and now Altagracia would take care of everything. The way she had when Maria was little.

Then a new set of letters appeared.

¿ENTIENDES LO QUE ESTÁS PIDIENDO, MARÍA?

Do you understand what you're asking, Maria?

Did she?

Maria hesitated. Spirits didn't have to follow the same rules as the living.

But Maria needed to fix this thing with Brandon. Fix it for

good. Altagracia was the only one who could help her.

"Yes." Maria's lip trembled. "I understand."

The next set of writing appeared almost immediately.

Dɪᴄʜᴏ ʏ ʜᴇᴄʜᴏ. ᴀ ʟᴀꜱ ꜱᴇɪꜱ ʏ ᴍᴇᴅɪᴀ. ᴄᴇʀᴄᴀ ᴅᴇʟ ʀᴏʙʟᴇ ᴀ ʟᴀ ᴏʀɪʟʟᴀ ᴅᴇʟ ʟᴀɢᴏ. ᴅᴇʙᴇꜱ ᴇꜱᴛᴀʀ ᴀʟʟí.

Then it is done. Six thirty. At the oak tree on the lake. You will go there.

Brandon had been going running by the lake in the mornings lately. He'd asked Maria to come with him, but Maria always said no. She hadn't been back to the lake since that night with Delilah.

Maria wondered how Altagracia knew Brandon ran in the mornings. Somehow the spirits knew everything.

Maria swallowed again as the last letters faded from the mirror, leaving no trace behind.

It was all set now.

She'd give him one more chance to change his mind. And if he didn't take it, then after tomorrow morning, Maria wouldn't ever have to worry again.

12

WHAT'S TO BE DONE?

The knocking at the door was like nothing Mateo had ever heard.

It wasn't really knocking. More like banging. It sounded really, really *angry*, like something out of a bad action movie.

Mateo rolled over, still groggy. If he ignored the sound, maybe the psychopath at the door would go away.

But there was no room to roll over. Brandon was splayed out over most of the twin bed.

Mateo groaned and looked at his phone. It was just before six in the morning. They were alone. Brandon's roommate rowed crew, so he left before dawn to work out with his teammates.

Mateo stretched out to loop his arm around Brandon, determined to go back to sleep. Miraculously, Brandon didn't move.

But when Mateo touched Brandon's shoulder, he felt him shaking.

Brandon was awake all right. Mateo leaned over to see that his eyes were open wide.

He was terrified.

Oh, crap. Brandon used to get panic attacks when he was a kid. Was some random early morning knocking really enough to set one off?

"Hey, relax," Mateo told him. "I'll get it. Don't worry."

Brandon didn't react. He didn't even move. Weird.

Mateo climbed out of bed, pulled on a pair of Brandon's pajama pants, and crossed to the door. The banging went on, the door shaking on its hinges. Who the hell would do this so early on a Saturday? Mateo doubted it was a dorm monitor—Ross or one of the others would have said something by now.

Mateo's hand was on the doorknob when he felt a flash of fear. Maybe he shouldn't open it.

No. That was stupid. Mateo wasn't a little kid anymore, hiding from La Llorona in the dark.

Mateo swung the door open, letting the light from the hallway flood the room. At first all he could see was a dim outline of someone standing on the other side. He blinked three times before he could make out who the figure was.

Maria Lyon.

"Hey there, Princess," Mateo said. "It's kinda early."

Maria blinked at him. Her fist was still raised, like he'd caught her midbang. "What are you doing here?"

"Exercising my right to spend the night in a classmate's room, provided said classmate is of the same sex," Mateo said, quoting their school handbook. He expected Maria to laugh, or smile knowingly, but her face just looked blank. "How can I help you, Ree?"

Maria shook her head. "I'm here to talk to Brandon."

Mateo looked back over his shoulder. Brandon had rolled over in bed. He was watching them, but his face was just as pale and stiff as before.

"I don't think he's feeling well," Mateo said. "Not sure he's up for talking."

"He'll be fine." Maria brushed past him and charged over to sit on the end of the bed. Brandon jumped back as if she'd burned him.

He didn't look fine at all.

Mateo pulled over Brandon's desk chair and sat in it backward, his legs stretched out on either side of the chair back, facing the bed.

Maria glanced up at him. "I need to talk to Brandon alone."

Mateo shrugged. "I'd rather stick around, if that's cool."

Maria glared at him, like she thought he'd get up if she looked sufficiently annoyed. He shrugged again. Leaving them alone together didn't seem right. Not with Brandon looking as pale as a ghost.

"Fine." Maria sighed and turned back to Brandon. "Listen. I wanted you to know I thought about what you said yesterday."

Brandon scooted back until he was sitting up in bed. A hint of a smile slid across his face. Mateo smiled too, relieved to see Brandon acting more like himself. "That's good."

Maria held his gaze. "I decided I'm not going to do it."

Brandon's smile dissolved.

"I was serious, Ree," he said. "I meant what I said."

"Are you absolutely sure of that?" Maria's smile wasn't friendly.

Neither of them looked in Mateo's direction, but he could tell by the frozen looks on their faces that they were extremely conscious of his presence. There was something going on here that they didn't want him to know about.

All Mateo knew was that Brandon had given her the ultimatum. He'd been pretty broken up about it the night before. There were tears. It had crushed Brandon, having to confront his best friend that way. He'd been afraid it would mean the end of their friendship.

Watching them now, Mateo had a feeling Brandon's fears had been spot-on.

Maria stood up and brushed off her jeans. She was wearing the same outfit she'd worn to classes the day before. Had she been up all night?

"Fine." Her eyes were on Brandon, her mouth set in a thin line. "Have it your way."

Mateo stood up too and met her by the door. He made a big show of swinging it open and ushering her out with a dramatic bow. Maria just gave him another tight-lipped smile.

"Don't let the door smack you on your way out, Princess," he said, then swung it fast enough that she had to do a little jump to get out of the way.

As soon as the sound of her footsteps faded, Mateo turned

back to Brandon. He looked even paler than he had before, and he'd pulled the sheet up to his chin like he was cold.

"What the hell?" Mateo said.

"I was sure she'd do it. I was sure she'd tell the truth." Brandon shook his head. "I just want Maria to be Maria again."

"Everyone at this damn school keeps so many damn secrets." Mateo sighed. It was too early in the morning for this. "Including you, apparently."

Brandon looked like he was about to cry again. Mateo sat in the desk chair and watched him. He didn't look as fragile as he had before. He just looked sad.

"You know you don't owe her anything anymore," Mateo said.

Brandon dipped his chin down, then looked up. He locked eyes with Mateo.

"Maria and Delilah went out that night," Brandon said. "The night of the accident. They snuck out and went to the bar in town and didn't get back until after lights-out."

Mateo stood up. "Wait. What?"

"Maria said some guy drugged their drinks." Brandon chewed on his thumbnail. Mateo had never seen him do that before.

"Why didn't she tell the police?" Mateo said.

"That's what I asked her. She said it wouldn't have mattered, and she didn't want to get in trouble."

That didn't make any sense. None of this did. He couldn't believe Brandon had bought this story. Did he really care about Maria so much that he'd let her get away with this bullshit?

Mateo shook his head. "We have to call the cops right now."

Brandon went pale again and pushed the sheet down around his waist. He was wearing an old *Star Wars* T-shirt he'd had since middle school. The thin fabric stretched across his chest and made him look like an overgrown kid.

"I can't." Brandon climbed out of bed slowly, holding on to the nightstand. "I'll find her later today after she's calmed down and talk to her again. I'll get her to go to the dean."

"And if she won't?"

Brandon bit his lip. "I'm going for a run." He pulled on his shorts. "Need to clear my head. You can come if you want."

Mateo shook his head. "No, thanks. When you get back, if you've come to your senses, let me know. I'll go with you to tell the dean."

"Whatever." Brandon laced up his sneakers.

As Mateo watched him leave the room, his shoulders shaking, he thought about telling Brandon to wait. He thought about apologizing. Saying that it was complicated, and they'd figure it out together.

He didn't say any of that, though. Instead Mateo watched him leave without a word.

"The stories they tell about this place are so stupid," Felicia chirped as she stumbled over the stone wall that bordered the lake path. "Did you know the Siward family weren't even the first owners? They're the ones everybody talks about, but really the town's named after this guy Joseph Lennox, and he's the one who actually built the plantation. Or, well, I guess his slaves did the building, since it was, like, the sixteen hundreds. Oh, crap—watch out, there's a root here!"

Felicia stumbled again, but her voice never lost its standard chirpiness. Brandon wished he were in the mood for chirping today.

Felicia had just been accepted as a student ambassador, and she wouldn't shut up about all the random school history stuff from her training. At least her chirping broke the silence. It was quiet outside this morning. Brandon ran the lake path as often as he could drag himself out of bed, and usually the air was full of noisy birds and crickets and mosquitoes that nipped at his ankles. Today they must've all still been asleep. The only sounds were the leaves crunching under their feet.

Brandon couldn't blame the birds and the crickets for leaving them alone. It was chilly out by the lake. For once, though, the constant thunderstorms had stopped. Instead a light, misty rain had coated them both before they'd even gotten to the lake path.

Felicia had seen Brandon on his way down the first-floor hallway and come trotting outside after him, her sneakers already in hand. She swore she'd been planning to go running anyway, but Brandon knew a tagalong when he saw one. He'd been tagging along his whole life.

He liked Felicia, though. She was funny, and she always looked at Brandon with these wide eyes that made him feel smart and important. She was short with a little baby fat, like him, and a few weeks ago she'd told him that she thought she was bisexual.

She had all the same freshman-year self-consciousness about that fact that Brandon remembered well. You could tell Felicia was going to be pretty in a couple of years, but right now she just looked awkward, with eyes that were too big for her face and brown hair that never stayed brushed. The other girls he knew, like Delilah and Emily and sometimes even Maria, looked right through Felicia when they passed her in the halls, but seeing her always made Brandon smile.

He'd told Felicia once that she was the little sister he'd never had. Felicia had smiled and bitten her lip and hugged him fiercely.

He had a feeling Felicia's actual brother, Austin, hadn't been much fun to grow up with.

"But then the whole Lennox family died in this fire that started in the church." Felicia's chirps were coming a little slower now, with pauses between words as she panted, trying to keep up with him. "Did you know that's what the jump rope rhymes are about, the ones we learn in elementary school? They're about that fire. It's crazy. Anyway, the Siwards bought the place after the fire. They got it on the cheap, because almost everything was burned."

"Uh-huh." Brandon wanted to speed up, but he didn't want to make Felicia feel bad. "Cool."

"Hey, do you smell something cooking? It smells really good out here all of a sudden."

Brandon didn't smell anything, but he saw something ahead, under the massive oak that dominated the far end of the lake. He couldn't tell what it was. All he saw was a big, dark shape.

For a second he thought it was the old church. It was supposed to still be on the grounds somewhere, though Brandon had never seen it. As he got closer, though, he knew it couldn't be the church. The shape was too low and narrow.

"Hey," he said to Felicia, since apparently she knew everything there was to know about Acheron. "What's that up there?"

"Where?" Felicia looked in the direction he pointed. "Oh, do you mean the big tree?"

"No, I . . ." How could she not see it? It was huge. It looked almost like some kind of animal crouching. Lying in wait. Brandon picked up his pace, skirting the low, crumbling stone wall to his right. He stumbled, held his arms out, and managed to stay upright.

Brandon wished his heart would stop pounding so hard. It made everything seem unreal.

The shape up ahead looked like it was getting bigger. Or closer.

He wasn't crazy. He was just still freaked about Maria. He had to keep moving, that was all.

"I'm going to run ahead a little ways," he called back to Felicia. "Do you mind? I'll meet you at the tree and then we'll take a break. Is that all right?"

"Sure." Felicia fell back to a trot.

Brandon sped up. This was faster than he usually ran in the mornings, but it felt good. His muscles strained to keep up the pace. He lifted his knees higher with each step. The harder he ran, the easier it was to forget that angry, guilty look on Maria's face.

He sped up again. The shape by the tree was still there.

It was just a shadow. The world was full of them. This wasn't some scary dream. There was no one else around. He was safe here.

He was a hundred yards from the tree when the shadow *moved*.

Brandon stumbled again, but he righted himself and kept running.

It was six thirty in the morning. The sun would be up soon, somewhere behind all those clouds. He didn't have anything to be afraid of.

Brandon ran faster. He was flying now. He'd almost reached the tree.

Soon he could stop and wait for Felicia. When she caught up to him he could tell her what he'd thought he'd seen. They could laugh about it together.

Ten yards to go.

The shadow was still there. It looked bigger than before. More solid.

Brandon kept going. Kept going a little farther. He was in an all-out sprint now, and closed the space between himself and the tree in a few leaps.

The shadow was gone. Brandon had outrun it. Relief flooded his chest. He smiled.

Then something slammed into his chest, knocking him to the ground.

Brandon lay panting on his back, his eyes closed. His head throbbed where it had hit the dirt.

His mind was foggy. A sharp sound rang in his ears. He smelled apples baking.

It felt like he was lying under a brick wall. But there was no wall at this part of the lake.

"Brandon!" Felicia was far behind him, her voice a shriek instead of a chirp. "Brandon, are you okay?"

Brandon tried to sit up, to call out to her that he was fine. That she didn't need to worry.

When he opened his eyes, Rafael was looking back at him.

Brandon tried to scream. No sound came.

Rafael smiled.

His eyes were solid black. He was bloodier than in the dreams. Dark red liquid streamed down his face, dripping onto his neck. The knife he held in front of Brandon's face was covered in slick red blood that dribbled down his arm.

Footsteps pounded behind them on the dirt path.

Then Brandon understood.

Rafael was going to hurt Felicia.

Brandon lifted his arms. His right arm wouldn't move, so he reached for Rafael with his left. He'd squeeze the life out of him if that's what it took.

His hand gripped nothing but air.

"Leave her alone!" Brandon tried to shout. His lips wouldn't move.

"Brandon!" Felicia shrieked again. She'd caught up with him. She was gripping his shoulders, lifting him up, shaking him.

Get away, he wanted to tell her. *Get away! He's dangerous!*

He still couldn't speak. He couldn't see Rafael anymore.

He couldn't see Felicia either. All he saw was darkness.

His eyes had closed again. He couldn't make them open.

"Stop it!" another girl's voice cried. "Let go! You're only hurting him worse!"

Maria.

Maria was here. Just like in his dream.

Brandon wanted to tell her to get away too. Rafael couldn't have gone far. He could still hurt either one of the girls, and—

Wait. Why was Maria here?

Felicia released his shoulders. Brandon sank back into the ground. It felt soft. Like a pillow.

Somewhere far away he heard Maria press three buttons on her cell phone. She was talking, but he couldn't make out the words.

Something wrapped around his palm. His left one, the one that could still feel. A warm hand squeezed his. Brandon tried to squeeze back, but he was too tired.

He went to sleep.

"Shut up!" Maria screamed. "Shut up, shut up, shut up!"

Felicia wasn't saying anything. She was just sitting there, crying and holding Brandon's hand like an idiot.

Maria was the one doing all the work. Calling the ambulance. Texting everyone she could think of to get someone down here from the house. The dorm monitors, the faculty, their friends—someone. Anyone.

Anyone who could fix this. Make Brandon get back up.

The birds were back, twittering away as though the whole world wasn't falling apart.

Do you understand what you're asking? the words in the mirror had asked her.

Had she understood?

Was *this* what Maria had asked for?

"No!" she screamed. Her cry sent a flurry of birds squawking out of the tree above.

Maria tried to remember what she'd said into the mirror last night. Her memory was foggy.

She'd wanted Brandon to forget about what he'd said. To leave her alone. She'd asked Altagracia to help her.

And Altagracia had.

Maria's knees gave way. She broke her fall with her hands, slamming them into the dirt path so hard her teeth dug into her lower lip, drawing blood.

"I don't think he's breathing," Felicia whispered.

"Shut up!" Maria shouted. "He's fine!"

Felicia only cried harder. She was still gripping Brandon's hand. He hadn't moved in a long time. Maria wanted to throw up.

"I saw him fall," Felicia whispered. "It looked like something ran into him. Did you see it?"

"Shut up!" Maria snapped. "There's no one out here but us! Where the hell is the ambulance?"

Maria looked down at her useless phone and threw it on the grass.

The doctors were supposed to be here by now. No one was doing anything right.

"Why are you here, anyway?" Felicia said. "No one else is even awake yet."

"Shut *up*!" Maria screamed for the last time.

She turned toward the house. Someone was running down the hill, finally. Far behind, another, slower figure was moving toward them. Maria could tell by her uneven gait that it was Lily.

Maria didn't want to see her. She didn't want to see anyone.

She wanted only Brandon.

Ross hurried around the bend toward them. Maria ran to meet him.

"Hurry up!" she screamed. "Where the hell is the ambulance?"

"It'll be here," Ross said. "I called too."

He fell onto his knees and put his hand on Brandon's neck.

"Stop that!" Maria bent over and knocked his arm away. "You don't need to check his pulse. He's *alive*, okay?"

Ross ignored her and put his hand back on Brandon's neck. Maria gave up and paced away from them.

Idiots. They were all idiots. This was all so stupid.

How could she have been so *stupid*?

Ross was moving now. Up and down. Doing CPR.

That was a waste. All of it was a waste.

A blaring sound almost made Maria scream again. She caught herself when she recognized it. Sirens, coming from the other side of the fence.

Maria left the others and ran toward the sirens. The people in the ambulance could fix this. They could put everything back how it was supposed to be.

Maria yanked open the service gate and waved her arms. The paramedics jogged toward her, moving way too slowly. Kits that looked like her father's fishing tackle box swung from their hands. Maria ducked behind a tree trunk to watch them work.

It was safer here. No one could see her. No one would know what she'd done.

Here, none of this was happening.

Brandon couldn't really be—

She hadn't—

She would never—

"There's no such thing," she whispered. She sank to the ground, pulled her knees up to her chest, and wrapped her arms around them. She bent her head so she wouldn't have to see what was happening on the other side of the trees. "There's no such thing."

That was how Lily found her a few minutes later. The paramedics were moving slower by then. One of them was talking quietly to Ross while the others strapped Brandon onto the stretcher. They were pulling a sheet over his face. By then, Maria had made up her mind.

No more hysterics. No more screaming. She knew what she had to do.

Maria knew it was Lily behind her from the sound of her

crutches in the grass. She didn't flinch when Lily put a hand on her shoulder.

"What's going on, Ree?" Lily whispered. "They're saying Brandon had a heart attack. Were you there? Did you see what happened?"

Maria didn't move.

"You're in shock," Lily said. "You need a doctor."

Lily stood up to signal the paramedics.

"No!" Maria's voice felt raw and scratchy. "No. I don't want them near me."

"Okay." Lily reached for Maria's hand. "Let's go back up to the house. You can tell me about it there."

"No." Maria pulled away. She lifted her head for the first time. There were tears in Lily's eyes. "I want to be left alone."

"Just tell me what happened. Had he been sick? I don't get it. Please, tell me what—"

"It was Altagracia."

Lily blinked. "It—what?"

"It was me." She whispered it so quietly Lily didn't hear.

Part of Maria wanted to collapse at Lily's feet, the way she had the night Delilah fell. She wanted to close her eyes and let Lily tell her what to do.

Instead she stayed where she was. Lily couldn't fix this. No one could.

Maria had done too much.

She stood up and faced the tree, its broad trunk solid and steady. Everlasting.

"Just leave me alone," Maria said.

"Okay, but—"

"Go *away*, Lily."

Lily stared at her. A single tear ran down her cheek. Maria turned so she couldn't see.

She'd lost everything.

She couldn't undo what she'd done. Her only choice was to forget all this. The only thing left to do . . . was win.

She could do it, too. She'd take all of this and tuck it away in a box somewhere. She'd put every ounce of energy she had into winning it all.

Homecoming queen. The league championships. The Kingsley Prize. She could probably be president someday if she wanted to.

It was all hers. Whatever it took, she'd do it. Then, at least, all of this would mean something.

After all . . . she'd already done the worst thing there was to do.

Maria crossed her arms. She ignored Lily's gentle touch on her elbow. After another long minute, Lily left.

The paramedics were gone by then too. They'd taken Brandon with them. Ross was walking back up the hill with his arm around Felicia's shoulders.

Maria finally had what she'd wanted.

She was all alone.

13

CONSIDER iT NOT SO DEEPLY

The room went dark. The needle sliced into Lily's finger.

"Damn." A bright spurt of blood poked through her skin. It looked black in the dim light.

Lily absently stuck her finger in her mouth while she hunted for a match. She'd been tightening a loose button on her homecoming dress when the building had lost power. Again. For the past week, ever since Brandon died, the building's power had been out almost as often as it was on.

After a minute, the taste of blood on her tongue made her retch. She yanked her finger out of her mouth and waved it in the air. Her cut stung.

She swore again and dug in her desk drawer for a Band-Aid. She didn't find one, but she did find an old matchbook from Porter's. She lit the rickety Target candelabra she kept next to her bed. A soft glow spread around her.

The blood still seeped from her finger. It made her sick to look at. She couldn't stand the sight or smell of blood, not since she'd found Delilah on the grass.

There were Band-Aids in the staff kitchen. Lily grabbed a crutch with one hand, the candelabra still gripped in the other. She leaned on her right leg, wincing at the pain, and held the candles out in front of her as she limped into the dark hall.

Lily was used to her crutches by now, but she hated them as much as ever. It had been almost seven years since she was first allowed to use them instead of her wheelchair, and that had been a year after the accident that had put her in it. She'd been on a trip with her church youth group, riding in the passenger seat of her friend's mother's minivan, when a pickup truck barreled into her car door.

Mostly, what she remembered about it was the way the other kids had screamed. They'd screamed so long and cried so hard it made Lily scream, too. Or that's what she'd thought. Everyone told her she hadn't made a sound, even when the police had to cut the van open to get her out.

The others got away with cuts and bruises, but not Lily. Lily, the doctors said over and over again, was lucky to be alive.

By the time she was allowed to ditch the wheelchair, Lily had missed close to a full school year, between the painful surgeries to fix her bones, reconstruct her ligaments, and make her legs somewhat functional again, and being stuck in the rehab facility with her tutors after that. Once she was finally deemed able to get around on crutches, Lily couldn't face the kids at her old Catholic day school. She'd begged her parents to send her away to Acheron. There, just like back home, everyone who looked at her would see the crutches before they saw her. But at least they wouldn't feel sorry for her, since they'd never seen her as anything else.

What all of them forgot—even Maria, sometimes—was that Lily wasn't paralyzed. She could feel her legs, all right.

They hurt. All the time.

It had been sometime after the second surgery—the one that made her ache so badly she'd maxed out her morphine drip and her parents had hired a hypnotist and gotten her an oxy prescription—that Lily realized she couldn't count on anyone else to make this better for her. Not her parents. Not their drugs. Certainly not her stupid hypnotist.

Not God, either. Lily had spent the first nine years of her life going to church and confession and believing God would take care of her. Then, when God had gotten His chance, He hadn't bothered.

There was nothing out there. Nothing up in the sky or below the dirt or walking alongside them on the ground.

There were just people. Good people, like her and Maria. Assholes, like the truck driver who'd slammed into the minivan and screwed up Lily's legs. And random people, like the other kids at Acheron, who she guessed were somewhere in between.

The random people didn't matter much to Lily. Not as long as the good people got rewarded and the assholes got what they deserved.

It was mostly her left leg that did the aching now. The right one still had issues, and bending it hurt like hell, but her left didn't need to wait for a reason to throb.

Lily had lived with the same pain for so long it felt like a part of her. The worst days, though, were when the pain was different. When it came faster, or harsher, or fiercer than she was used to. When it prickled instead of throbbed. When it attacked her right ankle instead of her left knee. When it woke her up at night instead of aching dully first thing in the morning. On those days, her standard-issue pain was replaced by something different and frightening, something that took over her body and left her without the slightest clue of when, or even if, it would release her.

Those times, her pain wasn't a part of her anymore. Those times, she was a part of *it*.

Lily's pain reminded her of what she'd lost. That she couldn't take anything for granted. That she had to work to make things right.

The quickest way to the staff kitchen was through the old dining hall next door. Lily hadn't been in the room since the night of the séance. When she pushed the heavy wooden door open, something brushed against her leg, making her jump, before she realized it was just one of the cats. Lily shook off her nerves and glanced around the room, holding up the candles.

The dining hall had been partially cleaned up since that night. The shards of glass had been swept away, but hastily—Lily could see fragments gleaming in the candlelight in the dark corner by the door. The table was still there, but the rickety rocking chair that had always inhabited the far corner of the room was gone. There was a jagged rip in the ceiling where the chandelier had hung. The chairs were still scattered around the edges of the room where they'd been moved for the cleaning. Maybe now they'd finally convert the room into something useful. Everyone always said they'd been afraid to renovate it because the chandelier was too valuable and fragile to move.

It was as cold as ever inside the room, the scuffed floor freezing against her bare feet, and Lily limped through it as quickly as she could to the relative warmth of the kitchen. The staff kitchen had been the "preparations room" back in the house's plantation days, the student ambassadors always said when they gave tours of the school. It was where the servants (twenty-first-century code for "slaves") had fixed up the food after it was brought inside from the kitchen before they served it to the Siward family.

Whenever Lily was in here, she pictured some Sally Hemings type spitting in her master's food. That's what Lily would've done if it were her.

She dug in the cabinet for the first-aid kit and bandaged her finger quickly. When she limped back into the darkened dining hall, something looked different. She held the candles higher. It took her a second to spot it.

It was the chairs. Three of them were standing in a neat row alongside the table.

What the hell? Lily was positive they'd all been pushed to the edges of the room a minute ago.

She'd been right next door. If someone had come in and

rearranged the room she would've heard. But there hadn't been a single scrape along that ancient wood floor.

She must've been mistaken when she walked through before. The chairs must've been arranged this way from the beginning.

A movement on the far side of the room made Lily's head jerk up. It was in the farthest corner, where her candlelight didn't reach. In the dark she could barely see what had moved.

Slowly, as her eyes readjusted to the dim light, she saw the faint outline of a person. A girl, wearing a long skirt. She must've been the one who'd moved the chairs.

"Jesus," Lily said. "You scared me. Are you looking for candles? There are more over in the kitchen."

The girl didn't move.

"Why are you standing in the dark?" The back of Lily's neck prickled.

The girl in the corner lifted her head slightly, but she didn't speak.

"Hey!" Lily took a step back. She stumbled.

Someone tapped on her shoulder, hard.

She whirled around. "Stop it!"

There was no one behind her.

She turned back around. The girl was gone too.

"What the hell?" Lily nearly tripped over her crutch as she made her way to the heavy double doors that led to the main foyer. When she pushed on it, the door gave way easily. Lily drew in quick, sharp breaths as she fell out into the hall.

It was dark outside the room. The only light was a single

candle at the far end of the main hallway. Lily held her candelabra out to illuminate the shadows.

A dark figure leaped in front of her. Lily screamed and dropped the candles, the flames flickering and going out.

"Grr!" Austin shouted, holding his black-gloved hands in front of him like claws. "Boo! Scared you!"

"Jesus freaking Christ, Austin!" Lily would've hit him if she hadn't had to grip the doorframe to keep from falling. "Why do you have to be such an asshole? What were you even doing in there?"

Austin's laugh was too long, too full. He was laughing so hard he couldn't speak.

"It was you, wasn't it?" Lily said. "You moved the chairs."

Austin picked up her extinguished candelabra and handed it to her.

"I wouldn't go in that dining hall if you paid me a bajillion dollars," he said. "God, the look on your face just now! People here act so funny when the lights go out."

Lily glared, but Austin just kept laughing.

"People act funny here all the time," Lily told him, and pushed him out of her way to limp back down the hall.

Lily turned to glare at him again as she left, but he wasn't watching her anymore. He was standing at the doorway to the old dining hall, gazing into the dark room.

Austin had come to Brandon's funeral. No one had expected him, but there he'd been, sitting in a pew with his sister Felicia, wearing a rumpled designer suit, with his hair half-combed.

He hardly talked to anyone, even during the long walk from the church to the cemetery, except to grumble, "This is messed up, man," over and over.

It figured that Austin got stoned even at funerals.

The school had planned to have a memorial on campus, but Brandon's parents said no. They wanted a funeral in their church back home and nothing more. Most of the students hadn't bothered to go, because the funeral was supposed to have been the same day as homecoming. But homecoming, which had already been pushed back once thanks to Delilah, had been delayed again. Now the dance was tomorrow night.

Everything else had been delayed, too. The league soccer championship had been rescheduled for next week, if it wound up happening at all. No one was sure what to expect anymore. Delilah still hadn't woken up, and there were murmurs about Acheron forfeiting the game to Birnam altogether.

Maria wouldn't hear any talk of a forfeit. Whenever anyone mentioned it, she muttered that no one would ever have tried to forfeit the *boys'* game, no matter how many people died. She was right, of course.

The problem was, it was hard to get Maria to say much of anything else now. She never wanted to talk to Lily. She never wanted to talk to anyone. When she did talk, she muttered, and Lily didn't understand most of it. She kept saying her old nanny's name, as though she were talking to *her*.

But Altagracia was dead. Long dead.

Lily wished she'd never bought that Ouija board. She wished

she'd never put these ideas in Maria's head. If it weren't for Lily she wouldn't be thinking about things like ghosts, and spirits, and supernatural beings coming to earth.

Doing things to people. Lurking in dark rooms.

Mostly, though, Lily just wished Maria would talk to her.

They still didn't know what had happened that day by the lake. The doctors said Brandon must've had an undiagnosed heart condition. There was no other way to explain a healthy seventeen-year-old having a cardiac arrest during his morning run.

Lily didn't think it was that simple. She wasn't the only one. The school had bumped up security, building brand-new campus guard stations that ruined the picturesque effect of the ancient campus lawns.

It didn't help that Felicia was going around telling anyone who would listen that something strange had happened that morning by the lake. She kept saying Brandon saw something up ahead, something weird, and that she thought she might've seen it too. Felicia was sure the "weird" thing—whatever it was—had killed Brandon.

Some of the seniors were whispering that something might've happened to Felicia herself that day. Something that had made her not quite right anymore.

There were other rumors, too. People said they'd seen or heard odd things the day Brandon died. One junior kept saying she'd heard humming on the front stairs. The same tune again and again. A lot of people said they'd been having weird dreams, about scary stories they'd heard as kids. One freshman had gone to the bathroom in the middle of the night and been so sure he saw a ghost's face in the mirror, he punched the glass. He'd had to get stitches at the health center.

Most of the stories made Lily roll her eyes. Some people wanted attention. And other people would believe anything.

Felicia, though . . . Everyone said she couldn't sleep through a single night without waking up screaming.

Lily had heard her once. The screaming had gone on for what felt like hours, but when Lily looked at her clock, it had only been a couple of minutes.

Everything was wrong. Time felt upside down.

She didn't know what Felicia thought had happened to Brandon. All Lily knew was that there was no logical reason for Maria to have been at the lake that morning. Not unless she'd known what was coming.

How could she have, though? If Brandon had some strange, undiagnosed illness, how would *Maria* possibly have known? Surely she didn't think a ghost told her?

There was no way to find out. Maria refused to talk about Brandon. Since the funeral, she'd refused to talk about pretty much anything.

It had been a two-hour drive, and the rain had poured the whole time. It was strange leaving town. Like something in a dream, or a movie. Acheron was the only world that really existed for any of them anymore.

Maria was the only one of their group who'd met Brandon's parents before, so at the cemetery she stood up front by the grave with them, leaving Mateo, Lily, Austin, and Felicia to stand awkwardly with the middle-aged mourners in cheap Kmart suits and fraying black skirt hems. The bottom corner of the front page of the *Lennox Daily News* had featured a close-up of Maria with her head bowed and her eyes closed, looking more beautiful than Lily had ever seen her. The headline said "Grieving a Life Too Brief."

Mateo had driven up for the funeral by himself in Tamika's brother's car, even though Dean Cumberland had offered him a ride along with Maria and Lily. No one seemed to know how Austin and Felicia had gotten there.

Mateo hadn't spoken a single word that day. He just stood there, still and silent, the rain pouring onto him and into the open grave below, while the others in the crowd grumbled to one another and huddled under umbrellas.

When they got back to campus a grief counselor met them in the common room and told them, in that condescending voice the guidance staff always used, that it was okay to talk about their feelings. Lily and Felicia nodded and thanked her. Mateo and Maria stared straight ahead and kept their mouths shut. Austin laughed out loud.

There was an hour left until lights-out. Lily needed to work on her dress, but she couldn't bear the thought of going back to that dark, frigid dorm room by herself. She set the candelabra down in a corner and swung over to the front door. A walk across the grounds would hurt her legs, but it would clear her head.

Lily waved to Tony, the security guard sitting in the booth

facing the lawn. He didn't wave back. Most of the new guard stations were on the opposite side of the house, facing the main driveway, since that was supposed to be the only way you could get onto campus from the outside. Only Tony, who'd been working at the school longer than anyone could remember, was watching the side facing the lake and the woods.

The Acheron kids liked Tony, and he liked them back. He joked around with them between classes, pretending to take out his Taser gun like the cops did on TV. Usually he worked the day shift, but with the new security measures his schedule had been flipped. The only way Tony could stay awake all night was by playing games on his computer, so he didn't see much going on outside his guard booth.

Lily dropped her hand and gazed out across the lawn. Maria had to be out here somewhere. She was always disappearing, alone, mumbling about needing to "work on something."

Lily couldn't imagine what. Maria used to study four hours a day, but Lily hadn't seen her touch a book since Brandon died.

Sometimes, at night, Lily lay awake in her bed listening to Maria whisper in her sleep, and she wondered if Maria was on drugs. If some night she was going to find Maria's broken body, the way she'd found Delilah's.

When she finally slept, Lily's dreams were always about blood.

What was Maria doing? What had she already done?

Had *she* done something to Brandon?

No. She wouldn't. He was her best friend. And nothing Maria could've done would trigger something as serious as a heart attack.

If it had really been a heart attack.

The truth was, Lily didn't want to know what had killed Brandon. If she was wrong . . . if Maria *had* done something . . . did that mean it was Lily's fault?

She remembered the conversation they'd had the night before he died very, very clearly.

We'll think of something, Lily had told Maria that night.

What if Maria *had* thought of something?

Before, when all this was just an idea, it had seemed simple. Like math. There were problems to be solved. Lily had always been very good at solving problems.

Now Brandon was dead. Delilah might die too. It wasn't just moves on a board anymore. This was real life.

Tears rolled down Lily's face as she approached the lake. She brushed them away and kept walking.

Maria hadn't cried the day of Brandon's funeral. Her best friend was gone and never coming back, but Maria's eyes had been dry all week.

The only time she'd seen Maria react to anything since then was that morning, when they'd gone to check the new list of Kingsley Prize finalists. It was supposed to go up by nine a.m., but the bulletin board by the dean's office was bare. Maria and Lily and half the senior class had waited until they were almost late for second period before a secretary finally poked her head through the door and told them the list's release had been "postponed indefinitely."

A few people wandered away, whining under their breath about how *everything* didn't have to be postponed just because one kid had bought it. Others walked off in silence, sneaking glances at Maria and looking away before she noticed.

Lily had heard snatches of another nasty rumor going around. According to this one, Maria had posed for that photo at the funeral on purpose. She'd known the prize committee would see it, and she was relying on the sympathy vote.

Lily thought Maria would cry when she saw the empty board. Or get angry. Or do *something*. Instead Maria blinked several times, closed her eyes, and inhaled deeply.

Lily tried to talk to her in their room later. She tried to tell her that she was sorry about Brandon. That she understood what he'd meant to Maria. That it was okay if Maria needed to cry, needed to lean on her, needed to open up about what she was feeling. Even if it wasn't something she wanted to tell anyone else.

Maria didn't answer. She lay on her back, staring at the ceiling through wide-open eyes.

It felt like life would go on exactly this way forever. College and the Kingsley Prize seemed like faraway, abstract things. Lily couldn't imagine ever living anywhere but here. She might as well spend the rest of her life limping across the gloomy Acheron campus. Shivering in her cold, cramped dorm room.

Fog was pouring off the lake tonight, the way it always did. Lily thought she saw someone else walking on the far side, but it was dark, and she couldn't be sure. She swung along the path on her crutches, taking care to stay on the opposite end of the lake from where Brandon had fallen.

Lily wasn't superstitious. She hated to remember what he'd looked like spread out on that stretcher, though. Lying so still.

Tiny waves lapped at the shores of the lake. That was strange. The water was usually still and silent.

The waves sounded musical. Almost like voices.

Then Lily realized the sounds *were* voices. Babbling the same notes again and again, the sounds echoing and overlapping.

The voices were low, mixed with the murmur of the waves, but Lily could make out rising, falling notes. Then garbled, distorted words.

Join us, the voices said. Three voices, maybe four, all the same.

Join us, they said again. *Come for a swim.* They giggled, like children.

Lily tried to laugh back. At herself, for hearing things.

She'd never swum in Acheron's lake. Everyone knew not to go in the water.

Even so, Lily found herself wandering toward the shoreline.

She'd loved swimming. Before her accident, she'd taken her team to the Virginia state finals year after year.

Looking out over the water, she remembered the way it used to feel. The ease of it. The weightlessness. The comforting swish of water closing over her.

Lily rolled her eyes at her own crazy imagination. Here she'd been scoffing at all the random people talking about mysterious humming and faces in the mirror, and now she thought the damn lake was talking to her.

If she wasn't careful she'd wind up just as crazy at the rest of them.

She turned to go back to the house. It was almost lights-out anyway. Maria would be back soon from wherever she'd run off to. In the meantime Lily had a homecoming dress to finish. She wanted to look good for the dance, even though she didn't have a date. She'd thought someone might ask her, but it hadn't happened, just like last year. When the boys at this school looked at her, all they saw was a giant pair of crutches.

She couldn't go to the dance as Maria's date, of course. She couldn't risk a rumor like that spreading back to her parents. She didn't want to give Delilah the satisfaction of knowing she still liked girls, either.

Oh. Wait. Right. Lily still hadn't gotten used to the idea that Delilah wasn't around to care about those things anymore.

Anyway, Lily was going to homecoming, whatever it took. She was acting class president now, and she had to play the part. Besides, getting dressed up and acting normal might be enough to snap Maria back to normal too.

But Maria wasn't in the room when Lily got back. The power was still out, too. Lily had navigated the candlelit hallway and the hordes of pajama-clad freshmen only to find her own room dark, freezing, and empty. So much for finishing her dress. She found her matches and lit the candles that had blown out while she was gone, and left them burning for Maria as she climbed into bed.

Maybe tonight she'd finally get some sleep. Even better, maybe Maria would climb into bed with her when she got back. Maybe they could pretend things were all right again.

Lily murmured the "maybes" to herself so long she almost convinced herself they were real.

Until she heard the scraping sound.

She was half-asleep by then, but her eyes jolted open right away.

It was coming from the window. There was only one in their room, above Lily's bed, right next to the wall their room shared with the old dining hall. Maria had a funny feeling about that window, so they always kept the curtains drawn and the window locked, despite the chill inside the room.

It had been more than a year since Lily had last heard that scraping sound. When she first moved into this room, in ninth grade, she'd heard it a few times, but it never lasted more than a minute. It sounded like a tree branch bending in the wind and dragging along the glass. Except there were no trees that close to the building.

The sounds had stopped when Maria moved into the room. How strange that tonight, of all nights . . .

Lily turned over, willing sleep to come back.

It didn't, but the sound at the window did. It lasted more than a minute this time. And it really didn't sound like a tree branch.

It sounded like fingernails. Scratching at the wall, trying to get in.

The sound didn't fade away like it had before, either. Instead it got louder, and louder. Until that scraping sound was the only thing in Lily's world.

14

TERRIBLE DREAMS THAT SHAKE US NIGHTLY

He was dreaming about La Llorona again.

Not about finding her in his bed. Mateo hadn't had that dream since Brandon was alive. When he dreamed about her now she was standing upright, pointing a long, bony finger at him, and wailing, "¡Aquí! ¡Aquí está mi hijo!"

Every time, he woke up with his head swimming and his heart pounding. He'd swear it wasn't going to happen again. He'd stay up all night drinking pot after pot of coffee if that was what it took.

It always happened anyway.

Tonight La Llorona was chasing him down the lake path. She moved unnaturally fast, gliding three feet over the ground. Her white veil hung all the way down to her feet. All he could see of her were the wild tangles of long black hair escaping from the edges of her veil and the pale, pointed fingers hanging below her billowy white sleeves.

She was going to catch him. There was no way he could outpace her.

He ran anyway. He pushed himself harder than he'd known he could.

He could win this. He could beat her. He could—

She caught him.

Mateo turned to fight, but he was tangled in her veil. Every time he swung a fist, all he reached was more soft fabric.

She wrapped her hands around his neck, around the back of his skull. Her grip was impossibly strong. Bony fingers dug into his flesh.

He stopped resisting. She banged his head into the dirt, pounding, again and again, the crashing sound echoing in his ears.

Blood bubbled out of the wounds in Mateo's neck and flowed down his back. His head throbbed. He was going to pass out. It would be a relief to pass out. But the banging didn't stop—the pounding, it would never stop, it—

He woke.

The dream was over.

The pounding hadn't stopped.

"Pendejo," he muttered. He rolled over toward the door and called, "Go away."

The knocking continued. Mateo glanced toward his roommate's bed, but it was empty.

The power had come back on in the night. The clock said it was ten o'clock on Saturday morning. Seven days and three and a half hours since Brandon had died.

Tonight was the homecoming dance.

Mateo still couldn't believe they hadn't canceled it. When he first heard it had been rescheduled he'd vowed he wasn't going to show up, but the assistant dean had stopped him in the hall and told him they were going to have a moment of silence at the dance, for Brandon. Mateo didn't have a choice anymore. If he skipped it he'd look like he didn't care at all.

And he cared. He cared more than he'd ever thought he could.

Mateo got out of bed, shivering in the ice-cold air-conditioning. He wanted to tell whoever was on the other side of the door to leave him the hell alone, but it was probably Felicia. She'd been stopping by a couple of times a day.

Mateo could never bring himself to say anything harsh to her. Not after . . .

He pulled a pair of cargo shorts on over his boxers, grabbed a fresh T-shirt, and swung open the door.

It wasn't Felicia. It was Ross.

Mateo dropped his eyes and pulled his T-shirt over his head. He knew, rationally, there was nothing Ross or anyone could've done, but regardless, Mateo couldn't stand to look at him now. It was hard to stay rational sometimes.

"Hey, man," Ross said. Lately he'd been saying "man" and "bro" to Mateo a lot. It was awkward. "How you holding up?"

Mateo shrugged.

"Can I come in?" Ross said. "I was hoping we could talk."

Mateo stepped to one side. Ross came in slowly, as if he was afraid Mateo would snap if he moved too fast. Like Mateo was a wild animal. No sudden movements or we might provoke the beast.

Ross sat down gingerly in Mateo's desk chair. Mateo sat on the trunk opposite him and picked up his phone so he'd have something to look at that wasn't Ross's face.

The Acheron staff had mostly been avoiding Mateo since Brandon died. When they talked to him, they said vague stuff like *How you holding up?* No one ever actually said *Sorry about your boyfriend dying.* It probably wouldn't have made a difference if they had, but their vagueness still grated at him.

Oh, well. Maybe they were doing him a favor. He wasn't even out to his family yet, and the idea of that changing someday scared him more than La Llorona ever could.

It wasn't just that Mateo's dad had burned the family's Ricky Martin CDs after Ricky came out, though if he didn't think about it too hard, that story was kind of funny.

No. What scared him was what had happened to his cousin Janisa.

Janisa had lived with her parents in San Juan until she was nineteen. Then, two years ago, she'd run away to the US to marry a girl she'd met on the internet. Now Janisa and her wife lived in Maryland, just one state away from Mateo's family. Last year, Mateo's little sister Cassie had asked if the family could invite

Janisa down for a visit. Mateo's mother had spat into the sink where she was washing dishes and said she didn't know what Cassie was talking about. There wasn't any Janisa in their family.

"I heard you left a message for Dean Cumberland," Ross said.

Mateo turned back to his phone and opened his email. Nothing except ads.

"Yeah," Mateo said. "I need to talk to him."

"How about you talk to me?" Ross said.

Mateo looked up. "I said I need to talk to *him*."

Ross nodded. The condescending patience on his face made Mateo shift his eyes down again.

"I know, but you've got to understand, he's got a lot going on right now," Ross said. "He's got a lot of worried parents to deal with, not to mention all the calls he's been getting from the media. So he asked me to talk to you instead. Or if you'd rather meet with a counselor, I can set that up."

One of those grief counselors? Yeah, right. Mateo wasn't going to go cry on the shoulder of some middle-aged lady in a too-tight blouse.

"Fine." Mateo shifted around on the trunk so he could see out the window. It looked so different in the daytime. The sun shone brightly on the hill where he'd spotted Delilah that night, spread out across the dark grass. "I think the police should reopen the case on Delilah."

Behind him, Ross coughed twice. "Pardon?"

"I have information that I think could make a difference." Mateo's eyes traced the pristine campus. The perfectly manicured lawn. The lake shimmering in the distance. "Delilah wasn't alone that night. She went to Lennox with someone else. She had drugs on her when she fell, but that same person took them out of her purse and flushed them down the toilet while Delilah was lying on the ground."

The feeling of a hand on his shoulder made Mateo leap to his feet. He had a fist pulled back, ready to throw a punch, when Ross took a big step backward and held up his hands.

"Whoa!" Ross said. "Sorry!"

All the adrenaline rushed out of Mateo at once. "Whatever, man." He sank back onto the chair.

"Listen," Ross said, his hands still raised. "I'm not going to lie. This is serious. If you confess now, though, maybe it won't be that big a deal. We'll call the police, and I'll let the dean know, and—"

"What?" Mateo stared at him. "I don't have anything to *confess*. It wasn't me. It was Maria Lyon."

Ross blinked. "What?"

"Maria went out with Delilah that night. She says some guys put drugs in their drinks, but then she took the drugs out of Delilah's purse after she fell. Which doesn't make any sense, right? Also, Maria hated Delilah. I mean, *hates* her. You know they used to be soccer co-captains before Delilah got made captain alone? Maria's still pissed about it. Also, she wants to win the Kingsley Prize. *And* she's been acting really shady ever since that night, like she's got something to hide."

"I get it." Ross put his hands down. "Did you see Maria

and Delilah together that night?"

"Well, no, not personally, but—"

"So did Maria tell you all this?"

"She told me about taking the drugs out of Delilah's purse. She told Brandon the rest."

"She told Brandon," Ross repeated. He sat back in the desk chair, slowly.

Mateo rubbed at his neck. The right side ached. He must've slept on it wrong while he was having that dream. "Yeah. Brandon told me the night before—uh."

The night before he died.

"Okay." Ross's eyes were fixed on Mateo's face. "I believe you."

"You do?" Mateo hadn't expected this.

"I believe that Brandon told you this story. But that's not the same thing as believing Maria did what you're accusing her of. Either way, I'll tell the dean. We can figure out what to do from there."

"Maria did do something wrong, though," Mateo said. "She's a liar. She should've told someone what she knew. There's something really wrong going on here, and Maria's right in the middle of it all. I don't know how, but she is. She was right there when—"

He stopped.

Why? For what *possible reason* had Maria been out by the lake when Brandon—

Mateo hadn't been there. Brandon had asked him to go and he'd said no.

He should've been there. Maybe he could've done something.

"Hey, man, it's all right." Ross's hand was on his shoulder again. Mateo was disgusted to realize he was crying.

"Can we be done now?" Mateo said. "Can you, like, go?"

"Are you sure you don't want to talk to a counselor?" Ross said.

"I am extremely damn sure."

"Well, you can always come and talk to me. Anytime, even if you just need a sounding board, you know, someone to lean on—"

"Christ almighty, please just go."

Ross nodded again. Then he was gone.

Dear lord.

What the hell was Mateo supposed to do now? Telling the dean about Maria was the only plan he'd had. It was supposed to make things better. Instead, he only felt worse.

He'd let Brandon go out there all alone. He'd fought with him, and then he'd let him go.

He kept waiting to wake up and have it not be true anymore. It always was. It would always be true.

It wasn't fair.

Mateo lay down on his bed and put his arm over his eyes to block out the light.

It didn't matter what he did now. Nothing he did would ever matter again.

Lily was back in the hall bathroom with Delilah.

It was the night of that room party. The last time Lily had

ever gotten drunk. The last time they'd kissed.

Lily knew she was dreaming. She knew it had been stupid to kiss Delilah the first time. She knew she shouldn't do it again. She didn't even *want* to.

She did it anyway.

This time, in the dream, Delilah didn't kiss her back. This time she pulled away just as Lily's lips brushed hers, and she started laughing.

Even though Lily knew it was a dream, even though she knew Delilah was in a coma and couldn't hurt her anymore, the laughter hurt anyway.

"Dyke," Delilah whispered. She laughed again.

Lily turned to go—out of this bathroom, out of this dream—but she stumbled on her crutches. Pain shot up her leg. It was strange how she could always feel pain, even in her dreams.

"Cripple," Delilah said, still laughing. "I'm going to tell everyone all about you. What a freak you are."

"Shut up," Lily whispered. She wanted to yell, but she could barely speak. "You aren't even real."

Delilah's laughter was deep and throaty, guttural. It got lower and lower as Lily struggled toward the door, until it turned into a howl.

"Shut *up*," Lily whispered again. She lunged for the door, ignoring the pain, but she couldn't move. Delilah had grabbed her around the waist from behind.

"Stop it!" Lily struggled. Delilah pinned her arms by her sides. Lily wondered if this was what it felt like to be paralyzed.

A sudden, blunt pain in the back of her head distracted her. Delilah had struck her. Lily tried to wrench her torso out of Delilah's grip, but she couldn't move an inch. Her head shrieked with pain. Then she felt a wrenching sensation in her leg and looked down. Bare white bone jutted out below her knee. Then a sharp slash came on both her wrists. Blood spurted out of her veins, running down to the floor in rivers.

"Oh God," Lily tried to cry, but her throat wouldn't make a sound.

"You don't even believe in God," Delilah told her through howls of laughter.

Lily opened her eyes. Delilah was gone.

She was in her room, on her bed, alone. But she could still hear Delilah laughing.

Lily's heart was beating so fast her chest ached. She tried to sit up, but she felt like she'd just swum the four-hundred-meter relay by herself.

The sun was filtering through the curtains high above her head. God, that window. Lily couldn't stand to look at it, but she still kept glancing up to make sure there was nothing on the other side.

What time was it? What *day* was it?

Lily propped herself up on her elbows and reached for her phone. Across the room her dress hung on the closet door, freshly ironed and pure white in the sunlight.

Right. It was the afternoon of the homecoming dance. As if Lily didn't have enough to deal with already.

She sat up slowly and blinked down at her phone screen. It was an hour before they had to leave for the dance. She should've already started getting ready. So should Maria.

Where *was* Maria? She was never in the room much anymore, but she *knew* today was homecoming. She knew how important it was.

Maria was guaranteed to win homecoming queen. She probably would've anyway with Delilah out of the picture, but now that her best friend was dead, not a single person would dare vote against her.

It was the same with the Kingsley Prize. Last week, the other finalists withdrew from the competition, leaving it all for Maria.

They'd gotten everything they wanted. Lily's dreams should be nothing but bunnies and rainbows.

If only Maria would start sleeping here again.

Lily shed her clothes and stepped into the shower. She only had time for a quick one, but she couldn't resist letting the steam rise up around her, luxuriating in the knowledge that they'd won. As long as no one else got in their way, they were golden.

If only this school weren't so damn full of distractions.

Lily climbed out of the shower, wrapped a towel around herself, and sat on the toilet to blow-dry her hair. She usually just threw it into a braid while it was still damp, but tonight she and Maria both needed to look perfect. They needed to *be* perfect. So she took her time, drying her hair carefully with a round brush so it would be neat and smooth before she curled it.

The hot air from the dryer combined with the humidity from

the shower, and Lily could feel herself starting to sweat. She stood up and dropped the towel, squeezing her eyes shut against the pain as she put her weight on her bad leg.

As soon as she closed her eyes, she saw Delilah's laughing face again. Lily stumbled, grabbing onto the sink to keep from falling.

What the hell was wrong with her? She scrubbed at her eyes with the back of her hand. This time she didn't see Delilah. She saw Brandon's body on the stretcher as they carried him away.

She stumbled again and gave up. She sat on the bathroom rug, her hands shaking as she struggled to aim the dryer.

What had happened to Brandon? She'd gone over it in her head a thousand times, but she couldn't come up with an explanation.

Had it really all been a coincidence? That seemed so unlikely.

Plus . . . the truth was, sometimes, Lily got nervous around Maria now.

It was silly. She loved Maria. She'd trust her with her life.

But a tiny voice whispered in her head sometimes, warning her to be careful around Maria. Just in case.

Lily finished drying her hair, got up, and reached for the curling iron. She stared into the steamed-over mirror as she wound the first lock of hair around the barrel.

Felicia had told her story to anyone who would listen. Brandon had died alone in the middle of the path. Maria hadn't shown up until afterward. There was no way she could've done anything to him.

So when Lily got there, why had Maria whispered, *It was me*?

Lily yanked the curling iron out of her hair so fast it hurt. Everything hurt today.

She blinked back tears while she finished her hair and came into the bedroom. It was still empty.

Maria's black dress hung untouched in the closet, her shoes still in their box. They had to leave in fifteen minutes. The candidates for homecoming court had to parade into the ballroom at the start of the dance. Once a year, they were all Miss America.

Everyone would be looking at Maria and Lily tonight. They had to do everything exactly right. They were already dangling over an edge Lily hadn't wanted to go near.

Lily pulled her dress out of the closet and peered at the soft white linen. The hanger shook in her hand.

Tonight was their last chance to make this right. If they still could.

Someone knocked on the door. Lily jumped so fast she nearly hurt her leg again, but she managed to pull on a robe and hop toward the door.

"Who is it?" she called.

"It's Ross."

Great.

Lily wiped her eyes and reached for the doorknob. It was time to play her part again.

She'd always been good at that. Until now, Maria had been too. They'd always followed exactly the same script. The script Lily had written.

Lily didn't know whose script Maria was following now. She only knew it wasn't hers.

Maria didn't sleep much anymore. When she did, she dreamed of Altagracia's funeral.

Her parents had told her Altagracia was buried near their home, in a Catholic cemetery in McLean. That was what she'd wanted, they said. Altagracia had grown up in Mexico and studied to be a teacher, but she'd left home at eighteen to get away from the husband she hadn't wanted to marry. She'd wound up in Virginia with no intention of ever going back.

In Maria's dream, though, Altagracia's funeral was in Mexico. In a tiny town with dirt roads and women in brightly colored dresses, weeping.

Hundreds of mourners walked in a long procession behind a priest and a group of men carrying a casket on their shoulders. The rain poured down, just like it had at Brandon's funeral, but no one seemed to notice except Maria.

They reached a graveyard at the top of the hill. The men lowered the casket to the ground and lifted the lid. Mourners filed up to look, one at a time. Maria was last.

As she approached the coffin the rain poured harder. Thunder rolled overhead. The clouds gathered until it was so dark it could've been nighttime. The rest of the crowd fell back as Maria reached the casket, until they were so far gone she couldn't see them anymore.

Maria looked down, ready to see Altagracia one last time.

Say good-bye. Beg forgiveness.

She didn't get a chance to say a word.

A figure floated out of the coffin and hovered in the air, upright. She was dressed in blue with a white veil covering her face. She was taller than Maria remembered her being.

Maria tried to stammer out her apology. The figure stood over her, immobile. Her blue dress sagged around her thin figure, yards of fabric draped over every inch of skin.

Finally she lifted her arms. Long, pale fingers slipped out of voluminous blue sleeves, gripping the edges of the veil to pull it back, exposing more pale flesh.

The figure tossed the veil aside. It wasn't Altagracia.

It was an old woman, with deeply crinkled lines around her eyes and sallow white skin. She had pencil-thin white eyebrows and a sharp, pointed nose. Her white-blond hair, streaked with dirt and blood, was wild around her face. Her eyes were a solid, shiny black with no white around the edges.

The figure opened her mouth, showing off a row of grimy, uneven teeth, and started to laugh. She laughed so hard she shook the very ground Maria stood on. Behind the old woman's head, the sky opened. A bolt of lightning flashed over their heads.

The rain picked up, pounding onto Maria's face and shoulders. It forced her to her knees, then all the way down until Maria was bowing to the woman in the veil, pressing her face into the mud. She was about to slip into the hole in the ground where the open casket lay.

The woman kept laughing through it all.

"You think you're alone now, Maria?" she rasped. "Soon you'll learn what it's like to *truly* be alone."

Maria opened her eyes.

The woman was gone. Above her, the sun was shining bright and hot. The ground beneath her was wet and scratchy.

Maria sat up slowly. It was getting harder to tell when she was dreaming and when she was awake.

She was outside, but there was no lightning or rain. Nothing but that unrelenting sun.

She was on the soccer field. The scratchy feeling was the just-mown grass, damp from the rain the night before. To her left was the lake, dark and still. She turned her head until it was outside her field of vision.

She wasn't at a gravesite. There wasn't any old woman.

She was in the real world. She was safe.

Safe.

Maria didn't know what "safe" meant anymore.

She'd thought Brandon would be safe.

No. She wasn't supposed to think about Brandon.

Not about how he'd looked by the lake.

Not about how he'd looked at her that day in the language lab. That mix of pity and revulsion when he'd seen what Maria really was.

That was all in the past. She was moving on.

Wait. What was she doing sleeping on the soccer field?

Oh, what did it matter.

Maria climbed to her feet and started back toward the house.

She kept her head to the side so she wouldn't have to see the stupid lake.

She fished her phone out of her pocket. Twelve texts, all from Lily. Maria started to text her back but gave up and put her phone away. She didn't know what to say.

Maria passed the spot where Delilah had fallen. She remembered how she'd looked that night. Her glassy eyes just before she started to climb the stairs. Her bloody hair on the grass.

Delilah was asleep now. Lying in bed, dreaming peaceful dreams. No one expecting her to do anything. It must be wonderful. Maria longed for that kind of sleep.

Maria glanced at the window to their room. She could see Lily inside, but Lily didn't see her. She was pacing back and forth on her crutches. It amazed Maria how fast Lily could move when she was determined.

Maria could just go back to the soccer field. Lie down again. Watch the day turn into night, then day again.

Instead, she trudged up the stairs and down the hall. Lily yanked open the door to their room before Maria could even reach for the knob.

She looked beautiful. She was wearing her vintage white linen dress with the poufy skirt. Her hair was out of its usual braid, piled up on top of her head in carefully messy curls that must've taken her an entire can of hairspray to get exactly right.

"How did you know I was out here?" Maria said.

"I heard your footsteps. You can hear every single thing in this damn house. Now get in here. We're going to be late."

Maria followed her in and sat down on her bed. She could just go back to sleep. Maybe there would be no more dreams this time. She could sleep the way Delilah did.

"Hurry up and put it on." There was a tone in Lily's voice Maria had never heard before. It sounded high-pitched, like she was about to cry. "Just *put it on*, Maria."

Lily held something in her hand. Maria's homecoming dress. She was shaking it back and forth on the hanger.

Oh, right. Tonight was homecoming. Maria blinked up at Lily. She couldn't think of anything to say.

"Look, please, I'm begging you." Lily really *was* about to cry. "Just put it on and comb your hair and try to act normal."

"What's the point?" Maria said. "It doesn't matter."

"It *does* matter, and the *point* is, people already think there's something up with you. If you aren't there tonight they'll know for sure. We're already going to be late, and that's bad enough." Lily yanked the short, flared black dress off its hanger. Maria's mother had ordered the dress online and had it shipped to the school last month. "You don't have time to shower, so just put on some deodorant and wash that dirt off your face."

There was dirt on her face? Maria ran a finger along her forehead and pulled it back. Sure enough, her fingertip was coated with dust.

"I can't pretend everything's normal," Maria said. "It hasn't been normal for three weeks. Not since we used that Ouija board."

"Right. I get it. It's *my* fault. Fine. Can you please get dressed so we can get out of this room?"

Lily glanced toward the window. She kept doing that.

"It isn't your fault." Maria tugged her dirty gray sweatshirt over her head and stood up to peel off her jeans. She went into the bathroom to wash her face, leaving the door open. "I'm the one Altagracia wanted."

"Altagracia," Lily repeated. She hopped into the bathroom on her right foot and leaned against the doorframe, rubbing her hands against the cold. "We're still talking about her, then."

"She's the one orchestrating everything." Maria patted a towel against her face, working out her thoughts as she spoke them aloud. "There are others, but she's in charge. She's the one who made the chandelier fall."

"Chandeliers fall, Maria. That thing was old. It isn't magic, it's *gravity*." Lily drummed her pink-painted nails on the doorframe. Lily's nails were usually perfect, but today they were ragged under the polish, as if she'd bitten them too far down to disguise it.

"I think they pushed Delilah, too." Maria turned the hot water on full blast and scrubbed at the dirt on her neck. Everything was falling into place, slowly. "Not Altagracia. One of the others. Delilah saw the spirits on the lake that night. Maybe one of them followed her inside."

"Maria, I'm begging you, please try to act normal tonight. You can't be talking like this. There aren't any ghosts in the lake. There aren't any ghosts at *all*." Lily tugged on the soft ends of her curled hair. "Nothing pushed Delilah. She was high. She jumped out a window."

Maria wished Lily would listen. It was all so simple if you just thought about it for a minute.

She didn't know how many spirits were at Acheron with them. All she knew was that Altagracia wasn't the only one. It had definitely been one of the others that had hurt Delilah.

Maria could feel the spirits now. It was only a weird tingly sensation, nothing she could've put a name to, but she knew when they were there.

Every time she walked past the old dining hall, she remembered that shadow she'd seen crouched on the ceiling. She didn't know who, or what, that shadow had been, but it wasn't Altagracia. The shadow spirit was something darker.

She tried to remember the stories Altagracia had told her. When she was little, she'd thought they were just that—stories. Now, though, she knew they were something more.

Altagracia had known about the spirits. She'd seen them herself, just as Maria had. When she told Maria about La Llorona, and all the others, she was trying to help Maria. To teach her what she knew. Then Altagracia had died before she could tell Maria everything she needed to learn.

Maria wished she'd told her something that could help her understand what she was feeling now. All these strange sensations that rippled under her skin.

"Don't you think it was weird how it happened?" Maria said. "You don't really think it's all a coincidence, do you? This whole thing, Delilah and Brandon both—it's been the spirits all along. They're helping me, but at the same time they're trying to get to me. I can't let them do that."

"Brandon?" Lily's high-pitched voice was back. "What do you know about Brandon?"

Maria splashed more water on her arms. The hot water from the faucet turned to steam when it hit the cold air, pouring out of the sink and into the room to surround Maria where she stood.

"You've got to tell me," Lily begged. "What are you talking about? *What happened to Brandon?*"

Maria tugged the black dress down over her head. "I don't know, exactly. There are too many spirits here. Dark spirits. They're trying to confuse us. I haven't figured out exactly what's going on, but—"

Lily was crying again, streaks forming in her once-perfect foundation. "Just stop it, okay? Mateo knows it was us."

Maria's head jerked up so fast she splashed water down the front of her dress. "He knows what?"

"What we did to Delilah. He knows—I mean, he *thinks*—you did something to Brandon, too."

"How do you know?" Maria stood, frozen, watching Lily.

"Ross came by looking for you. I told him you weren't here, so he asked if I knew anything about it. He wouldn't say what Mateo told him, but I figured it out. I think he's going to call the police."

"Mateo doesn't know." Maria hoped she sounded more confident than she felt. "No one can prove anything."

She was certain of that last part. Spirits didn't leave behind the sort of evidence that worked in a courtroom. Mateo could have his theories, but there was no proof he could use against Maria.

There was one thing he could do, though. He was already doing it. Spreading rumors about her. Saying Maria was using what had happened to make herself look better. To make people pity her.

If those rumors went far enough—if they got back to the prize committee—Maria would be out of the running for sure. All of this would have been for nothing.

"We need a plan," Lily said. "Let's talk all this through tonight, after the dance."

"Just leave it to me, all right? I'll handle this. I'll handle all of it."

"Don't. Please. I can't—"

Lily let go of the doorframe and waved a frustrated hand at Maria. She lost her balance and plummeted forward. Maria rushed forward and caught her just before her head slammed into the tile counter. Lily pulled free of her grip as soon as she could, grabbing the countertop and jerking herself back upright, her face contorted with pain.

"Oh my God, are you all right?" Maria pushed her back, trying to make her lean against the wall so the weight would be off her legs. It wasn't like Lily to lose control like that. "Lie down. I'll go to the health center and get you something for the pain."

"No." Lily shook her head so fast another curl came loose. "We don't have time."

"It's just a stupid dance. No one will notice if we're late."

Or if they didn't show up at all. That idea sounded wonderful to Maria, actually. If they skipped the dance, she'd have more time to figure out what to do about Mateo.

"Oh, they'll notice." Lily's sigh was almost a laugh. "We have to go. Trust me. Everyone is going to be looking at you tonight, Maria. We can't let them down."

15

THE VERY PAINTING OF YOUR FEAR

They had to have the moment of goddamn silence while he was still standing on the goddamn stage.

They'd just crowned the homecoming court. If Mateo had put a single second's thought into the homecoming court before this moment, he probably could've predicted how it would go down, but he hadn't. He hadn't paid the slightest bit of attention to what was happening at the dance either. By the time he arrived it had already been going on for an hour. So when they called his name from the microphone, his first thought was that they'd figured out he was carrying a flask in his suit jacket and were calling him up to see the dean.

The goddamn dean. The dean, who had pulled Mateo aside when he first got there and told him that he'd spoken with "the authorities" about what Mateo had told Ross that morning, and that there wasn't enough evidence to pursue it. Case closed.

"I know it's hard to accept, son," the dean had said, "but what's happened at this school has been nothing but a series of tragic accidents. I know when you're young you want there to be a bad guy you can fight back against, but the truth is, in this world, sometimes bad things just happen. Even to nice people like your good friend Brandon."

There were so many things Mateo wanted to say then. All he could choke out was "Brandon and I weren't *good friends*."

The dean just patted him on the shoulder and motioned for him to go into the ballroom.

Mateo was on his own. No one would believe him. Brandon had been the only other person who knew what was going on, and Brandon was gone.

It was all awfully convenient for Maria.

Now, on the stage, the dean was smiling that same condescending smile. Mateo wasn't sure who he hated more, Maria or Dean Cumberland.

When the dean called Mateo's name, announcing him as the damn homecoming king, of all the stupid-ass things, there had been dozens of arms pushing Mateo forward. All the rich, pretentious assholes in tuxedos and shiny strapless dresses. Clapping and smiling and wiping away fake tears.

Mateo had stumbled up onto the stage, because that's the direction all those arms were pushing him, and the dean had put a crown on his head. While he was still trying to understand what was happening, the dean called out *Maria's* name as homecoming queen, and then she was up there too.

Then the dean said that instead of the traditional homecoming-king-and-queen dance they were going to have a moment of silence, and Mateo figured it out.

This wasn't about the dance. This was the school trying to show how bad they felt about Brandon. Mateo hadn't bothered to vote for homecoming court, but he bet his name and Maria's had been the only ones on the damn ballot sheet.

It would've been Delilah if it hadn't been for the drugs and the coma, but with the queen bee out of commission, they'd gone with the girl who'd put her there. Because Maria was the next-best thing, and besides, everyone thought Maria and Brandon had been BEST FRIENDS FOREVER OMG.

Brandon was more popular than he'd ever been. Girls were wiping invisible tears. Even the guys who'd spent the past three years whispering *F.F.* (for "Fat Fag") to one another whenever Brandon passed them in the locker room were bowing their heads somberly tonight.

This whole school was one giant waste of space.

They were only a couple of seconds into the moment of god-damn silence, and Mateo was waiting for the dean to lead them in a rousing sing-along of "Kumbaya," when the power went out. A few girls gasped. Behind them, the dean gave a start.

The background generator lights flicked on, casting a dim glow over the tiny, stuffy room. The ballroom was on the second floor of the main house, but it never got used except for home-coming and prom and the big reception for alumni donors every spring. There was just enough light in the room for Mateo to see the faces of everyone he hated.

The worst of them all, Maria, wasn't bothering to cry. He was thankful for that. He couldn't stand to see insincere tears in those dark brown eyes. To see her pretending she'd ever given a crap about Brandon.

He couldn't stand to see her there at all, looking so fake and so pretty in her little black dress. She'd probably picked it to match the color of her goddamn soul.

In the front row, Lily was sobbing. Caitlin and Emily stood on either side of her, rubbing her back, dabbing at their cheeks.

The room was full of girls just like them. Guys too. Wearing the fancy clothes their parents had bought them, their hair coiffed and their eyes fixed on their shoes, wondering how long they had to keep acting solemn. Acting like they cared about a guy they'd have hardly given the time of day if Princess Maria hadn't made them.

At the back of the room Kei and Ryan were standing by the punch bowl, passing a phone back and forth between them. Watching football? Texting townie girls? Playing Candy Drop? Well, at least they weren't putting on an act like the rest of these failures.

Mateo wished they'd all give it a rest. Even Dean Cumberland, who could never remember Brandon's name when he was alive, was wiping his eyes. Probably sad he'd wasted all that scholarship money on some kid who hadn't even made it to graduation.

It was all Mateo could do not to shout. Call them on their hypocrisy. Show them for the phonies they were.

He might have even done it. He'd lost track of how much whiskey he'd drunk that night, and he was past the point of caring what anyone at this school thought of him anymore.

But Maria did it first.

"It wasn't me," she said.

Her words were quiet. Mateo turned to face her.

She wasn't looking at him. She was staring straight out in front of her into the empty air. Looking at something Mateo couldn't see.

They could all see him. Maria was certain of it. Hovering above the room over everyone's heads. Covered in blood.

Why was he covered in blood? It had been a bloodless death.

She'd been there. She'd seen it.

He floated just beneath the high ceiling, his eyes black and solid. Red seeped from the hole in his chest where his heart had been.

"It wasn't me," she said again. Louder, to make sure he heard. "I didn't mean to! I didn't know what it was going to do!"

Brandon cocked his head. He stared at her with those empty eyes. His face had the same disappointed look he'd had in the language lab that day.

He knew exactly what she'd done.

"Please! I'm sorry!" Maria fell to her knees. Her tights tore on the rough surface of the stage, the skin underneath ripping open.

She reached out to Brandon. "Please. Forgive me. I'm so sorry. I'm so, so sorry."

Brandon just cocked his head at her again.

"It's not—she's not—it's not what it looks like, it's—"

Oh God.

It didn't matter what Lily said. No one was listening to her.

Every eye was fixed on Maria. Who was standing on the stage with her eyes bright and her hair wild around her face, talking to no one in the middle of the room.

Lily had to do something. Maria was acting like a complete freak.

She pushed through the crowd and climbed the steps as fast as she could, her leg twisting as she rounded the corner, the pain seizing her. She ignored it and swung past Mateo to where Maria still knelt on the stage. Lily bent down, her leg screaming, and wrapped her arm around Maria's shoulders. She tried to pull her up, but Maria wouldn't budge.

"Please." Lily looked up at Dean Cumberland. "She isn't feeling well. Can I take her to the health center?"

The dean didn't say anything. Lily wasn't sure he'd even heard her. He was staring at Maria, his fist clutched over his open mouth.

Lily tugged at Maria's shoulders, but it was useless. She was frozen.

Desperate, Lily turned to Mateo. "Please. Help me get her out of here."

Mateo didn't seem to hear her either. The look on his face was almost a smile.

Could Brandon hear her?

Why wasn't he saying anything? Altagracia had spoken to her. She'd written on the mirror. Why would Brandon have come here unless he had a message for her?

Maybe he'd come to tell Maria he hated her. That it was all her fault. That she was doomed to hell for all eternity.

"Say something," Maria pleaded.

Brandon just stared back at her.

There was a weight on her shoulders. Lily. Maria shook her off.

The tiara on Maria's head tipped to one side, fell onto the stage, and cracked in half. The pieces rolled off with a clatter that rang out sharply in the silent hall.

"Tell me what this means," Maria begged him. "Tell me why you're here. Tell me why there's so much blood."

Something stirred below her. People talking. Whispering. Moving toward her. Maria ignored it all.

"Tell me," she pleaded again.

She was falling apart.

Maria was breaking into little crazy pieces right in front of his face.

Mateo should've been relishing this moment. He'd thought no one would ever believe him when he told them what she'd done. Now here she was, taking care of the whole thing herself.

He couldn't relax, though. He didn't like that look on Maria's face at all.

She didn't look like she was hiding anything. She just looked sad.

"Don't you understand?" Maria's voice rang out clearly, the crowd below hanging on her every word. "I didn't mean to. I didn't know what would happen. I didn't think anyone would get hurt."

Lily—poor, poor Lily—reached around Maria like she was going to clap her hand over Maria's mouth. Maria pulled out of her grasp and rose to her feet, still reaching out into the empty air in front of her.

Mateo ached to know what she was seeing.

He ached to see it for himself.

Brandon still wouldn't answer her.

He must think she didn't mean what she was saying. That she was only playing for the crowd, the way the rumors said. That all she cared about was getting people's pity.

She had to tell him. She had to make him understand.

Maria leaned forward and swept her arm out wide, gesturing to the roomful of people, to the stupid dance, and raised her voice.

"None of this is important," she called. Brandon didn't give any sign that he'd heard her, but below, the crowd's whispers grew. "Don't you see? This doesn't matter. I don't care about any of this."

Brandon's black eyes still looked right at her. Into her.

He could see everything she'd ever done. Every thought she'd ever had.

"Please," she whispered. Brandon's eyes shone. "I'm so sorry."

Brandon vanished.

The power came back on.

"Please! She just needs to go to the health center!"

Lily's begging sounded overwrought even to her own ears. Maria was on her feet now, her face pressed into Lily's bare shoulder and her arm wrapped tight around Lily's waist. All Lily could think about was what they must look like to all those silent people watching below.

"I'll take her," Lily said. "She'll be fine. She's tired, that's all. She's been so upset about Brandon."

"She needs jail, is what she needs," Mateo said to the dean. "Did you hear what she said about somebody getting hurt? About blood? And what was that bull about the moment of silence not mattering? What the hell is *wrong* with her?"

"She isn't making sense." Lily focused on Dean Cumberland. She didn't know how much argument she had left in her. If the dean didn't agree, Lily might just collapse onto the stage in tears herself. "She hasn't been sleeping. She needs to get some rest. Sir, please."

The dean seemed to still be in a daze.

"Yes, take her to the health center," he finally muttered, waving Lily on.

"No!" The look in Mateo's eyes was fierce.

The dean didn't seem to hear Mateo. He grabbed the dean's arm.

"Look, she's obviously on something." Mateo sounded just as desperate as Lily. "At least take her to the hospital and get her tested."

"No!" Lily said. "She didn't take anything. Sir, please!"

Lily wished she hadn't climbed onto this stage at all. No one would've thought she had anything to do with Maria or Maria's crazy. Now it was way too late.

"It's not anything," Lily went on when the dean looked unconvinced. "I swear. I've been with her all day and she didn't take anything. I'll just bring her to the health center and they'll check her out."

The dean looked at Lily as if he were seeing her for the first time. His eyes slid down to her crutches. Then he looked up at her face again and nodded.

Lily looped her arm around Maria's shoulders. She didn't bother looking to Mateo, or anyone else, for help this time.

Maria hadn't said any single word since the lights came back on.

Lily twisted around and unwrapped Maria's arm from her waist. Maria stumbled, catching her skinned knee on Lily's dress. When she stepped back again, there was a smear of blood on Lily's white linen skirt. Lily managed not to retch at the sight.

She drew back, trying to steer Maria down the steps on her crutches. The dean had to help her. The ballroom was tiny, already too small for the hundred students squeezed into it, but even so everyone fell back to make a path for Maria and Lily to get out of the room. As if they didn't want Maria to touch them.

Lily couldn't blame them.

The feeling of all those eyes on Maria, on both of them—the girls gazing at her and biting their lips, the guys smirking—it made Lily's skin crawl. She wanted to sink down into the floor.

She knew, rationally, that the people in the crowd were thinking about Maria. About the spectacle she'd made up on the stage during what was supposed to be a moment of silence for her dead best friend. They were wondering whether Maria was on something or whether she'd just gone crazy. Emily, standing at the front of the crowd in her red one-shoulder gown, was watching Maria with one eyebrow quirked up, as if she found the whole thing mildly funny.

Lily was sure, though, that they were thinking about her too. Trying to figure out why Lily had gotten involved. Mulling over how strange it was for roommates to touch each other the way Maria had clung to her on the stage. Remembering that they'd shown up for the dance together, without dates.

Putting together the pieces. Figuring out the truth.

Lily didn't even know what the truth was anymore.

She didn't know what Maria had just seen. She didn't want to know.

She led Maria out of the ballroom, trying not to touch her more than she had to. Maria's entire body was quivering.

None of this mattered anymore anyway. Not with those

things Mateo was going around saying.

Lily glanced back at him one last time as she pushed Maria through the door and out into the hall.

He was still watching them. Everyone was.

They couldn't hide anymore.

ACT 4

when the
hurley-burly's
done

16

FOUL WHISPERINGS ARE ABROAD

Tap. Tap. Tap.

Lily pulled her grandmother's quilt over her head, blocking out the light.

Lily didn't believe in ghosts. It was the same as with God. There was no logical reason to accept the idea that something she couldn't see or hear or touch—some vague idea she was supposed to take purely on faith—had any power over her.

Between the atheism and the lesbian thing, Lily was a terrible Catholic. Even before she'd added murder to her list of sins.

But that was reality for you. If there had been some benevolent force watching over them, there was no way it would've let Lily and Maria wind up where they were now.

Tap. Tap. Tap.

Lily didn't know what had moved the planchette that night.

All she knew was that it wasn't a spirit. Because there was no such thing.

She didn't know what she'd heard that night at the window. She didn't know who Maria thought she'd seen in the ballroom, or how she thought she'd been talking to her dead nanny, or what she thought had killed Brandon. She didn't know why she'd found her favorite photo of her and Maria lying on the floor with the glass cracked over Lily's face.

All she knew was that none of it had anything to do with imaginary creatures of any kind. This was the real world, not some crappy horror movie.

Tap. Tap. Tap.

Lily had scored a 2380 on her SATs. She hadn't done that by believing in fairy tales.

But now Lily was afraid.

Not of ghosts. There was a rational explanation for all the things that kept happening. Whatever that rational explanation might be—*that* was what Lily was afraid of.

But the only rational explanations she could think of all led to Maria.

Lily knew Maria as well as she knew herself. There were a lot of people Maria didn't particularly like, but she wasn't capable of actually *hurting* anyone.

The problem was, Maria hadn't been herself lately.

Tap. Tap. Tap.

The student health center had decided to keep Maria for a few hours to make sure she slept. They hadn't run a drug test—Lily doubted they had the equipment for that—but they'd said Maria's pupils weren't dilated, she didn't have a nosebleed, she knew who the president was, and she was probably just stressed about exams coming up.

Lily agreed. Yes, that was probably it.

The nurse said she'd give Maria something to help her sleep through the night, and that Lily should go on back to the dance. Lily told Maria to call her if she needed anything, but Maria didn't seem to hear. She was lying on the cot, her face tipped toward the ceiling, her eyes moving back and forth like she was watching something Lily couldn't see.

Lily had no intention of going back to the dance. Instead she'd gone straight to her room and yanked her homecoming dress over her head, tearing off the top button in the process. She'd thrown it over Maria's desk chair and collapsed on her bed.

More than an hour had passed since then, but none of their friends had come to check on them. No one wanted to be around Maria. Lily didn't want to either, but no one ever asked what Lily wanted.

Now she was huddled on the bed, shivering under her grand-mother's quilt.

Because—the sound at the window. It was back again.

Scratching. Tapping. Like fingernails, dragging back and forth across the wood, stopping every so often to deliver short little raps. Three of them, always, all in a row.

Tap. Tap. Tap.

It was louder than it had been last time she'd heard it. Tonight it was so loud everyone upstairs in the ballroom could surely hear it. So loud the whole building should've been shuddering on its foundations.

Lily was shaking harder than she could ever remember shaking before.

She'd been shivering there for an hour, listening to the sound getting louder, waiting for it to turn into something normal. A raccoon rubbing against the siding. The ancient heating system malfunctioning.

No matter how long she waited, it still sounded like enormous, claw-shaped hands scraping eagerly at the window frame.

Lily peeked out from the edge of the blanket. She could see the window in the candlelight, but the glass was hidden behind the curtains. All she had to do was draw them back and she'd have her answer.

She was still working up her nerve when the scratching sound was replaced with a slow, steady thumping.

Then louder. A fist, pounding on the window, hard as thunder.

It sounded exactly like the knocking they'd heard that first night in the old dining hall. The knock that sounded like it was coming from everywhere and nowhere all at once.

Lily shrank back onto the bed. There was no way she was touching those curtains now.

It was getting louder. Then louder still.

Scratching. Knocking. Crashing. Like some wild, ferocious animal trying to tear through the wall.

When Lily heard a sharp, sudden thud right above her, she dove back under the covers, pulling the pillow over her head to shut it out.

Nothing is happening. I'm only having a nightmare. I'll wake up tomorrow and realize how stupid I've been.

As though they could hear her thoughts, the sounds started to lessen. Slowly. Over another hour, or two, or three—Lily had lost count—the constant, insistent knocking gave way to the occasional tap or scrape. Sometimes an entire minute would pass without a single sound at all.

Finally, the sounds ceased altogether.

After ten minutes of silence, Lily's breathing started to slow.

Then the window latch slid open.

Oh, Jesus Christ.

Lily was beyond reason now.

Oh God, please help me. Please make this stop. Please make this go away. This isn't real—make this not real, please, please. . . .

The window squeaked as it slid up in its tracks.

Lily shut her eyes as tight as she could and ordered every muscle in her body to still. She held her breath. Maybe the thing wouldn't see her if she didn't move.

She waited to feel the flow of warm air from the window. For the thump of something lowering itself onto the floor. She hoped whatever it did, it would do it fast.

She waited.

A minute passed. Then another.

She couldn't hold her breath any longer. But when she allowed the air to softly enter her body then flow back out again, nothing happened.

There was no thump. No warm air, either.

The room was silent.

Had she imagined it all?

Lily's heart was pounding harder than she'd have thought possible. There was no use waiting any longer.

She had to get out of this room. She had to leave her blanket cocoon and face whatever was in here with her.

Except there *couldn't* be anything.

Lily knew better than that. She *knew*.

She took a deep breath. Then she threw the blankets from her head before the fear could immobilize her again.

A blurry white shape stared at her from the other side of the room.

She started to scream. Then she clapped her hand over her mouth.

It was just her crumpled homecoming dress, hanging from Maria's chair.

Hold it together, Lily, she told herself. *You've made it this far. You can't lose it now.*

She darted her eyes around the room, but nothing else seemed out of place. The window was shut and locked.

She got out of bed, taking care not to look at the spot on the floor just under the window. She was sure there was nothing there, but she didn't want to look right now, that was all.

Lily had to do something. She had to get the hell out of this room.

She pulled on a pair of sweatpants, headed for the main entrance of the house, and pushed the front door open, letting the humid air wash over her. It had stopped raining.

There wasn't a soul outside, not even a stray groundskeeper or lonely freshman. Everyone was still at the dance. Out of habit, she waved a trembling hand toward Tony in the security guard's booth, but she was too far away to see if he waved back. It didn't matter either way. On dance nights, students were allowed outside two hours past their usual curfew as long as they stayed on campus.

The hill next to the house rose up in Lily's eyes. The Siward family cemetery plot stood at the top. Lily had only been up there once, with her tour group when she'd first started at Acheron. Lily wasn't good at climbing hills.

Before she knew what she was doing, though, Lily was hoisting herself up to the very top. She was trembling, but she pushed on, ignoring the pain in her legs.

The graveyard was tiny, bordered by a low stone wall that would've crumbled away decades ago if the school landscapers hadn't kept it up. At one end was a statue of a woman, her face too eroded to make out the features. A veil was draped over her head, and she clasped a bouquet of roses in her hand. Below her, a dozen ancient tombstones perched at odd angles. A single chestnut tree stood opposite the statue.

Lily remembered that tree from her tour. It looked old, but it wasn't. It had been planted when the school was created in the 1950s. The original cemetery tree had been cut down for firewood during the Civil War. The Union soldiers who'd occupied the house, the student ambassador told them, had torched pretty much everything they could find. Trees. Furniture. The clothes and books and kids' toys the Siward family had left behind when they were forced to evacuate. It was a miracle the Northern army had left the house standing at all.

Lily stepped over the low stone wall and lowered herself onto it unsteadily. Her legs ached from the climb. One of the dorm cats climbed onto the wall beside her and rested its head in her lap. Lily petted it absently and squinted to read the old tombstones. One had a tiny drawing carved above the indistinguishable letters. It might've been a bird or an angel. Had the grave belonged to a child?

A low chuckle from behind the tree almost made Lily scream again.

"What's the matter, Lily Boiten?" Austin's head popped out from behind the trunk. He slunk around and settled onto the stone wall next to Lily, stretching out to rest his feet on the tombstone with the carved drawing.

"You like it up here too?" Austin's eyes were red and glassy in the moonlight. "Usually we have the place to ourselves."

We? Lily looked back more carefully toward the tree. Sitting on the wall right next to it was Austin's kid sister, Felicia. In the darkness, Lily hadn't even noticed her.

Felicia was wearing jeans and a sweatshirt and had dark

circles under her eyes. Austin was still in his rumpled black tuxedo jacket over a black shirt, a loose purple bow tie dangling around his open collar.

The cat scowled and jumped off the wall when Austin sat down, leaving the three of them alone.

Lily gave Felicia a little halfhearted wave. Felicia didn't wave back. Her eyes were fixed on Lily's face. Lily tried not to find that creepy.

"What'd you come up here for, Lily Boiten?" Austin reached into his pocket, but when he pulled his hand out it was empty. "Sorry, I'm all out."

"I don't want any of your *stuff*, Austin," Lily said.

Austin pointed at the statue of the woman with the roses. "You came up here to hang with her, then, right? She's totally your type."

Lily flinched. She glanced over to see if Felicia was laughing, but Felicia's face was completely still.

Austin was probably just making another of his stupid jokes. But what if he'd seen her and Maria up on the stage and figured it out? What if everyone had? Tomorrow, at breakfast, was everyone going to look at her and know?

"So, Lily Boiten," Austin said, distracting her before she could work herself into a full panic. "You remember that night you came and bought those two pills from me?"

Lily froze.

She'd counted on Austin, in his perpetually stoned haze, to forget about that. She'd counted on him not to be a risk.

"What about it?" Lily glanced behind her, calculating how fast she could get down the hill. It would be hard with her legs still hurting this way.

"You were acting really funny that night." Austin lifted his feet into the air and thumped them back down onto the tombstone. Lily shifted, remembering the lectures she'd heard as a kid when she visited her grandparents' graves about being respectful of the dead.

"I still can't figure out why you wanted that stuff," Austin went on. "I haven't even seen you drink a beer since, like, sophomore year."

Lily shrugged, trying to act like this was no big deal. "I wanted to unwind."

"You? Unwind? Yeah, okay." Austin laughed. "Anyway, it's weird how they said Delilah did acid that same night. Where would she've gotten it? I know I didn't have any. I didn't even remember I had those two pills I gave you. Not until you asked and I saw them stuck in the bottom of my bag."

"Yeah, weird." Lily tried to stand up, but her legs hurt too much.

"Anyway, welcome to our spot, Lily Boiten." Austin leaned in close. "Fee and me, we like to come up here sometimes. Get a break from all the crazy down the hill. Nice to go someplace quiet, where you can hear yourself think."

"It was quiet until *you* got here." Felicia looked pointedly at Austin.

"Yeah, well, things went cuckoo in that ballroom. Had to get away from that shit before I lost it. You too?" Austin directed the question to Lily.

A trickle of sweat formed behind her right ear. "I don't know what you're talking about."

"Oh." Austin dropped his feet to the ground. He looked disappointed. "Never mind. You seemed so freaked, I thought maybe you saw it too."

He didn't sound like he was talking about her and Maria, but Lily had to be sure. "Saw what?"

He shrugged. Then he glanced at Felicia.

"Tell her if you want." Felicia shrugged. "I don't see the point in hiding it."

Austin hesitated another moment. Finally, he turned to Lily.

"You seriously didn't see it?" he said. "You didn't think there was anything *out of the ordinary* in that ballroom? Besides your friend acting like a psycho, I mean?"

He'd said "friend." She was safe. Lily exhaled.

"I seriously didn't see anything," Lily said. "And Maria wasn't acting like—"

"You didn't feel the air change?" Austin interrupted her. "You didn't see the lights go fuzzy?"

"I saw the power go out. Is that what you mean?" Maybe Austin was stoned after all.

He shook his head. His face had gone from disappointed to frustrated. When he spoke again, it was in a mutter so low Lily could barely hear him. "No one at this godforsaken school ever sees them but me."

"Sees what? What are you talking about?"

"He's talking about *them*." Felicia's voice was crisp and clear. It made Lily shiver.

She remembered that night she'd sat up listening to Felicia's screams. She wondered if Felicia's dreams were like her own.

"Have *you* seen them?" Lily whispered.

Felicia shook her head. "No. But I've heard them . . . at the window."

Oh, hell. Oh, *hell*.

"Does it come from up here?" Lily whispered. Felicia glanced at her but didn't answer. "The sound at the window?"

"No. *They* aren't in the cemetery." Austin swept his arm out over the graves. "This place is the only safe spot in this whole damn campus. It's consecrated ground. The dead people up here, even that creepy statue chick with the flowers, they're all off in heaven someplace. Or hell. Wherever. Either way, they don't bother us. The messed-up ones are all down the hill. And in the woods."

The sweat trickled down Lily's neck. It sounded like Maria wasn't the only one who believed in ghosts.

Austin was speaking rapidly, without his usual slur. He pulled out a lighter and flicked it on. His fingers shook. "This place is cursed as hell, man."

Lily felt shaky too. She hadn't sensed anything in the ballroom, but Maria clearly had. She turned back to Felicia. "You've heard them before?"

Felicia nodded.

"At the window?" Lily pressed. "The scratching?"

Felicia nodded again, slowly this time.

That meant Lily *wasn't* crazy. But she didn't want to think about what else it might mean.

"I've seen them lots of times," Austin said. "And one of them . . . the girl on the lake . . . I only saw that girl once, but it was enough to last the rest of my life. She had freaky big black eyes. She talked to me, too. Told me to come swimming."

Lily's palms were slick. She wiped them off on her pants and tried to catch Felicia's eye, but her face was blank again.

"I cannot wait, man." Austin lit a cigarette and took a long puff. "I cannot wait to graduate and get the hell out of this place."

"What else have you seen?" Lily asked him.

Austin looked up, startled. Lily realized she'd grabbed his arm. She didn't let go.

"Are there . . . others?" she asked him.

Austin looked at her hand and took another puff. "Is this why you wanted stuff that night? To drown it all out?"

"Uh." Lily hesitated. But Austin nodded, as if he understood.

"Anyway, after what happened to Bran . . ." Austin glanced over at Felicia, then cut himself off. "Up until then, I didn't think they could actually hurt us. But now I'm not spending another second down at that school that I don't absolutely have to."

"What do you mean?" Lily's heart was pounding so loud she was sure he could hear it. "Brandon had a heart problem."

"Sure he did." Austin inhaled another whiff of smoke. Felicia's face was stony.

Lily gazed around at the darkened tombstones. This was why she'd come up here, wasn't it? To see if it could be true? If there really were dead people who rapped on windows and sent photo frames crashing to the ground?

"What else have you seen?" Lily asked again.

"Once I saw a shadow moving outside my room." Austin kept his eyes fixed on the tombstone under his feet. His voice shook. "And I've heard rustling outside my door, near the top of the stairs. Sometimes I go in my room and I swear there's stuff there I've never even seen before. But mostly I just, like, *feel* it. You know? Like at the dance tonight. It'll get really cold all of a sudden, and the air goes funny. It's like looking into a cloud, or a fog, except you're inside."

A fog. Lily wondered again about the capsules Austin had given her. These sounds. These feelings.

"And then there are all those stories," Austin said slowly.

"Hey." Felicia's eyebrows shot up. "It's time to stop talking."

"What stories?" Lily said.

"Oh, you know," Austin said. "The townies tell them. Like the one about that dead teacher."

"Seriously," Felicia said. "Stop. We can't trust her with this."

Lily pressed on, hoping Austin wouldn't listen to his sister. "What teacher? When?"

"Well, it was in the fifties."

Lily nodded. That explained a lot.

No one ever talked about Acheron in the fifties. Back then, the school had been exclusive, Christian, and all white. The holdouts were trying to come up with ways to keep their kids from having to go to school with black people, no matter what the Supreme Court had to say about it. Eventually, they lost, but not without a serious fight.

The Acheron brochures never mentioned why the school was founded. They just said, "Acheron Academy is proud to maintain a diverse student body."

"She was a student teacher," Austin said. "They say she was acting really weird—talking to people who weren't there, stuff like that. Then she jumped out a window on the fourth floor. The one at the top of the stairs."

Lily's breath hitched. That was the window Delilah had jumped from.

"What happened to her?" Lily asked.

Austin drew a flat hand across his throat in a slicing motion. Lily shivered.

"There are a ton of others. Stories about what happened to the old plantation owners before the Siwards, and to their slaves. That's why I wear this goth crap." Austin tugged on the front of his black T-shirt. "I figure they go after people who're scared of them. If I act like I'm into all this prince-of-darkness stuff, maybe they'll leave me alone."

Felicia laughed. "Yeah. That'll totally work."

"That's ridiculous." Lily tried to smile at Felicia in agreement, but Felicia was back to ignoring her again.

Austin shrugged. "Yeah, well, I never want to see that chick on the lake for the rest of my life. I don't care what I've gotta do."

Lily wondered about those voices she'd heard, telling her to come for a swim. She didn't want to hear them again either.

Well, maybe she did. Just a little bit.

Austin peered at Lily. "So now it's your turn. What really happened in that ballroom?"

"I, um—"

Lily couldn't tell them. She couldn't trust anyone except Maria.

If she could still trust Maria.

"I don't know," she said. "I don't—I only—look, you guys, I just want everything to get back to normal."

Austin laughed. "Normal?"

"You know what I mean."

"Well, I hate to break it to you, but that's not how it works." Austin put out his cigarette on the damp stone wall with a low sizzle. "Whatever's down the hill—they're the ones pulling the strings, not us. Which means there isn't any such thing as 'normal' around here."

17

COME LIKE SHADOWS, SO DEPART

Maria could feel them all around her now.

Altagracia. The others, too.

The one at the top of the stairs. The one on the lake. The one who whispered through the mirrors. They were all different. They were all powerful.

Acheron seeped with it. The stench of death, and rot, and power. How had she never noticed before?

When the spirits were present, it was little more than a feeling. She couldn't have explained it. It wasn't anything you could see or smell or touch. It was like . . . falling but never hitting the ground. That glorious sensation, of nothing beneath you but empty air.

Maria understood the spirits now.

Altagracia wanted to help her. She already had. She'd do whatever Maria asked.

The other spirits were darker. Their intentions weren't so clear.

They were the ones who'd pushed Delilah. Who'd drowned people in the lake.

Those spirits did as they chose. Took what they wanted.

And what they wanted now was Maria. They'd sent Brandon as a warning.

But they couldn't have her. She wouldn't let them.

Altagracia had taught her well. She knew what she had to do.

It had been easy to talk the health center nurse into letting her leave early. But the Ouija board was in shards, and she couldn't go back to the mirror in her bathroom without Lily getting in the way. She'd tried to go to the old dining hall, but the door wouldn't budge, even when she threw herself against it with all her strength.

So she'd come to the woods, beyond the borders of the lake. She'd always felt something dark here. Tonight it felt darker still.

She'd come looking for the spot where Brandon died. Spirits always lingered at the site of a death. If Maria could find Altagracia by the lake path, she could find out what the spirit knew. Seek her advice. Renew her protection.

But Maria had been out here for hours, and she still hadn't found the oak tree she'd hidden behind that day. Everything looked different from how it had that morning. Upside down and inside out. She'd wandered from tree to tree, and now she'd gone too deep into the woods to be at the right place.

Still, her legs propelled her forward even when her sense said to turn back. Leaves and branches were all she could see in every direction. Shadows flitted from one tree trunk to another each time she turned her head. Her black dress was sticky with sweat and tree sap.

She couldn't see the glint of moonlight off the lake any longer, but she could hear the water lapping at the shore. A strange, unfamiliar sound. The lake was usually still as glass.

Maria reached for a trunk to steady herself and felt a strange, rough pattern under her fingers. She looked up. Twisted branches wound toward the sky, higher than she could see.

This tree was old. Gnarled. Ancient. Maria turned and saw another tree that looked just like it, and another. Behind her was a trunk so massive she couldn't see around it. It had to be eight feet wide.

But there weren't any ancient trees on this campus. The plantation grounds had been destroyed in the fire three centuries ago. Then the Union soldiers had chopped down every tree the fire had spared. The trees that made up the woods now had been put here by the school's landscapers in the 1970s. Yet the trees she was facing looked like they'd been standing since the dawn of time.

Something else caught Maria's eye then. A sight she'd never seen before. A tall, dark shape stood at one end of the grove. It almost looked like a building—but it couldn't be. There weren't any buildings this far out on campus.

Maria moved toward the shape, picking her way carefully

through the grass in her bare feet, her gold high-heeled sandals looped over her little finger.

She squinted against the glimmer of moonlight, trying to get a better view of the shape. She rubbed her eyes. She hadn't slept much lately, and it was making her vision blurry. Making her see things that weren't there.

A shadow flitted to her right. Maria tried to follow it with her eyes, but it was gone. Instead she glimpsed another shadow in the distance. A dark shape standing under a tree. Tall, lean. A human shape.

"Altagracia?" Maria hated how small her voice sounded. How much fear it held. "Is that you?"

The shadow tilted to the right. Like it was swaying in the breeze.

Not swaying. Swinging.

Swinging from a tree branch.

Maria clapped a hand over her mouth to keep from crying out. She could see the thin shadow of the rope. The dark figure in the distance swung in the wind.

This couldn't be real.

The figure in the distance moved. It wasn't a gentle sway this time. This time, the figure jerked in Maria's direction. The wind picked up to a gust.

The other spirits. They were trying to scare her again.

Maria turned away and tried to make herself stop trembling.

She wasn't a little kid anymore. If the spirits wanted to frighten her, it would take more than a shadow in the distance.

She turned her attention back to the trees. She still hadn't found the right spot. She peeked around a trunk, looking for anything else that was familiar.

The wind stopped suddenly. The air grew unnaturally still.

Something pricked at the back of Maria's neck. She turned slowly.

The figure wasn't hanging from the tree anymore.

It was on the ground. It was halfway to where Maria stood.

It was still moving.

Maria turned and ran.

She ran toward the tall, dark shape at the end of the grove. There was a point at the top of the structure. Maybe she could hide behind it.

Maria picked up her pace, her legs pumping, crunching down on twigs that broke and cut into the soles of her feet. She hit a tree root and tripped, cursing as she caught herself with her hands and scrambled to her feet. She looked over her shoulder, but she couldn't see the figure anymore.

She turned back. That was when she got her first good look at the building.

It was the church. The old one-room family church that had belonged to the original plantation. One of the only structures to survive the Civil War. It was supposed to have a trapdoor with a secret passage that led to the river where the Siward family could escape during Indian raids. Maybe Maria could hide behind the trapdoor.

She looked behind her. She couldn't see the figure anymore,

but it was still there. It had to be. The feeling was still pricking at the back of her neck. Maria reached the front of the church, panting, and ran from one end of the building to the other, looking for a way inside. The outside of the church was shabby, with old, peeling white paint. Most of the windowpanes were broken, showing a dark and dusty interior.

Finally she found a heavy, scarred door. There was no doorknob, so she pushed against the middle of the door. It swung open easily, its bottom scraping against the unpolished wood floor.

Maria ran across the threshold and shoved the door closed behind her, then darted to the nearest window. She peered out into the gray light of the woods. She couldn't see the hung figure anymore.

Was it gone? Would she be safe in the church?

No. It didn't work that way. Spirits didn't care about shut doors or broken windows. Still, though, it felt better to have walls on all sides of her.

It was dark inside the church, despite the early morning light filtering through the trees. Maria groped around the doorframe for a light switch, but she didn't expect to find one, and she didn't. Instead she turned on her phone. She didn't have a signal here, but the screen gave off a faint light. Maria held it up to illuminate the room.

The inside of the church felt smaller than it looked from the outside. Dust swirled in every direction, stinging Maria's eyes and settling onto the gauzy black fabric of her dress. The brick floor was covered with a thick layer of dirt and dead insects that coated her feet and made her itch. The walls were gray and covered in dark shadows and smears. There were no pews, just a bare wood altar along the opposite wall holding a rusty bowl and a single candlestick. Maria walked toward it, holding up her phone to get a better look.

When she was a few feet from the altar, she felt it. The sensation under the soles of her feet had changed. She was standing on a cracked wooden square.

She crouched down to look. Dust flew up and she swept it aside, coughing. Her fingers wrapped around a metal handle.

The trapdoor.

Maria could sense warmth coming from it. Something on the other side of this door was humming at her, the way the Ouija board had that night.

LEAVE. NOW.

The words were strong and startling in her head.

For a moment she thought it was Altagracia, but it wasn't the cold, distant voice of a spirit. This voice was warm, afraid, and very close by.

This wasn't Altagracia. This was *her*. Maria's own instincts, telling her she should get out of this place.

But she had to find out what was coming. This was her only chance to get answers.

Maria couldn't let fear control her. She'd done so much already. She'd go as far as she had to.

She pulled the handle. It moved easily, just like the front

door. Too easily for something that hadn't been opened in centuries. Behind the door was nothing but heat, darkness, the smell of old smoke, and that overpowering fear.

Maria held her phone light toward the opening, but all she could see was swirling dust. She hesitated only long enough to drop her shoes on the dirty floor and slide the phone back into her pocket before she swung one leg over the side. When nothing happened, she slid her other leg in, until she was sitting on the edge of the hole.

The humming feeling was louder than ever. It called for Maria to drop all the way in.

She hesitated.

Even if that story about the secret passage was only a school legend, this had to at least be some sort of storage room, or a priest's quarters, didn't it? People must've been able to get in and out of it when the church was built. Surely the hole was shallow enough that she could jump in and land on her feet.

But what if it wasn't? What if Maria fell and broke her neck? No one would ever find her here. She'd starve to death while she waited.

She swung one foot in a slow circle, exploring the surroundings as best she could. Then she felt it. A hard, smooth surface to her left side. An earth wall with a depression in it. She slid her foot down farther and felt another depression, and another.

A ladder, carved into the wall.

Maria angled her body toward it and slid down, her toes getting a firm grip on the ladder's rungs. As she descended, it got darker and darker and hotter and hotter until the soles of her feet struck something hard and rough. A very old wooden floor. It was free of dirt, but something crunched under her heel. The floor was covered in tiny, jagged pebbles and sticks. Thousands of them, reaching all the way to the walls on either side.

Maria didn't bother to turn on her phone here. The air was heavy with stale heat, dust, a lingering smell of smoke, and something else. Something thicker. Slowly, her eyes adjusted to the darkness.

There was a faint light coming from somewhere far away. The end of the tunnel, maybe. Maria wondered if the sun had risen.

But it wasn't light enough to get a good look at her surroundings. All she could see were the walls on either side of her. The space was narrow, barely wide enough for her to walk without turning sideways, and long, made of hard, packed earth. A few yards on, something glinted in the faint light.

Whatever it was up ahead—that was it. The reason Maria was here. This was what had hummed to her.

Maria moved toward the light. Small piles of sticks were gathered against the bases of the walls every few feet. There were dark splotches on every surface, like the ones she'd seen on the walls of the church above. The sticks and pebbles dug into her feet, breaking the skin and leaving bloody smears on the stones behind her.

She kept her eyes fixed on the light ahead. It looked like the flame of a tiny candle, perched on the wall on her left side.

This was it. This flame—it was a spirit.

Altagracia.

Maria straightened her shoulders. She wouldn't show her fear, the way she had with that shadow in the woods. She wouldn't let the spirits see how weak she was.

The flame grew brighter as she approached. When she was close enough to get a good look, she bit her lip not to show her surprise.

There was no candle. Just a ball of flame hanging in the air.

Maria swallowed. Keeping her voice as steady as she could, she said, "I am here."

The flame flared higher.

"Altagracia?" Maria said. The flame was bright. Brighter than a candle flame had any right to be. "I have questions."

The flame flickered and began to fade.

"Wait." Maria panicked and switched to Spanish. "Lo siento. Soy yo María."

I'm sorry. It's me, Maria.

The flame brightened and grew. Maria shielded her eyes.

A voice whispered to her left, too quiet for her to make out the words. Maria darted her eyes toward the sound but she didn't see anything. "Altagracia?"

The voice whispered again. Maria still couldn't make it out. Then it giggled.

It didn't sound like Altagracia. It sounded like a child. An uneasy feeling stirred in Maria's chest.

"¿Quién es?" Maria asked. *Who's there?*

The answer came in a rumbling man's voice, so loud and deep Maria's knees buckled.

"GET OUT!" the man roared.

The ball of flame flared up. It was as big as Maria's head, radiating heat toward her face. She took a step back, but the heat didn't lessen.

"Who are you?" she said in English, her voice barely above a squeak.

The child's voice giggled again.

The flame flared. Smoke billowed up, making Maria cough. In the center of the flame was a dark spot with a strange shape. It grew longer, higher. It was too dim to make out the features, but the shape looked almost like the outline of a human face.

Brandon.

The flame was going to form Brandon's face. She knew it.

Sweat dripped down Maria's forehead. She didn't know if it was the fire or the fear.

She couldn't stand to look at him again.

"Altagracia? Are you here?" Maria looked back in the direction she'd come. She couldn't see more than a few feet away, despite the light from the flame.

Surely she could find her way if she needed to. Climb back up that ladder. Hoist herself into the church.

But it didn't matter. Maria took a long, deep breath. That thing, the flame, these voices, Brandon—none of them could touch her. She was alive. She was stronger than the dead.

"I demand to speak with Altagracia!" Maria hoped she

sounded bold. Like she wouldn't take no for an answer.

The next voice she heard was a woman's, but it wasn't Altagracia.

This voice moaned low, the same sounds over and over. At first Maria didn't think she was speaking actual words. After a minute, the moans became clearer.

"Please." The woman's voice was fragile, like she might break at any moment. "Please. Please don't."

"Listen to me!" Maria shouted. Somewhere in this mess was Altagracia. Maria couldn't let the others scare her away before she got her answers. "Tell me what I want to know!"

More voices came.

Men. Women. Children. All speaking at once. They were talking fast, racing over each other, some in English, some in Spanish, some in other languages. Their words were too garbled for her to understand.

The voices multiplied until Maria couldn't tell them apart. There must have been hundreds. She couldn't tell if Brandon was among them.

Panic stirred in her. She'd never faced more than one spirit at a time.

It was too much. There were too many.

Maria turned to run.

Another flame shot up from the ground, blocking her path back to the church. The sweat was pouring down her face.

"Let me go!" she shouted.

The flames shot up toward the ceiling.

Fire.

That was why it was so hot. Why the smoky smell still lingered.

The fire three hundred years ago—it had started in this tunnel.

The Siwards. Their slaves.

Hundreds had died here.

The pebbles under her feet—that was what was left of them.

Maria stumbled at the realization, at the crunch of crumbled bones under her feet. She turned to run the other way. She couldn't stay here, not with—

The fragments under her feet were moving.

Maria scrambled backward until she felt heat at her back.

The fire. It was on all sides of her now.

She bent down and curled her hands over her head to protect her face from the flames. That was when she saw it.

The bone fragments on the ground in front of her. They were moving to form shapes. No, not shapes, lines. Like the lines that had faded into the steam on her bathroom mirror.

The spirits were writing to her again. In Spanish.

BIENVENIDA, MARÍA.

Welcome, Maria.

Maria pushed back the panic in her chest and waited until her breathing steadied. She stood as tall as she could and straightened her shoulders.

"I order you to tell me what you know," Maria said.

The pebbles spilled out of their neat rows, and the flame on the wall in front of her dimmed. For a long moment there was no sound in the tunnel. Even the fire behind her burned in silence.

Then came the sharp, horrible sound of laughter.

Maria took a long breath and stood her ground. She knew what she had to say. Altagracia had taught her years ago. It had all seemed like a game then, but she must've known Maria would need to know someday.

"Tell me what my future holds," Maria said. "Or an eternal curse will fall on you!"

The laughter came again. With it, the pebbles began sliding back into neat lines. It took longer than before for the letters to form.

AUNQUE TENGAS EL PODER, MARÍA, NO SABES USARLO. NO ERES COMO NOSOTRAS.

Although you may have power, Maria, you don't know how to use it. You are not like us.

Power. Altagracia had told Maria the spirits only had as much power as you gave them.

"That's of no use to me," Maria said. "I command you to tell me my future. Do I have anything to fear?"

MATEO PÍFANO.

She'd known Mateo was a threat. Still, seeing it spelled out right in front of her sent a chill down Maria's spine.

"Thank you," she said, trying not to let her new apprehension show. "Next, I order you to—"

The ball of flame flared high before she could finish. The fire covered half the wall now.

The spirits in this tunnel were strong. Too strong.

Maria had made them that way. She'd invited them in with that damn Ouija board, but she'd never bound them back.

She didn't have much time.

"What do I need to do?" Maria cursed the begging note that crept into her voice.

The pebbles moved quickly this time.

LA SANGRE QUIERE SANGRE.

Blood will have blood.

Maria swallowed. She'd thought it might come to this.

She had to kill Mateo.

The spirits were right. It was the only way. Mateo was the last thing standing between Maria and what the spirits had promised her.

She'd killed already. What difference would one more death make?

It was funny, the way she used to think it mattered what she did and didn't do. It was funny, how she used to care.

"Where?" she whispered. "When?"

EN DUNSINANE. CUANDO EL SOL SALGA POR EL OESTE

At Dunsinane. When the sun rises in the west.

Maria blinked. Was that a riddle?

Dunsinane was the official name of Acheron's football field, even though no one actually called it that anymore. It was huge, much bigger than the soccer field, with massive metal bleachers and bright lights on giant poles.

Maria didn't know what "when the sun rises in the west" meant, though. Was she supposed to wait for an eclipse? She didn't have that kind of time. Mateo was probably telling all sorts of lies about her right now.

Whatever. None of that mattered. Now that she knew what lay ahead it was time to move forward, not back. She wasn't going to waste precious time worrying about it the way she had with Brandon.

"Thank you," she said again. Altagracia had told her it was important to show respect to the spirits after they'd spoken with you. Now she just had to get rid of them, like she should've done with the Ouija board. "I dismiss you, spirits."

The pebbles started moving again.

They shouldn't do that. Not after she'd released them.

"Thank you, again, for speaking with me." Maria tried hard to keep her voice steady. "I dismiss you!"

She could hear that rumbling laughter again. It was coming from all around her.

The flames beside her grew and spread. Maria tried to move, but her legs wouldn't budge.

She had to stay calm. Keep thinking.

The ball of flame contracted, then blazed brighter than ever. Maria's eyes closed against her will.

She could see it.

Hundreds of people gathered in this tight, dark space. Screaming. Running.

Families, clutching at each other's hands. Old people,

stumbling, getting trampled under the flowing crowd.

She saw a little girl with her hair in braids. The back of the girl's dress was on fire. She was crying as she ran.

There was nowhere for them to go. The smoke and flames were everywhere.

Maria's body quivered. The spirits would see her fear. They'd use it against her.

"You can't keep me here!" Maria shouted over the roar of the flames and the screams of the dead. "I'm alive! You have no power over me!"

The screams faded. The dead people running past her faded too, into shadows, then empty darkness.

Maria opened her eyes.

All those piles of bones. People the spirits had drawn to this tunnel before her.

Maria wasn't like them. She was going to win. Her fate wasn't up to the spirits to decide.

She knew all their tricks now. She could feel them as sure as she'd felt that spirit on the stairs. The one with the rustling skirts, humming Altagracia's tune. This fire was no more real than the shadow who'd chased her through the woods, or the face in her bathroom mirror.

Maria closed her eyes, the fire shining bright behind her eyelids, and stretched out her hand toward the far end of the tunnel. The heat was sharper than ever. Sweat dripped from her fingertips.

The burn never came.

Maria opened her eyes. Her hand was right in the flames. It felt hot enough to be real, but her skin was still intact. No burns, no blisters.

She stepped closer. The heat on her face was almost unbearable.

Maria closed her eyes again and stepped right into the fire. Still, she didn't burn. She took another step, and another, and—

It was over. A breeze flowed past her face. Behind her eyelids there was only darkness.

Maria opened her eyes and turned around.

She was staring into a dark, empty pathway lined with dirt. She'd beaten them.

She was smarter than the spirits. Stronger.

A soft line shone from the far end of the tunnel. Maria blinked against it. Her eyes had become accustomed to the darkness.

But up ahead, the sun had risen.

18

THEN THE CHARM iS FiRM AND GOOD

Someone was screaming.

Lily couldn't move. Couldn't even open her eyes. All she could see was blood.

She bolted upright and winced. She'd fallen asleep on the stone wall by the cemetery, half bent over. Her left leg jolted out at a horrible angle, and her right was mashed underneath her. She pried her eyes open and groped for her crutches as she blinked against the light. Her clothes were soaked with dew, but the sky above her was still dark.

How long had she slept? She couldn't remember anything that happened after Austin and Felicia went back down the hill.

The screaming came again. It sounded exactly like Maria's had that night. It was coming from inside the house, near their dorm room.

Lily moved down the hill as fast as she dared on her crutches, stumbling every few feet, sending a fresh wave of pain up each leg. She reached the main entrance and yanked the door open, ready to collapse from the effort.

A crowd of freshmen, some in pajamas, some still in their dance clothes, were gathered in the first-floor hall near the girls' bathroom. The screams were coming from behind the bathroom door. Two girls broke away from the crowd and ran toward Lily.

Lily froze. She waited to see what they would do to her.

Then she realized they hadn't even noticed she was there. Their eyes were fixed on the staircase behind her.

Lily flattened herself against the wall, pain stabbing into her leg. The girl in front, Katie, ran right past her.

"Ross!" Katie shouted, her footsteps pounding on the stairs. "Somebody! We need help!"

The second girl started to follow Katie up the steps. She brushed her hair out of her eyes. That was when Lily recognized Felicia.

"What's going on?" Lily's voice came out desperate.

Before Felicia could answer, footsteps thundered down the stairs. Katie and Ross rushed past Lily carrying a first-aid kit, then shoved their way through the crowd gathered around the bathroom door. An abbreviated wail sounded from inside the room before Ross slammed the door, pushing the rest of the group out into the hall. Now that Lily was closer, the screams didn't sound at all like Maria's.

"After your princess roommate pulled her little stunt at the dance . . ." Felicia angled her head toward the cemetery and lowered her voice. "Everybody went berserk. Apparently a bunch of girls from my English class just tried to hold a séance in the bathroom. They read that the best way to summon ghosts was to prick your finger. By the time I came in to stop them they already had a knife out. Next thing I know, there's blood spraying out everywhere."

Lily's stomach lurched. She couldn't stop herself from picturing it. All that blood, arcing across the bathroom.

The other freshmen had noticed Lily and Felicia talking. A few edged toward them. Probably eavesdropping. The last thing Lily needed was more rumors spreading.

But the looks on their faces were clear enough. They could tell there was something wrong with her.

Lily shrank back against the wall. After what happened at the dance, had the whole *school* figured out that she was with Maria?

The bathroom door burst open. Three freshmen reeled back as Ross and Katie ran forward, pulling another girl between them. Her face was ashen, her lips formed into a silent cry. A piece of gauze was taped to the girl's forearm, but bright red liquid had already seeped through the bandage. It spilled out onto the floor behind them as Ross and Katie pulled her toward the health center.

Lily's stomach dropped again. As soon as Katie and Ross were gone she bent forward, her hands on her knees, and retched. She couldn't remember the last time she'd eaten, so there was nothing to come up, but Felicia and the other freshmen looked at her warily, with whispers and giggles.

She had to get back to her room. Lily pulled herself upright, avoiding the others' gazes, and began the long, slow walk. She tried not to put any weight on her left leg, but she winced every time she leaned too hard on her right.

A group of juniors ran past her talking about the Kingsley Prize. For a second she thought about calling after them and asking for help, but—

Wait. Why were they talking about the Kingsley Prize? The second-round list couldn't have gone up yet. It was a Saturday. Or was it Sunday already?

It didn't matter. The juniors were long gone now.

Lily trudged toward the end of the hall. All she wanted to do was lie down in her own bed and sleep until whenever morning came. She hadn't been to her room since she'd heard those sounds by the window, but she'd probably imagined that whole thing.

Besides, Maria might be back from the health center by now. Lily wouldn't have to be alone.

But Maria wasn't there when Lily pushed open the door. The room was cold, dark, and empty.

Well, maybe some extra sleep in the health center was just what Maria needed. You never knew. Lily was tired too. Maybe when she woke up everything would be back to normal.

Even though her left leg felt like it was burning, Lily hopped to the window before she lay down. Everything looked the same as always. The windowpane was shut tight, the lock still in place. She couldn't see any marks on the frame, inside or out. There was nothing on the wall or floor beneath the window.

It was just like she'd thought. Those scratching nails, that horrible knocking—it had only been a nightmare. An unbelievably vivid scene her worthless imagination had conjured up.

Lily collapsed onto the bed, shoved a pile of pillows under her legs, took three Advil from the bottle on her nightstand, and slept.

She thought she slept, anyway.

She must have. Because when the phone rang and her eyes creaked open, she could feel herself blinking back forgotten dreams.

Her phone wasn't on the nightstand, where she usually left it. It was on Maria's bed, sliding along the comforter with each vibration. The pain in Lily's legs had faded to a dull ache, but she couldn't face the thought of standing. She pulled a pillow over her head and ignored the sound until it finally stopped.

She fell asleep again. And this time, she remembered her dream.

She was on the stage at the dance. Maria was clutching her, just as she'd done then. The students gathered below didn't watch with silent frowns, though, the way they had at the real dance. In her dream, they pointed at Lily and smirked behind their hands.

"I knew," Emily said from the front row. She didn't bother to whisper. Her voice was loud and clear enough for the whole room to hear. "I knew about her all along."

"Me too," Caitlin said, with a giggle. "Didn't everyone?"

The rest of the crowd answered with giggles of their own. The mocking stares and shrieks and laughter went on, and on, until they turned into a piercing, insistent noise loud enough to wake Lily with a start.

It was her phone again. An awful, high-pitched ringtone she didn't remember hearing before.

Lily sat up in bed, scrubbing at her eyes, and looked out the window. It was still pitch-black.

That couldn't be right. It had been nearly dawn when she came down from the cemetery, hadn't it?

Maybe there was a storm coming up. Deep clouds blocking the sun.

There was something weird on the window frame, too. Something she hadn't seen before. Lily leaned over to get a better look.

There were uneven grooves in the wood inside the frame. Right above her bed.

Scratch marks. As if something had been inside her room— right over her bed—scrambling in from the outside.

No.

She'd checked the window frame when she'd come in. It had been smooth and even.

She must still be dreaming.

Lily backed away from the window as the phone kept ringing. It should've gone to voice mail after four rings, but the shrill sound continued, bouncing as it vibrated, sliding dangerously close to the edge of Maria's bed.

Lily slapped her cheek, trying to wake herself up. It didn't work, but her cheek throbbed. Her legs did too.

This wasn't a dream.

Lily moved farther back and gathered her crutches. She crossed the room to Maria's bed and picked up her phone. A blinking icon told her she had a new text message. She clicked through to read it.

THEY ALL KNOW.

She didn't recognize who the text was from. It didn't even look like a real phone number. It said 555-555-5555.

Either way, the text was creepy. It reminded her of that terrible dream from before.

Her phone was still letting out that awful noise. Lily hit the Off button, but it kept ringing. She must not have pushed hard enough.

She pressed the button again. This time the phone switched to another ringtone. A long, constant, high-pitched buzzing.

The sound climbed into Lily's ears. Pain churned through her body.

Lily brought her fist down on the Off switch, but the buzzing didn't stop. It was getting higher with each passing second. More like a screech than a buzz. Lily turned on the phone display and hit numbers randomly, trying to make it shut up, but nothing happened.

Then the display cut off altogether and another text appeared from the same number. All in caps, it read:

WE ARE HERE, LILY. WE ARE STILL HERE.

Lily shrieked, the sound disappearing into the blare from the phone.

She dropped the phone onto the thick carpet. The screeching only got louder.

She clapped her hands over her ears and moved toward the door. When she tried the knob, it wouldn't budge.

She pounded on it. Surely someone would hear her and call for help. They must've already heard the phone's god-awful screeching.

No one came.

The ringing phone was so loud it felt like it was coming from inside her head.

Lily bent down, pain shooting up her legs in protest, and tugged at the edge of the carpet nearest the door. If she could pull it up she could slide the phone underneath the bottom edge of the door. Push it out into the hallway, where someone would hear and get help.

The carpet wouldn't budge. It was glued down too tight. Lily could only pull up a tiny corner. She pushed it back, yanking it with all her strength, while the phone kept shrieking in her ears, getting louder still.

It was no use. She could only get that corner. It was barely enough to slide a match under the door, but it was enough for Lily to get her first good look at the floor underneath the carpet.

It was a black-and-white diamond pattern. The same pattern that was in the old dining hall next door.

Lily jerked her head back toward the window.

It was right next to the wall that separated the room from the dining hall. So close it didn't make sense to put a window there.

Not unless it had once been a window somewhere else.

Not unless this room—*her* room—had been part of the dining hall when the house was built.

No.

Oh God, no.

The dining hall. The Ouija board. Where all this had started. Where these *things*—whatever they were—had first entered their lives.

How long had the *things* been creeping into her dreams at night? How long had they been whispering into her ears as she slept?

Lily climbed to her feet. Her legs hurt so much it was like walking through fire to make her way to the window, but she did it anyway, yanking on the latch to unlock it. She'd throw the phone outside. She didn't care if it shattered on the sidewalk.

The window glass wouldn't move. It was sealed as tight as the door.

The screeching turned into a series of high, sharp sounds. They matched perfectly with the beat of Lily's heart. She bent down, the pain in her left leg excruciating, and picked the phone up off the floor.

It was hot. White-hot. She'd have blisters on her hands from the burns.

That was all right. It would be over soon. She had an idea.

She moved toward the open bathroom door, yanked up the toilet seat lid, and dropped the phone into the water. It sank to the bottom.

Silence. Blessed, blessed silence.

It was over.

Lily had bowed her head to say a prayer of thanks when a sudden noise behind her made her jump.

Water. She turned around.

The faucet was on full blast. Piping-hot water filled the sink. Steam poured out into the room.

A loud, low sound shook the bathroom. The water in the toilet bubbled and fizzed. Something red floated through the water toward the surface.

It was Delilah's lip gloss tube. The bloodstains on the plastic still looked as fresh as they had the night Lily found her in the grass.

Lily screamed.

The lip gloss sank back into the water. In its place, Lily's phone floated to the top of the toilet bowl, the screen facing up. It blinked back on with another text.

TURN AROUND, LILY.

She turned.

Streaks of blood dripped down the bathroom mirror.

Lily turned again, ready to run, but the bathroom door swung closed. The old brass lock slid into place.

"Leave me alone!" Lily pounded on the bathroom door, even though she knew if no one had heard her before, they wouldn't hear her now. "I'm sorry! Just let me go, please!"

The faucet in the sink cut off. The shower came on in its

place. Burning-hot water splashed out past the shower curtain, stinging Lily's skin.

She turned away to hide her face. The sink was overflowing, even though the water had stopped running. Her cell phone floated on the surface of the flooding water in the basin. A new text had appeared on the phone's screen.

BLOOD WILL HAVE BLOOD.

Lily reached into the water. It was boiling hot. Welts were already forming on her skin. She grabbed the phone and yanked back the shower curtain, ready to hurl the phone at the hard tile of the shower walls.

Behind the curtain, a pair of bulging red eyes glowed out at Lily from the dark.

Lily screamed. She screamed, and screamed, and screamed.

She turned and grabbed the brass doorknob, ignoring the way it burned her skin. It wouldn't move. She pounded on the door, on the counter, on anything she could reach. She banged her boiling-hot phone onto the ceramic of the overflowing sink. Anything that might stop this. Anything that might bring help.

No help came.

Instead, she felt a heavy presence behind her.

She turned slowly. All she could see was steam rising from the shower. There was no sign of those glowing red eyes.

Then the steam was coming toward her. Enveloping her.

A deep gash appeared on the back of Lily's hand. Blood dripped down her skin onto the white tile.

She sank down to the floor, every bit of her hurting. She bent her head into her knees.

"Leave me alone," she begged.

A six-inch razor blade she'd never seen before appeared in her hand.

A slash bit into her left wrist. Then her right. She tried to drop the razor, but it stayed in place, grasped tightly between her fingers.

"Please," she said.

The next slash came to the side of Lily's neck.

"Please." Lily wrapped her arms around her knees. Blood seeped into the fabric of her sweatpants. "Somebody help me."

The power went out. The room was black.

"Please." Lily looked up into the darkness. "Please. Leave me alone. I—"

The mist evaporated.

A cough bubbled up in her throat, then died on her lips.

She lay down, the blood smearing onto her cheek, soaking into her hair. She closed her eyes.

So much blood.

That was when the laughter started. It was soft at first. Faint. Then, slowly, it grew louder. More erratic. "Hysterical" wasn't the right word for it. "Malevolent" was closer.

Please let it stop, Lily pleaded to no one. *Please, just leave me alone. Please, just let it be quiet.*

But it didn't stop. Instead it got louder, and louder. She couldn't clap her hands over her ears this time, though. She couldn't move at all.

Where was the laughter even coming from? The shower? The door? The old dining hall on the other side of her bedroom wall?

Or was *Lily* the one laughing?

She opened her eyes and climbed unsteadily to her feet. The room was still black, but she could see the faint outline of her face in the bathroom mirror.

Sure enough, she was smiling.

ACT 5

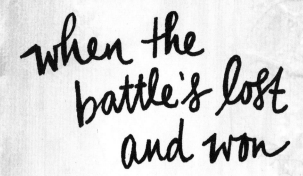

when the
battle's lost
and won

19

HERE'S THE SMELL OF THE BLOOD STILL

Brandon was standing by the lake.

No. Not by it. On it. Hovering inches above the water.

The sun had been up for a few hours but it was shrouded in fog. Mateo had been doing speed drills in the dim light on the soccer field. He was a hundred yards from the lake, but if he ran he could be there in no time.

So he ran. The closer he got, the better he could see Brandon. He didn't look like himself.

His eyes were too dark. He wasn't smiling. And there was a strange glow around him.

It was the glow that made Mateo slow down.

The lake wasn't still like it usually was. The surface was trembling. Little waves lapped at the shore.

Mateo's sneaker was only a few inches from the water's edge when Brandon changed.

He grew taller. The glow around him brightened. For a moment it was so bright Mateo couldn't see him at all.

Then it wasn't Brandon anymore.

It was La Llorona.

She was soaking wet. Her long white dress was heavy and dripping. Her veil fell thick over her face. Her sleeves were spread wide, her long white fingers curled into hooks.

She floated toward Mateo across the water.

This was either a dream or a hallucination. Either way, there was no point running. There was nothing on that lake.

Brandon was dead. La Llorona was a dumb story somebody made up a thousand years ago. There was no way this was real.

But whatever she was, she was getting closer.

Mateo pulled the brim of his baseball cap down over his eyes. *Wake up, asshole. Wake up wake up wake up. Wake the hell up RIGHT NOW!*

He tripped over his sneaker and fell to the ground, scrambling backward on his elbows. A sharp pain slid up his ankle.

La Llorona began to lift the hem of her long white veil. Her fingers gripped the fabric so tightly he could see the skin straining over her knuckles.

She pulled the veil up to her chest, then higher, showing the deep, dark hollows of her neck. Black veins ran under the cool gray skin.

Somehow, Mateo knew he shouldn't—couldn't—see her

face. He threw his arm over his eyes, thrust out his leg, and kicked with all the strength he had.

His foot connected with something not quite solid. Not quite human. He kicked again.

"Stay the hell away from me!" he shouted.

This time, his foot swung in the empty air. He opened his eyes.

Nothing. There was nothing there. All he could see was the glassy surface of the still lake.

The waves were gone. So was she.

Mateo stayed motionless on the bank, waiting for his heartbeat to slow.

Was that a dream?

It must've been. He must've fallen asleep here on the lakeshore.

He couldn't actually remember waking up, but he must have. He'd had a crazy, stupid nightmare, and that was it.

So why couldn't he stop shaking?

Mateo pushed himself up slowly. His ankle throbbed. He'd gotten a sprain last year that felt just like this. He'd have to wrap it when he got back to his room. It was lucky soccer season was over.

Lucky. Right. He'd just sprained his ankle while having a dream about getting chased by a fake ghost after hallucinating his dead boyfriend.

Mateo had shitty, shitty luck.

He winced as he stood and climbed the hill back to the house.

It looked like it was going to storm again. The grounds were all but deserted, and the house was dark and quiet when he pushed the front door open. The power was out again.

As he started to climb the stairs to his room he heard someone above him. It sounded like heavy fabric rustling up at the top of the steps.

He was on the third floor when he saw her. Lily Boiten was climbing the stairs.

It hurt her. You could tell from the look on her face. But there she was, a floor ahead of him on the steep staircase, straining even more than usual in the flickering candlelight.

"Hey, Lily," he called after her. He hated her twisted, pained expression. "Hang on a sec. I'll help you."

Lily kept walking. He'd have thought she was just being obstinate, but she didn't even look up when he spoke. She must not have heard.

"Lily, wait up," he called again.

She still didn't look at him, but her lips were moving. Like she was talking to herself.

"All right, fine." Mateo wiped the sweat gathering under his cap with the hem of his old Birnam Academy district championships T-shirt and picked up his pace, ignoring the pain in his ankle with each step.

He caught up with Lily on the fourth floor. She was leaning down to look out the dormer window at the top of the stairs. Her hair was out of its usual braid. The frizz of curls around her face and the dirty sweatshirt she was wearing made her look so different from the Lily he knew that Mateo wondered for a second if he'd mistaken someone else for her.

Then he heard her voice. She was whispering so low he could barely make out the words.

"You're being hysterical," Lily whispered. With her Southern accent, the sounds came out slow and thick. "No one will know we had anything to do with it."

"Lily?" Mateo kept his voice low too. He didn't want to startle her, not when she was leaning that far out the wide-open window.

Wait. That was strange. That window was always kept locked since—since Delilah.

"She doesn't deserve your pity." Lily was still whispering, like she hadn't heard Mateo this time either. "Come straight back when you're done. I'll wait up."

Mateo stepped forward and put his hand on her shoulder. "Lily?"

Lily leaned forward. Too far forward.

He leaped toward her, grabbing her by the shoulders and wrenching her back inside. He expected her to resist, but she didn't, and he wound up pulling too hard. They both fell backward onto the hard wood landing.

Lily's face screwed up with pain, but she didn't make a sound. Something rolled out of her pocket.

"Sorry, sorry." Mateo stood and reached for Lily's hand to help her up. To his surprise, she took it, bracing herself on the wall with her other arm and climbing to her feet. He gathered up her crutches from where they'd fallen and passed them to her. She took them, but her eyes looked faraway.

"What the hell were you doing at that window?" he asked her. "How did you even get it open?"

"I'm sorry," Lily whispered. She stared up at him with those cold blue eyes of hers. "I'm so, so sorry."

"What are you doing up here, anyway?"

Lily's eyes were fixed on a point on the floor. Mateo followed her gaze and saw the thing that had fallen out of her pocket. It looked like a plastic toy. He bent to pick it up. Something wet rubbed off it onto his fingers. He wiped his hand on his T-shirt, leaving a red stain behind.

"What—" he started, then jumped back when he recognized it. It was Delilah's old lip gloss case. He'd seen her play with it countless times.

There was blood on it.

"Where did you find this?" Mateo wanted to shake her. "Did you get it from Maria?"

"I'm sorry," Lily whispered again.

"Don't be sorry, just tell me." Mateo was talking so fast he tripped over the words. "Why do you have this?"

"I'm sorry about Brandon, too." She held her hands out in front of her face, studying them. "How did I get out of the bath-room?"

"What are you talking about?" Mateo couldn't decide whether to call the cops or take her to the health center, but he tried, once again, to sound gentle. "Why were you leaning out the window, Lily?"

She mumbled so low he had to lean in close to hear.

"I was just following her," she whispered.

"Following who?" The corridor was empty.

Lily shook her head. "She had a candle."

This was useless. "Tell me what's going on, Lily."

Lily didn't move. Her face didn't change expression, but there was a new undertone in her voice that made goose bumps form on Mateo's skin. "I could ignore them before, but they're stronger now. It's getting harder."

"'They'?" Mateo said. "Who's 'they'?"

"There was blood before." Lily stretched out her arms in front of her again and turned them over, examining her smooth, pale skin. "Where did all the blood go?"

If Lily was really as crazy as she was acting, she needed more help than Mateo could give her. Well, the nurses at the health center would know what to do.

"Tell you what," Mateo said. "I'll walk you back down to your room."

Lily didn't move. When Mateo put a gentle hand on her back, though, she came with him easily enough.

"Have you ever seen the girl?" Lily asked as they climbed down the stairs. It was slow going. She leaned on Mateo so hard he felt his ankle buckling. He wished he'd had time to wrap it up before he'd run into her.

"Can't say that I have," he said.

"The little girl who skips on the lake. Sometimes there are others with her. Sometimes she tells you to come for a swim."

Mateo stopped walking. "Who are you talking about? Not—not La Llorona?"

"I don't know her name." Lily stopped too. "That other one had the candle on the stairs. The one in blue. She's the one who told me about the blood. About how pretty it would look on the grass."

What? "Whose blood, Lily?"

Lily ignored him. Her breath was coming in huffs. They were nearing the second-floor landing.

"I went to the cemetery last night," Lily said. "I just want them all to leave me alone. I just want Maria to be Maria again."

Mateo nearly fell again.

Those words. That was exactly what Brandon had said the morning he died.

God, Lily was just as much of a victim as the rest of them.

"Listen, Lily," Mateo whispered, "you've got to stay away from Maria. Something's not right with her. I know she's your girlfriend and you think you love her or whatever, but—"

Lily started crying. "She's not my—we're not—does *everyone* know?"

Oh. Shit. He wasn't helping her at all. He was probably making things worse.

"Crap, I'm sorry," he said. "I only know because Brandon told me. I don't think anyone else knows. It's okay. Please don't cry."

Lily sobbed. Mateo patted her arm and sighed again.

"You need to go to the health center," he said. She scowled, and he quickly added, "For your legs. I can tell they hurt worse than usual. They can give you something for that."

Lily shook her head. She leaned back against the wall and held out her hands in front of her again, turning them over and over. Tears streamed down her face.

She definitely needed help. For more than just her legs.

Mateo put his arm around her waist. It was a shame the school was too busy being historically accurate to put in a damn elevator. Lily let him steer her down the stairs and to the path outside that led to the health center.

He turned to shut the door to the house. Maybe he should stay with Lily for a while. She seemed like she might break at any moment.

But when he turned back, Lily was gone.

Someone else was standing in her place.

The fog was so thick Maria could barely see the house, but she knew it was ahead of her. She was almost at the top of the hill now. She'd had to limp the whole way in her scratched bare feet. Her shoes were still on the dirty floor of the clapboard church.

She'd thought it was dawn when she left the woods, but it must have been later. There was a tiny patch of sky that was brighter than the rest, and it was nearly overhead. How long had she been in the forest? Did time work differently when the spirits were in control?

When she reached the crest of the hill, the house emerged from the fog all at once. It was so dim the white wooden siding looked gray. Maria stared up at the four stories of wood and brick and wondered how it must've looked to the people who'd died in that tunnel all that time ago. If any of them had ever stared up at the building like she was now, hating it as much as she did.

Not that it mattered what Maria hated or didn't hate.

No one was around when she pushed open the front door. The chill in the empty front hallway made her shiver. Her dress and her bare legs and arms were caked with dirt from the church, the tunnel, the woods.

Where was everyone? It was usually impossible to be alone in this place. Maria rubbed the goose bumps on her shoulders as she gazed up and down the corridors.

No matter. First she had to find Lily. Then she needed to plan.

When Maria turned the key to her door, though, their room was empty. Even the bathroom was dark and silent. Maria pulled her phone out of her pocket and texted Lily, but the text took forever to send, and then a red message popped up on her screen: "Not Deliverable."

All right, fine. Maria would do this on her own. That was how she'd been doing everything anyway.

On her way back from the woods, she'd had an idea. Just a little something to shake things up. Get Mateo off his game. She sat down at her computer and started typing.

She'd just hit Send on the email when someone knocked on her door. It was Emily, with an odd look on her face.

"Hi there, Maria," Emily said. There was a quirk to her smile that Maria didn't like at all. "How are you, uh, feeling?"

Maria didn't have time for this. "What do you want, Emily?"

"I thought you'd want to know they just posted the new Kingsley list. It's outside Cumberland's office."

"What?" Maria shook her head. "They weren't supposed to post the next round for another week at least."

Emily shrugged, that smile still in place. She took in Maria's dirt-smeared dress. "Nice look, by the way."

Maria pushed past Emily into the hall and charged toward the dean's office. Emily kept pace beside her.

"Have you seen Mateo?" Maria said.

Emily laughed. Maria didn't see what was funny.

"Not since last night," Emily said. "Any particular reason you want to see him?"

Maria shook her head. They were almost at the office. The crowd looking up at the list was five people thick. Maria was ready to fight through them to get close enough, but when they saw her they parted easily, making a path, giggling. When she got to the front, she saw why.

The list was only two lines long. *Maria Lyon* was the second name on it. *Mateo Pífano* was first.

"Mateo?" Maria read the letters over and over. Maybe they'd spell out something different if she looked long enough. "He can't win. He didn't even apply."

"He sent in his application a couple of weeks ago," Emily said behind her. Maria could still hear the smile in her voice.

"Right before the deadline."

"No." Maria didn't believe her. Couldn't.

"They already took Delilah off," a guy muttered to her right. "Wonder if Mateo's gonna be the next one to have an *accident*."

"Shh! Careful," a girl muttered back, lower. "She can hear you."

"No," Maria said again.

Mateo wasn't getting that spot. It was hers.

Hers.

She turned around. Everyone was watching her. A few of them edged away when they saw her looking. Caitlin and Ryan were off to one side, whispering, their fingers covering their lips. Austin watched silently from the back of the group. Emily looked straight at Maria with obvious delight in her eyes.

Maria was surrounded by liars.

"He *can't* be ahead of me." Maria was horrified to discover that her eyes were wet. "His rank isn't good enough."

Maria'd had the class rankings memorized since freshman year. Mateo was fourth in their class, behind Delilah, Lily, and Maria.

"It isn't just about rank. He had soccer and the GSA and everything. Plus, there's also, you know . . ." Emily lowered her voice to a stage whisper. "Affirmative action."

More giggles from the group.

"And he wrote this essay for a gay writing contest," Tamika added. "It won an award or something."

No.

No.

Maria fought the urge to stamp her foot on the hardwood floor.

She had suffered. *She* had sacrificed.

Mateo was *not* going to beat her.

He didn't deserve to. Certainly not for being *gay*, of all things.

"I have to go," Maria announced. She started to push back through the group, but once again, they parted for her. As she walked away, she heard more giggles.

Maria hadn't been sucking up to these people for the past nine years only for them to disrespect her now.

And she definitely hadn't emptied that capsule into Delilah's drink so *Mateo* could win.

It was just like the spirits said. He was her biggest threat. She had to get rid of him.

"Text me if you see Mateo," she called from the edge of the crowd. She didn't bother to force a smile. "I want to, you know, *congratulate* him."

No one answered. They all just stared at her.

Fine. Whatever.

Maria brushed past the last of them and went straight to the old dining room. She pushed on the tall, creaky door, and it swung open immediately.

Inside, the room was dark and cold. The dim light from outside wasn't strong enough to penetrate the old, thin windows, but the breeze was. Maria shivered and wished she'd thought to change out of her wet dress.

The darkness, though—that was a comfort. The darkness was a friend.

She texted Mateo. She made sure her texts were friendly. She asked him to come and meet her.

He didn't answer right away, so she texted a few more times. Between texts, Maria smiled up at the ceiling. At the hole where the chandelier had been. She looked for the jagged edges of the spirit who had crouched there that first night. The one who'd first told Maria what she could be.

"Yo soy suya," Maria said to the empty room. She closed her eyes. "Dime qué hacer y lo haré. He hecho bastantes preguntas. Estoy lista para actuar."

I am yours. Tell me what to do and I'll do it. I'm through asking questions. I'm ready to act.

There was no answer.

Maria opened her eyes. Had she done something wrong?

That's when she spotted something gleaming on the dining table. Something that hadn't been there when she came into the room.

She moved slowly forward. Reached out a trembling hand. Slid one finger along the length of it. Then she lifted it, grasping its handle in her fist. It was long and thin.

The blade was shiny, even though the knife itself looked like an antique. Maria had never seen a real dagger before, but it was exactly as she'd have pictured one, with a slick ivory handle and a blade that looked too short to really do much damage.

But she was certain it could.